ENID BLYTON

FIVE ON A TREASURE ISLAND

Illustrated by Betty Maxey

CW00952485

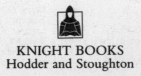

KNIGHT BOOKS
Hodder and Stoughton

This Famous Five Two-in-One Special Edition
was first published in 1986
Revised edition 1992

Five on a Treasure Island

First published in a single volume by
Hodder and Stoughton, 1942

First Knight Books single volume
edition 1967

Printed and bound in Great Britain
for Hodder and Stoughton Children's
Books, a division of Hodder and
Stoughton Ltd., Mill Road, Dunton
Green, Sevenoaks, Kent TN13 2YA.
Editorial Office: 47 Bedford Square,
London WC1B 3DP) by Cox &
Wyman Ltd., Reading, Berks. Photoset
by Rowland Phototypesetting Ltd.,
Bury St Edmunds, Suffolk.

British Library C.I.P.

Blyton, Enid
  Five on a treasure island. –
  (Blyton, Enid. Famous Five).
  I. Title
  823'.9'1J   PZ7.B629

A Knight Two-in-One Special Edition

FIVE ON A TREASURE ISLAND
FIVE GO ADVENTURING AGAIN

The Famous Five are Julian, Dick,
George (Georgina by rights), Anne and
Timmy the dog.

This book brings together their first
two exciting adventures

Join the Famous Five . . .

Contents

1 A great surprise   7
2 The strange cousin   15
3 A peculiar story – and a new friend   23
4 An exciting afternoon   33
5 A visit to the island   43
6 What the storm did   53
7 Back to Kirrin Cottage   61
8 Exploring the wreck   69
9 The box from the wreck   77
10 An astonishing offer   87
11 Off to Kirrin Island   95
12 Exciting discoveries   103
13 Down in the dungeons   113
14 Prisoners!   123
15 Dick to the rescue!   131
16 A plan – and a narrow escape   139
17 The end of the great adventure   147

1 A great surprise

'Mother, have you heard about our summer holidays yet?' said Julian, at the breakfast-table. 'Can we go to Polseath as usual?'

'I'm afraid not,' said his mother. 'They are quite full up this year.'

The three children at the breakfast-table looked at one another in great disappointment. They did so love the house at Polseath. The beach was so lovely there, too, and the bathing was fine.

'Cheer up,' said Daddy. 'I dare say we'll find somewhere else just as good for you. And anyway, Mother and I won't be able to go with you this year. Has Mother told you?'

'No!' said Anne. 'Oh, Mother – is it true? Can't you really come with us on our holidays? You always do.'

'Well, this time Daddy wants me to go to Scotland with him,' said Mother. 'All by ourselves! And as you are really getting big enough to look after yourselves now, we thought it would be rather fun for you to have a holiday on your own too. But now that you can't go to Polseath, I don't really quite know where to send you.'

'What about Quentin's?' suddenly said Daddy. Quentin was his brother, the children's uncle. They had only seen him once, and had been rather frightened of him. He was a very tall, frowning man, a clever scientist who spent all his time studying. He lived by the sea – but that was about all that the children knew of him!

'Quentin?' said Mother, pursing her lips. 'Whatever made you think of him? I shouldn't think he'd want the children messing about in his little house.'

'Well,' said Daddy, 'I had to see Quentin's wife in town the other day, about a business matter – and I don't think things are going too well for them. Fanny said that she would be quite glad if she could hear of one or two people to live with her for a while, to bring a little money in. Their house is by the sea, you know. It might be just the thing for the children. Fanny is very nice – she would look after them well.'

'Yes – and she has a child of her own too, hasn't she?' said the children's mother. 'Let me see – what's her name – something funny – yes, Georgina! How old would she be? About eleven, I should think.'

'Same age as me,' said Dick. 'Fancy having a cousin we've never seen! She must be jolly lonely all by herself. I've got Julian and Anne to play with – but Georgina is just one on her own. I should think she'd be glad to see us.'

'Well, your Aunt Fanny said that her Georgina would love a bit of company,' said Daddy. 'You know, I really think that would solve our difficulty, if we telephone to Fanny and arrange for the children to go there. It would help Fanny, I'm sure, and Georgina would love to have someone to play with in the holidays. And we should know that our three were safe.'

The children began to feel rather excited. It would be fun to go to a place they had never been to before, and stay with an unknown cousin.

'Are there cliffs and rocks and sands there?' asked Anne. 'Is it a nice place?'

'I don't remember it very well,' said Daddy. 'But I feel sure it's an exciting kind of place. Anyway, you'll love it! It's called Kirrin Bay. Your Aunt Fanny has lived there all her life, and wouldn't leave it for anything.'

'Oh Daddy, do telephone to Aunt Fanny and ask her if we can go there!' cried Dick. 'I just feel as if it's the right place somehow. It sounds sort of adventurous!'

'Oh, you always say that, wherever you go!' said Daddy, with a laugh. 'All right – I'll ring up now, and see if there's any chance.'

They had all finished their breakfast, and they got up to wait for Daddy to telephone. He went out into the hall, and they heard him dialling.

'I hope it's all right for us!' said Julian. 'I wonder what Georgina's like. Funny name, isn't it? More like a boy's than a girl's. So she's eleven – a year younger than I am – same age as you, Dick – and a year older than you, Anne. She ought to fit in with us all right. The four of us ought to have a fine time together.'

Daddy came back in about ten minutes' time, and the children knew at once that he had fixed up everything. He smiled round at them.

'Well, that's settled,' he said. 'Your Aunt Fanny is delighted about it. She says it will be awfully good for Georgina to have company, because she's such a lonely little girl, always going off by herself. And she will love looking after you all. Only you'll have to be careful not to disturb your Uncle Quentin. He is working very hard, and he isn't very good-tempered when he is disturbed.'

'We'll be as quiet as mice in the house!' said Dick.

'Honestly we will. Oh, goody, goody – when are we going, Daddy?'

'Next week, if Mother can manage it,' said Daddy.

Mother nodded her head. 'Yes,' she said, 'there's nothing much to get ready for them – just bathing suits and jerseys and jeans. They all wear the same.'

'How lovely it will be to wear jeans again,' said Anne, dancing round. 'I'm tired of wearing school tunics. I want to wear shorts, or a bathing suit, and go bathing and climbing with the boys.'

'Well, you'll soon be doing it,' said Mother, with a laugh. 'Remember to put ready any toys or books you want, won't you? Not many, please, because there won't be a great deal of room.'

'Anne wanted to take all her fifteen dolls with her last year,' said Dick. 'Do you remember, Anne? Weren't you funny?'

'No, I wasn't,' said Anne, going red. 'I love my dolls, and I just couldn't choose which to take – so I thought I'd take them all. There's nothing funny about that.'

'And do you remember the year before, Anne wanted to take the rocking-horse?' said Dick, with a giggle.

Mother chimed in. 'You know, I remember a little boy called Dick who put aside one teddy bear, three toys dogs, two toy cats and his old monkey to take down to Polseath one year,' she said.

Then it was Dick's turn to go red. He changed the subject at once.

'Daddy, are we going by train or by car?' he asked.

'By car,' said Daddy. 'We can pile everything into the boot. Well – what about Tuesday?'

'That would suit me well,' said Mother. 'Then we

could take the children down, come back, and do our own packing at leisure, and start off for Scotland on the Friday. Yes – we'll arrange for Tuesday.'

So Tuesday it was. The children counted the days eagerly, and Anne marked one off the calendar each night. The week seemed a very long time in going. But at last Tuesday did come. Dick and Julian, who shared a room, woke up at about the same moment, and stared out of the nearby window.

'It's a lovely day, hurrah!' cried Julian, leaping out of bed. 'I don't know why, but it always seems very important that it should be sunny on the first day of a holiday. Let's wake Anne.'

Anne slept in the next room. Julian ran in and shook her. 'Wake up! It's Tuesday! And the sun's shining.'

Anne woke up with a jump and stared at Julian joyfully. 'It's come at last!' she said. 'I thought it never would. Oh, isn't it an exciting feeling to go away for a holiday!'

They started soon after breakfast. Their car was a big one, so it held them all very comfortably. Mother sat in front with Daddy, and the three children sat behind, their feet on two suitcases. In the luggage-place at the back of the car were all kinds of odds and ends, and one small trunk. Mother really thought they had remembered everything.

Along the crowded London roads they went, slowly at first, and then, as they left the town behind, more quickly. Soon they were right into the open country, and the car sped along fast. The children sang songs to themselves, as they always did when they were happy.

'Are we picnicking soon?' asked Anne, feeling hungry all of a sudden.

'Yes,' said Mother. 'But not yet. It's only eleven o'clock. We shan't have lunch till at least half-past twelve, Anne.'

'Oh, gracious!' said Anne. 'I know I can't last out till then!'

So her mother handed her some chocolate, and she and the boys munched happily, watching the hills, woods and fields as the car sped by.

The picnic was lovely. They had it on the top of a hill, in a sloping field that looked down into a sunny valley. Anne didn't very much like a big brown cow who came up close and stared at her, but it went away when Daddy told it to. The children ate enormously, and Mother said that instead of having a tea-picnic at half-past four they would have to go to a tea-house somewhere, because they had eaten all the tea sandwiches as well as the lunch ones!

'What time shall we be at Aunt Fanny's?' asked Julian, finishing up the very last sandwich and wishing there were more.

'About six o'clock with luck,' said Daddy. 'Now who wants to stretch their legs a bit? We've another long spell in the car, you know.'

The car seemed to eat up the miles as it purred along. Tea-time came, and then the three children began to feel excited all over again.

'We must watch out for the sea,' said Dick. 'I can smell it somewhere near!'

He was right. The car suddenly topped a hill – and there was the shining blue sea, calm and smooth in the evening sun. The three children gave a yell.

'There it is!'

'Isn't it marvellous!'

'Oh, I want to bathe this very minute!'

'We shan't be more than twenty minutes now, before we're at Kirrin Bay,' said Daddy. 'We've made good time. You'll see the bay soon – it's quite a big one – with a funny sort of island at the entrance of the bay.'

The children looked out for it as they drove along the coast. Then Julian gave a shout.

'There it is – that must be Kirrin Bay. Look, Dick – isn't it lovely and blue?'

'And look at the rocky little island guarding the entrance of the bay,' said Dick. 'I'd like to visit that.'

'Well, I've no doubt you will,' said Mother. 'Now, let's look out for Aunt Fanny's house. It's called Kirrin Cottage.'

They soon came to it. It stood on the low cliff overlooking the bay, and was a very old house indeed. It wasn't really a cottage, but quite a big house, built of old white stone. Roses climbed over the front of it, and the garden was full of flowers.

'Here's Kirrin Cottage,' said Daddy, and he stopped the car in front of it. 'It's supposed to be about three hundred years old! Now – where's Quentin? Hallo, there's Fanny!'

2 The strange cousin

The children's aunt had been watching for the car. She came running out of the old wooden door as soon as she saw it draw up outside. The children liked the look of her at once.

'Welcome to Kirrin!' she cried. 'Hallo, all of you! It's lovely to see you. And what big children!'

There were kisses all round, and then the children went into the house. They liked it. It felt old and rather mysterious somehow, and the furniture was old and very beautiful.

'Where's Georgina?' asked Anne, looking round for her unknown cousin.

'Oh, the naughty girl! I told her to wait in the garden for you,' said her aunt. 'Now she's gone off somewhere. I must tell you, children, you may find George a bit difficult at first – she's always been one on her own, you know, and at first may not like you being here. But you mustn't take any notice of that – she'll be all right in a short time. I was very glad for George's sake that you were able to come. She badly needs other children to play with.'

'Do you call her "George"?' asked Anne, in surprise. 'I thought her name was Georgina.'

'So it is,' said her aunt. 'But George hates being a girl, and we have to call her George, as if she was a boy. The naughty girl won't answer if we call her Georgina.'

The children thought that Georgina sounded rather exciting. They wished she would come. But she didn't. Their Uncle Quentin suddenly appeared instead. He was a most extraordinary looking man, very tall, very dark, and with a rather fierce frown on his wide forehead.

'Hallo, Quentin!' said Daddy. 'It's a long time since I've seen you. I hope these three won't disturb you very much in your work.'

'Quentin is working on a very difficult book,' said Aunt Fanny. 'But I've given him a room all to himself on the other side of the house. So I don't expect he will be disturbed.'

Their uncle looked at the three children, and nodded to them. The frown didn't come off his face, and they all felt a little scared, and were glad that he was to work in another part of the house.

'Where's George?' he said, in a deep voice.

'Gone off somewhere again,' said Aunt Fanny, vexed. 'I told her she was to stay here and meet her cousins.'

'She wants a good talking to,' said Uncle Quentin. The children couldn't quite make out whether he was joking or not. 'Well, children, I hope you have a good time here, and maybe you will knock a little common-sense into George!'

There was no room at Kirrin Cottage for Mother and Daddy to stay the night, so after a hurried supper they left to stay at a hotel in the nearest town. They would drive back to London immediately after breakfast the next day. So they said good-bye to the children that night.

Georgina still hadn't appeared. 'I'm sorry we haven't seen Georgina,' said Mother. 'Just give her our love and tell her we hope she'll enjoy playing with Dick, Julian and Anne.'

Then Mother and Daddy went. The children felt a little bit lonely as they saw the big car disappear round the corner of the road, but Aunt Fanny took them upstairs to show them their bedrooms, and they soon forgot to be sad.

The two boys were to sleep together in a room with slanting ceilings at the top of the house. It had a marvellous view of the bay. The boys were really delighted with it. Anne was to sleep with Georgina in a smaller room, whose windows looked over the moors at the back of the house. But one side-window looked over the sea, which pleased Anne very much. It was a nice room, and red roses nodded their heads in at the window.

'I do wish Georgina would come,' Anne said to her aunt. 'I want to see what she's like.'

'Well, she's a funny little girl,' said her aunt. 'She can be very rude and haughty – but she's kind at heart, very loyal and absolutely truthful. Once she makes friends with you, she will always be your friend – but she finds it very difficult indeed to make friends, which is a great pity.'

Anne suddenly yawned. The boys frowned at her, because they knew what would happen next. And it did!

'Poor Anne! How tired you are! You must all go to bed straight away, and have a good night. Then you will wake up quite fresh tomorrow,' said Aunt Fanny.

'Anne, you *are* an idiot,' said Dick, crossly, when his aunt had gone out of the room. 'You know quite well

what grown-ups think as soon as we yawn. I did want
to go down on the beach for a while.'

'I'm so sorry,' said Anne. 'Somehow I couldn't help
it. And anyway, *you're* yawning now, Dick – and
Julian too!'

So they were. They were as sleepy as could be with
their long drive. Secretly all of them longed to cuddle
down into bed and shut their eyes.

'I wonder where Georgina is,' said Anne, when she
said good-night to the boys, and went to her own
room. 'Isn't she odd – not waiting to welcome us – and
not coming in to supper – and not even in yet! After all,
she's sleeping in my room – goodness knows what
time she'll be in!'

All the three children were fast asleep before
Georgina came up to bed! They didn't hear her open
Anne's door. They didn't hear her get undressed and
clean her teeth. They didn't hear the creak of her bed as
she got into it. They were so tired that they heard
nothing at all until the sun awoke them in the
morning.

When Anne awoke she couldn't at first think where
she was. She lay in her little bed and looked up at the
slanting ceiling, and at the red roses that nodded at the
open window – and suddenly remembered all in a rush
where she was! 'I'm at Kirrin Bay – and it's the
holidays!' she said to herself, and screwed up her legs
with joy.

Then she looked across at the other bed. In it lay the
figure of another child, curled up under the bedclothes. Anne could just see the top of a curly head, and
that was all. When the figure stirred a little, Anne
spoke.

'I say! Are you Georgina?'

The child in the opposite bed sat up and looked across at Anne. She had very short curly hair, almost as short as a boy's. Her face was burnt a dark-brown with the sun, and her very blue eyes looked as bright as forget-me-nots in her face. But her mouth was rather sulky, and she had a frown like her father's.

'No,' she said. 'I'm not Georgina.'

'Oh!' said Anne, in surprise. 'Then who are you?'

'I'm George,' said the girl. 'I shall only answer if you call me George. I hate being a girl. I won't be. I don't like doing the things that girls do. I like doing the things that boys do. I can climb better than any boy, and swim faster too. I can sail a boat as well as any fisher-boy on this coast. You're to call me George. Then I'll speak to you. But I shan't if you don't.'

'Oh!' said Anne, thinking that her new cousin was most extraordinary. 'All right! I don't care what I call you. George is a nice name, I think. I don't much like Georgina. Anyway, you look like a boy.'

'Do I really?' said George, the frown leaving her face for a moment. 'Mother was awfully cross with me when I cut my hair short. I had hair all round my neck; it was awful.'

The two girls stared at one another for a moment. 'Don't you simply hate being a girl?' asked George.

'No, of course not,' said Anne. 'You see – I do like pretty frocks – and I love my dolls – and you can't do that if you're a boy.'

'Pooh! Fancy bothering about pretty frocks,' said George, in a scornful voice. 'And dolls! Well, you *are* a baby, that's all I can say.'

Anne felt offended. 'You're not very polite,' she said. 'You won't find that my brothers take much notice of you if you act as if you know everything.

They're *real* boys, not pretend boys, like you.'

'Well, if they're going to be nasty to me I shan't take any notice of *them*,' said George, jumping out of bed. 'I didn't want any of you to come, anyway. Interfering with my life here! I'm quite happy on my own. Now I've got to put up with a silly girl who likes frocks and dolls, and two stupid boy-cousins!'

Anne felt that they had made a very bad beginning. She said no more, but got dressed herself too. She put on her grey jeans and a red jersey. George put on jeans too, and a boy's jersey. Just as they were ready the boys hammered on their door.

'Aren't you ready? Is Georgina there? Cousin Georgina, come out and see us.'

George flung open the door and marched out with her head high. She took no notice of the two surprised boys at all. She stalked downstairs. The other three children looked at one another.

'She won't answer if you call her Georgina,' explained Anne. 'She's awfully funny, I think. She says she didn't want us to come because we'll interfere with her. She laughed at me, and was rather rude.'

Julian put his arm round Anne, who looked a bit doleful. 'Cheer up!' he said. 'You've got us to stick up for you. Come on down to breakfast.'

They were all hungry. The smell of bacon and eggs was very good. They ran down the stairs and said good-morning to their aunt. She was just bringing the breakfast to the table. Their uncle was sitting at the head, reading his paper. He nodded at the children. They sat down without a word, wondering if they were allowed to speak at meals. They always were at home, but their Uncle Quentin looked rather fierce.

George was there, buttering a piece of toast. She scowled at the three children.

'Don't look like that, George,' said her mother. 'I hope you've made friends already. It will be fun for you to play together. You must take your cousins to see the bay this morning and show them the best places to bathe.'

'I'm going fishing,' said George.

Her father looked up at once.

'You are not,' he said. 'You are going to show a few good manners for a change, and take your cousins to the bay. Do you hear me?'

'Yes,' said George, with a scowl exactly like her father's.

'Oh, we can go to the bay by ourselves all right, if George is going fishing,' said Anne, at once, thinking that it would be nice not to have George if she was in a bad temper.

'George will do exactly as she's told,' said her father. 'If she doesn't, I shall deal with her.'

So, after breakfast, four children got ready to go down to the beach. An easy path led down to the bay, and they ran down happily. Even George lost her frown as she felt the warmth of the sun and saw the dancing sparkles on the blue sea.

'You go fishing if you want to,' said Anne when they were down on the beach. 'We won't tell tales on you. We don't want to interfere with you, you know. We've got ourselves for company, and if you don't want to be with us, you needn't.'

'But we'd like you, all the same, if you'd like to be with us,' said Julian, generously. He thought George was rude and ill-mannered, but he couldn't help rather liking the look of the straight-backed, short-haired little girl, with her brilliant blue eyes and sulky mouth.

George stared at him. 'I'll see,' she said. 'I don't make friends with people just because they're my cousins, or something silly like that. I only make friends with people if I like them.'

'So do we,' said Julian. 'We may not like *you*, of course.'

'Oh!' said George, as if that thought hadn't occurred to her. 'Well – you may not, of course. Lots of people don't like me, now I come to think of it.'

Anne was staring out over the blue bay. At the entrance to it lay a curious rocky island with what looked like an old ruined castle on the top of it.

'Isn't that a funny place?' she said. 'I wonder what it's called.'

'It's called Kirrin Island,' said George, her eyes as blue as the sea as she turned to look at it. 'It's a lovely place to go to. If I like you, I may take you there some day. But I don't promise. The only way to get there is by boat.'

'Who does the funny island belong to?' asked Julian.

George made a most surprising answer. 'It belongs to *me*,' she said. 'At least, it *will* belong to me – some day! It will be my very own island – and my very own castle!'

3 A peculiar story – and a new friend

The three children stared at George in the greatest surprise.

George stared back at them.

'What do you mean?' said Dick, at last. 'Kirrin Island can't belong to you. You're just boasting.'

'No, I'm not,' said George. 'You ask Mother. If you're not going to believe what I say I won't tell you another word more. But I don't tell untruths. I think it's being a coward if you don't tell the truth – and I'm not a coward.'

Julian remembered that Aunt Fanny had said that George was absolutely truthful, and he scratched his head and looked at George again. How could she be possibly telling the truth?

'Well, of course we'll believe you if you tell us the truth,' he said. 'But it does sound a bit extraordinary, you know. Really it does. Children don't usually own islands, even funny little ones like that.'

'It *isn't* a funny little island,' said George, fiercely. 'It's lovely. There are rabbits there, as tame as can be – and the big cormorants sit on the other side – and all kinds of gulls go there. The castle is wonderful too, even if it *is* all in ruins.'

'It sounds fine,' said Dick. 'How does it belong to you, Georgina?'

George glared at him and didn't answer.

'Sorry,' said Dick, hastily. 'I didn't mean to call you Georgina. I meant to call you George.'

'Go on, George – tell us how the island belongs to you,' said Julian, slipping his arm through his sulky little cousin's.

She pulled away from him at once.

'Don't do that,' she said. 'I'm not sure that I want to make friends with you yet.'

'All right, all right,' said Julian, losing patience. 'Be enemies or anything you like. We don't care. But we like your mother awfully, and we don't want her to think we won't make friends with you.'

'Do you like my mother?' said George, her bright blue eyes softening a little. 'Yes – she's a dear, isn't she? Well – all right – I'll tell you how Kirrin Castle belongs to me. Come and sit down here in this corner where nobody can hear us.'

They all sat down in a sandy corner of the beach. George looked across at the little island in the bay.

'It's like this,' she said. 'Years ago my mother's family owned nearly all the land around here. Then they got poor, and had to sell most of it. But they could never sell that little island, because nobody thought it worth anything, especially as the castle has been ruined for years.'

'Fancy nobody wanting to buy a dear little island like that!' said Dick. 'I'd buy it at once if I had the money.'

'All that's left of what Mother's family owned is our own house, Kirrin Cottage, and a farm a little way off – and Kirrin Island,' said George. 'Mother says when

I'm grown-up it will be mine. She says she doesn't want it now, either, so she's sort of given it to me. It belongs to me. It's my own private island, and I don't let anyone go there unless they get my permission.'

The three children stared at her. They believed every word George said, for it was quite plain that the girl was speaking the truth. Fancy having an island of your very own! They thought she was very lucky indeed.

'Oh Georgina – I mean George!' said Dick. 'I do think you're lucky. It looks such a nice island. I hope you'll be friends with us and take us there one day soon. You simply can't imagine how we'd love it.'

'Well – I might,' said George, pleased at the interest she had caused. 'I'll see. I never have taken anyone there yet, though some of the boys and girls round here have begged me to. But I don't like them, so I haven't.'

There was a little silence as the four children looked out over the bay to where the island lay in the distance. The tide was going out. It almost looked as if they could wade over to the island. Dick asked if it was possible.

'No,' said George. 'I told you – it's only possible to get to it by boat. It's farther out than it looks – and the water is very, very deep. There are rocks all about too – you have to know exactly where to row a boat, or you bump into them. It's a dangerous bit of coast here. There are a lot of wrecks about.'

'Wrecks!' cried Julian, his eyes shining. 'I say! I've never seen an old wreck. Are there any to see?'

'Not now,' said George. 'They've all been cleared up. Except one, and that's the other side of the island. It's deep down in the water. You can just see the broken mast if you row over it on a calm day and look down into the water. That wreck really belongs to me too.'

This time the children really could hardly believe George. But she nodded her head firmly.

'Yes,' she said, 'it was a ship belonging to one of my great-great-great-grandfathers, or someone like that. He was bringing gold – big bars of gold – back in his ship – and it got wrecked off Kirrin Island.'

'Oooh – what happened to the gold?' asked Anne, her eyes round and big.

'Nobody knows,' said George. 'I expect it was stolen out of the ship. Divers have been down to see, of course, but they couldn't find any gold.'

'Golly – this does sound exciting,' said Julian. 'I wish I could see the wreck.'

'Well – we might perhaps go this afternoon when the tide is right down,' said George. 'The water is so calm and clear today. We could see a bit of it.'

'Oh, how wonderful!' said Anne. 'I do so want to see a real live wreck!'

The others laughed. 'Well, it won't be very alive,' said Dick. 'I say, George – what about a bathe?'

'I must go and get Timothy first,' said George. She got up.

'Who's Timothy?' said Dick.

'Can you keep a secret?' asked George. 'Nobody must know at home.'

'Well, go on, what's the secret?' asked Julian. 'You can tell us. We're not sneaks.'

'Timothy is my very greatest friend,' said George. 'I couldn't do without him. But Mother and Father don't like him, so I have to keep him in secret. I'll go and fetch him.'

She ran off up the cliff path. The others watched her go. They thought she was the most peculiar girl they had ever known.

'Who in the world can Timothy be?' wondered Julian. 'Some fisher-boy, I suppose, that George's parents don't approve of.'

The children lay back in the soft sand and waited. Soon they heard George's clear voice coming down from the cliff behind them.

'Come on, Timothy! Come on!'

They sat up and looked to see what Timothy was like. They saw no fisher-boy – but instead a big brown mongrel dog with an absurdly long tail and a big wide mouth that really seemed to grin! He was bounding all round George, mad with delight. She came running down to them.

'This is Timothy,' she said. 'Don't you think he is simply perfect?'

As a dog, Timothy was far from perfect. He was the wrong shape, his head was too big, his ears were too pricked, his tail was too long and it was quite impossible to say what kind of a dog he was supposed to be. But he was such a mad, friendly, clumsy, laughable creature that every one of the children adored him at once.

'Oh, you darling!' said Anne, and got a lick on the nose.

'I say – isn't he grand!' said Dick, and gave Timothy a friendly smack that made the dog bound madly all round him.

'I wish *I* had a dog like this,' said Julian, who really loved dogs, and had always wanted one of his own. 'Oh, George – he's fine. Aren't you proud of him?'

The little girl smiled, and her face altered at once, and became sunny and pretty. She sat down on the sand and her dog cuddled up to her, licking her wherever he could find a bare piece of skin.

'I love him awfully,' she said. 'I found him out on the moors when he was just a pup, a year ago, and I took him home. At first Mother liked him, but when he grew bigger he got terribly naughty.'

'What did he do?' asked Anne.

'Well, he's an awfully chewy kind of dog,' said George. 'He chewed up everything he could – a new rug Mother had bought – her nicest hat – Father's slippers – some of his papers, and things like that. And he barked too. I liked his bark, but Father didn't. He said it nearly drove him mad. He hit Timothy and that made me angry, so I was awfully rude to him.'

'Did you get told off?' said Anne. 'I wouldn't like to be rude to your father. He looks fierce.'

George looked out over the bay. Her face had gone sulky again. 'Well, it doesn't matter what punishment I got,' she said, 'but the worst part of all was when Father said I couldn't keep Timothy any more, and Mother backed Father up and said Tim must go. I cried for days – and I never do cry, you know, because boys don't and I like to be like a boy.'

'Boys do cry sometimes,' began Anne, looking at Dick, who had been a bit of a cry-baby three or four years back. Dick gave her a sharp nudge, and she said no more.

George looked at Anne.

'Boys don't cry,' she said, obstinately. 'Anyway, I've never seen one, and I always try not to cry myself. It's so babyish. But I just couldn't help it when Timothy had to go. He cried too.'

The children looked with great respect at Timothy. They had not known that a dog could cry before.

'Do you mean – he cried real tears?' asked Anne.

'No, not quite,' said George. 'He's too brave for that. He cried with his voice – howled and howled and looked so miserable that he nearly broke my heart. And then I knew I couldn't possibly part with him.'

'What happened then?' asked Julian.

'I went to Alf, a fisher-boy I know,' said George, 'and I asked him if he'd keep Tim for me, if I paid him all the pocket-money I get. He said he would, and so he does. That's why I never have any money to spend – it all has to go on Tim. He seems to eat an awful lot – don't you, Tim?'

'Woof!' said Tim, and rolled over on his back, all his shaggy legs in the air. Julian tickled him.

'How do you manage when you want any sweets or ice-creams?' said Anne, who spent most of her pocket-money on things of that sort.

'I don't manage,' said George. 'I go without, of course.'

This sounded awful to the other children, who loved ice-creams, chocolates and sweets, and had a good many of them. They stared at George.

'Well – I suppose the other children who play on the beach share their sweets and ices with you sometimes, don't they?' asked Julian.

'I don't let them,' said George. 'If I can never give them any myself it's not fair to take them. So I say no.'

The tinkle of an ice-cream man's bell was heard in the distance. Julian felt in his pocket. He jumped up and rushed off, jingling his money. In a few moments he was back again, carrying four fat chocolate ice-cream bars. He gave one to Dick, and one to Anne, and

then held out one to George. She looked at it longingly, but shook her head.

'No, thanks,' she said. 'You know what I just said. I
haven't any money to buy them, so I can't share mine
with you, and I can't take any from you. It's mean to
take from people if you can't give even a little back.'

'You can take from us,' said Julian, trying to put the
ice into George's brown hand. 'We're your cousins.'

'No, thanks,' said George again. 'Though I do think
it's nice of you.'

She looked at Julian out of her blue eyes and the boy
frowned as he tried to think of a way to make the
obstinate little girl take the ice. Then he smiled.

'Listen,' he said, 'you've got something we badly
want to share – in fact you've got a lot of things we'd
like to share, if only you'd let us. You share those with
us, and let us share things like ices with you. See?'

'What things have I got that you want to share?'
asked George, in surprise.

'You've got a dog,' said Julian, patting the big
brown mongrel. 'We'd love to share him with you,
he's such a darling. And you've got a lovely island.
We'd be simply thrilled if you'd share it sometimes.
And you've got a wreck. We'd like to look at it and
share it too. Ices and sweets aren't so good as those
things – but it would be nice to make a bargain and
share with each other.'

George looked at the brown eyes that gazed steadily
into hers. She couldn't help liking Julian. It wasn't her
nature to share anything. She had always been an only
child, a lonely, rather misunderstood little girl, fierce
and hot-tempered. She had never had any friends of
her own. Timothy looked up at Julian and saw that he
was offering something nice and chocolatey to

George. He jumped up and licked the boy with his friendly tongue.

'There you are, you see – Tim wants to be shared,' said Julian, with a laugh. 'It would be nice for him to have three new friends.'

'Yes – it would,' said George, giving in suddenly, and taking the chocolate bar. 'Thank you, Julian. I will share with you. But promise you'll never tell anyone at home that I'm still keeping Timothy?'

'Of course we'll promise,' said Julian. 'But I can't imagine that your father or mother would mind, so long as Tim doesn't live in their house. How's the ice? Is it nice?'

'Ooooh – the loveliest one I've ever tasted!' said George nibbling at it. 'It's so cold. I haven't had one this year. It's simply DELICIOUS!'

Timothy tried to nibble it too. George gave him a few crumbs at the end. Then she turned and smiled at the three children.

'You're nice,' she said. 'I'm glad you've come after all. Let's take a boat out this afternoon and row round the island to have a look at the wreck, shall we?'

'Rather!' said all three at once – and even Timothy wagged his tail as if he understood!

4   An exciting afternoon

They all had a bathe that morning, and the boys found that George was a much better swimmer than they were. She was very strong and very fast, and she could swim under water, too, holding her breath for ages.

'You're jolly good,' said Julian, admiringly. 'It's a pity Anne isn't a bit better. Anne, you'll have to practise your swimming strokes hard, or you'll never be able to swim out as far as we do.'

They were all very hungry at lunch-time. They went back up the cliff-path, hoping there would be lots to eat – and there was! Cold meat and salad, plum-pie and custard, and cheese afterwards. How the children tucked in!

'What are you going to do this afternoon?' asked George's mother.

'George is going to take us out in a boat to see the wreck on the other side of the island,' said Anne. Her aunt looked most surprised.

'*George* is going to take you!' she said. 'Why, George – what's come over you? You've never taken a single person before, though I've asked you to dozens of times!'

George said nothing, but went on eating her plum-pie. She hadn't said a word all through the meal. Her father had not appeared at the table, much to the children's relief.

'Well, George, I must say I'm pleased that you want to try and do what your father said,' began her mother again. But George shook her head.

'I'm not doing it because I've got to,' she said. 'I'm doing it because I want to. I wouldn't have taken anyone to see my wreck, not even the Queen of England, if I didn't like them.'

Her mother laughed. 'Well, it's good news that you like your cousins,' she said. 'I hope they like you!'

'Oh yes!' said Anne, eagerly, anxious to stick up for her strange cousin. 'We do like George – and we like Ti . . .'

She was just about to say that they liked Timothy too, when she got such a kick on her ankle that she cried out in pain and the tears came into her eyes. George glared at her.

'George! Why did you kick Anne like that when she was saying nice things about you?' cried her mother. 'Leave the table at once. I won't have such behaviour.'

George left the table without a word. She went out into the garden. She had just taken a piece of bread and cut herself some cheese. It was all left on her plate. The other three stared at it in distress. Anne was upset. How could she have been so silly as to forget she mustn't mention Tim?

'Oh, please call George back!' she said. 'She didn't mean to kick me. It was an accident.'

But her aunt was very angry with George. 'Finish your meal,' she said to the others. 'I expect George will go into a sulk now. Dear, dear, she *is* such a difficult child!'

The others didn't mind about George going into a sulk. What they did mind was that George might refuse to take them to see the wreck now!

They finished the meal in silence. Their aunt went to see if Uncle Quentin wanted any more pie. He was having his meal in the study by himself. As soon as she had gone out of the room, Anne picked up the bread and cheese from George's plate and went out into the garden.

The boys didn't scold her. They knew that Anne's tongue very often ran away with her – but she always tried to make up for it afterwards. They thought it was very brave of her to go and find George.

George was lying on her back under a big tree in the garden. Anne went up to her. 'I'm sorry I nearly made a mistake, George,' she said. 'Here's your bread and cheese. I've brought it for you. I promise I'll never forget not to mention Tim again.'

George sat up. 'I've a good mind not to take you to see the wreck,' she said. 'Stupid baby!'

Anne's heart sank. This was what she had feared. 'Well,' she said, 'you needn't take me, of course. But you might take the boys, George. After all, they didn't do anything silly. And anyway, you gave me an awful kick. Look at the bruise.'

George looked at it. Then she looked at Anne. 'But wouldn't you be miserable if I took Julian and Dick without you?' she asked.

'Of course,' said Anne. 'But I don't want to make them miss a treat, even if *I* have to.'

Then George did a surprising thing for her. She gave Anne a hug! Then she immediately looked most ashamed of herself, for she felt sure that no boy would have done that! And she always tried to act like a boy.

'It's all right,' she said, gruffly, taking the bread and cheese. 'You were nearly very silly – and I gave you a kick – so it's all square. Of course you can come this afternoon.'

Anne sped back to tell the boys that everything was all right – and in fifteen minutes' time four children ran down to the beach. By a boat was a brown-faced fisher-boy, about fourteen years old. He had Timothy with him.

'Boat's all ready, George,' he said with a grin. 'And Tim's ready, too.'

'Thanks,' said George, and told the others to get in. Timothy jumped in, too, his big tail wagging nineteen to the dozen. George pushed the boat off into the surf and then jumped in herself. She took the oars.

She rowed splendidly, and the boat shot along over the blue bay. It was a wonderful afternoon, and the children loved the movement of the boat over the water. Timothy stood at the prow and barked whenever a wave reared its head.

'He's funny on a wild day,' said George, pulling hard. 'He barks madly at the big waves, and gets so angry if they splash him. He's an awfully good swimmer.'

'Isn't it nice to have a dog with us?' said Anne, anxious to make up for her mistake. 'I do so like him.'

'Woof,' said Timothy, in his deep voice and turned round to lick Anne's ear.

'I'm sure he knew what I said,' said Anne in delight.

'Of course he did,' said George. 'He understands every single word.'

'I say – we're getting near to your island now,' said Julian, in excitement. 'It's bigger than I thought. And isn't the castle exciting?'

They drew near to the island, and the children saw

that there were sharp rocks all round about it. Unless anyone knew exactly the way to take, no boat or ship could possibly land on the shore of the rocky little island. In the very middle of it, on a low hill, rose the ruined castle. It had been built of big white stones. Broken archways, tumbledown towers, ruined walls – that was all that was left of a once beautiful castle, proud and strong. Now the jackdaws nested in it and the gulls sat on the topmost stones.

'It looks awfully mysterious,' said Julian. 'How I'd love to land there and have a look at the castle. Wouldn't it be fun to spend a night or two here!'

George stopped rowing. Her face lit up. 'I say!' she said, in delight. 'Do you know, I never thought how lovely that would be! To spend a night on my island! To be there all alone, the four of us. To get our own meals, and pretend we really lived there. Wouldn't it be grand?'

'Yes, rather,' said Dick, looking longingly at the island. 'Do you think – do you suppose your mother would let us?'

'I don't know,' said George. 'She might. You could ask her.'

'Can't we land there this afternoon?' asked Julian.

'No, not if you want to see the wreck,' said George. 'We've got to get back for tea today, and it will take all the time to row round to the other side of Kirrin Island and back.'

'Well – I'd like to see the wreck,' said Julian, torn between the island and the wreck. 'Here, let me take the oars for a bit, George. You can't do all the rowing.'

'I can,' said George. 'But I'd quite enjoy lying back in the boat for a change! Look – I'll just take you by this rocky bit – and then you can take the oars till we come

to another awkward piece. Honestly, the rocks around
this bay are simply dreadful!'

George and Julian changed places in the boat. Julian
rowed well, but not so strongly as George. The boat
sped along rocking smoothly. They went right round
the island, and saw the castle from the other side. It
looked more ruined on the side that faced the sea.

'The strong winds come from the open sea,' explained George. 'There's not really much left of it this
side, except piles of stones. But there's a good little
harbour in a little cove, for those who know how to
find it.'

George took the oars after a while, and rowed
steadily out a little beyond the island. Then she
stopped and looked back towards the shore.

'How do you know when you are over the wreck?'
asked Julian, puzzled. 'I should never know!'

'Well, do you see that church tower on the mainland?' asked George. 'And do you see the tip of that hill
over there? Well, when you get them exactly in line
with one another, between the two towers of the castle
on the island, you are pretty well over the wreck! I
found that out ages ago.'

The children saw that the tip of the far-off hill and
the church tower were practically in line, when they
looked at them between the two old towers of the
island castle. They looked eagerly down into the sea to
see if they could spy the wreck.

The water was perfectly clear and smooth. There
was hardly a wrinkle. Timothy looked down into it
too, his head on one side, his ears cocked, just as if he
knew what he was looking for! The children laughed
at him.

'We're not exactly over it,' said George, looking

down too. 'The water's so clear today that we should be able to see quite a long way down. Wait, I'll row a bit to the left.'

'Woof!' said Timothy, suddenly, and wagged his tail – and at the same moment the three children saw something deep down in the water!

'It's the wreck!' said Julian, almost falling out of the boat in his excitement. 'I can see a bit of broken mast. Look, Dick, look!'

All four children and the dog, too, gazed down earnestly into the clear water. After a little while they could make out the outlines of a dark hulk, out of which the broken mast stood.

'It's a bit on one side,' said Julian. 'Poor old ship. How it must hate lying there, gradually falling to pieces. George, I wish I could dive down and get a closer look at it.'

'Well, why don't you?' said George. 'You've got your swimming trunks on. I've often dived down. I'll come with you, if you like, if Dick can keep the boat round about here. There's a current that is trying to take it out to sea. Dick, you'll have to keep working a bit with this oar to keep the boat in one spot.'

The girl stripped off her jeans and jersey and Julian did the same. They both had on bathing costumes underneath. George took a beautiful header off the end of the boat, deep down into the water. The others watched her swimming strongly downwards, holding her breath.

After a bit she came up, almost bursting for breath. 'Well, I went almost down to the wreck,' she said. 'It's just the same as it always is – seaweedy and covered with limpets and things. I wish I could get right into the ship itself. But I never have enough breath for that. You go down now, Julian.'

So down Julian went – but he was not so good at swimming deep under water as George was, and he couldn't go down so far. He knew how to open his eyes under water, so he was able to take a good look at the deck of the wreck. It looked very forlorn and strange. Julian didn't really like it very much. It gave him rather a sad sort of feeling. He was glad to go to the top of the water again, and take deep breaths of air, and feel the warm sunshine on his shoulders.

He climbed into the boat. 'Most exciting,' he said. 'Golly, wouldn't I just love to see that wreck properly – you know – go down under the deck into the cabins and look around. And oh, suppose we could really find the boxes of gold!'

'That's impossible,' said George. 'I told you proper divers have already gone down and found nothing. What's the time? I say, we'll be late if we don't hurry back now!'

They did hurry back, and managed to be only about five minutes late for tea. Afterwards they went for a walk over the moors, with Timothy at their heels, and by the time that bedtime came they were all so sleepy that they could hardly keep their eyes open.

'Well, good-night, George,' said Anne, snuggling down into her bed. 'We've had a lovely day – thanks to you!'

'And *I've* had a lovely day, too,' said George, rather gruffly. 'Thanks to *you*. I'm glad you all came. We're going to have fun. And won't you love my castle and my little island!'

'Oooh, yes,' said Anne, and fell asleep to dream of

wrecks and castles and islands by the hundred. Oh, when would George take them to her little island?

5 A visit to the island

The children's aunt arranged a picnic for them the next day, and they all went off to a little cove not far off where they could bathe and paddle to their hearts' content. They had a wonderful day, but secretly Julian, Dick and Anne wished they could have visited George's island. They would rather have done that than anything!

George didn't want to go for the picnic, not because she disliked picnics, but because she couldn't take her dog. Her mother went with the children, and George had to pass a whole day without her beloved Timothy.

'Bad luck!' said Julian, who guessed what she was brooding about. 'I can't think why you don't tell your mother about old Tim. I'm sure she wouldn't mind you letting someone else keep him for you. I know my mother wouldn't mind.'

'I'm not going to tell anybody but you,' said George. 'I get into awful trouble at home always. I dare say it's my fault, but I get a bit tired of it. You see, Daddy doesn't make much money with the learned books he writes, and he's always wanting to give mother and me things he can't afford. So that makes him bad-tempered. He wants to send me away to a good school but he hasn't got the money. I'm glad. I don't want to go away to school. I like being here. I couldn't bear to part with Timothy.'

'You'd like boarding school,' said Anne. 'We all go. It's fun.'

'No, it isn't,' said George obstinately. 'It must be awful to be one of a crowd, and to have other girls all laughing and yelling round you. I should hate it.'

'No, you wouldn't,' said Anne. 'All that is great fun. It would be good for you, George, I should think.'

'If you start telling me what is good for me, I shall hate you,' said George, suddenly looking very fierce. 'Mother and Father are always saying that things are good for me – and they are always the things I don't like.'

'All right, all right,' said Julian, beginning to laugh. 'My goodness, how you do go up in smoke! Honestly, I believe anyone could light a cigarette from the sparks that fly from your eyes!'

That made George laugh, though she didn't want to. It was really impossible to sulk with good-tempered Julian.

They went off to bathe in the sea for the fifth time that day. Soon they were all splashing about happily, and George found time to help Anne to swim. The little girl hadn't got the right stroke, and George felt really proud when she had taught her.

'Oh, thanks,' said Anne, struggling along. 'I'll never be as good as you – but I'd like to be as good as the boys.'

As they were going home, George spoke to Julian. 'Could you say that you want to go and buy a stamp or something?' she said. 'Then I could go with you, and just have a peep at old Tim. He'll be wondering why I haven't taken him out today.'

'Right!' said Julian. 'I don't want stamps, but I *could*

do with an ice. Dick and Anne can go home with your
mother and carry the things. I'll just go and tell Aunt
Fanny.'

He ran up to his aunt. 'Do you mind if I go and buy
some ice-creams?' he asked. 'We haven't had one
today. I won't be long. Can George go with me?'

'I don't expect she will want to,' said his aunt. 'But
you can ask her.'

'George, come with me!' yelled Julian, setting off to
the little village at a great pace. George gave a sudden
grin and ran after him. She soon caught him up and
smiled gratefully at him.

'Thanks,' she said. 'You go and get the ice-creams,
and I'll have a look at Tim.'

They parted, Julian bought four ice-creams, and
turned to go home. He waited about for George, who
came running up after a few minutes. Her face was
glowing.

'He's all right,' she said. 'And you can't imagine
how pleased he was to see me! He nearly jumped over
my head! I say – another ice-cream for me. You really
are a sport, Julian. I'll have to share something
with you quickly. What about going to my island
tomorrow?'

'Golly!' said Julian, his eyes shining. 'That would be
marvellous. Will you really take us tomorrow? Come
on, let's tell the others!'

The four children sat in the garden eating their ices.
Julian told them what George had said. They all felt
excited. George was pleased. She had always felt quite
important before when she had haughtily refused to
take any of the other children to see Kirrin Island – but
it felt much nicer somehow to have consented to row
her cousins there.

'I used to think it was much, much nicer always to do things on my own,' she thought, as she sucked the last bits of her ice. 'But it's going to be fun doing things with Julian and the others.'

The children were sent to wash themselves and to get tidy before supper. They talked eagerly about the visit to the island next day. Their aunt heard them and smiled.

'Well, I really must say I'm pleased that George is going to share something with you,' she said. 'Would you like to take your dinner there, and spend the day? It's hardly worthwhile rowing all the way there and landing unless you are going to spend some hours there.'

'Oh, Aunt Fanny! It would be marvellous to take our dinner!' cried Anne.

George looked up. 'Are you coming too, Mother?' she asked.

'You don't sound at all as if you want me to,' said her mother, in a hurt tone. 'You looked cross yesterday, too, when you found I was coming. No – I shan't come tomorrow – but I'm sure your cousins must think you are an odd girl never to want your mother to go with you.'

George said nothing. She hardly ever did say a word when she was scolded. The other children said nothing too. They knew perfectly well that it wasn't that George didn't want her mother to go – it was just that she wanted Timothy with her!

'Anyway, I couldn't come,' went on Aunt Fanny. 'I've some gardening to do. You'll be quite safe with George. She can handle a boat like a man.'

The three children looked eagerly at the weather the next day when they got up. The sun was shining, and everything seemed splendid.

'Isn't it a marvellous day?' said Anne to George, as they dressed. 'I'm so looking forward to going to the island.'

'Well, honestly, I think really we oughtn't to go,' said George, unexpectedly.

'Oh, but why?' cried Anne, in dismay.

'I think there's going to be a storm or something,' said George, looking out to the south-west.

'But, George, why do you say that?' said Anne, impatiently. 'Look at the sun – and there's hardly a cloud in the sky!'

'The wind is wrong,' said George. 'And can't you see the little white tops of the waves out there by my island? That's always a bad sign.'

'Oh, George – it will be the biggest disappointment of our lives if we don't go today,' said Anne, who couldn't bear any disappointment, big or small. 'And besides,' she added, artfully, 'if we hang about the house, afraid of a storm, we shan't be able to have dear old Tim with us.'

'Yes, that's true,' said George. 'All right – we'll go. But mind – if a storm does come, you're not to be a baby. You're to try and enjoy it and not be frightened.'

'Well, I don't much like storms,' began Anne, but stopped when she saw George's scornful look. They went down to breakfast, and George asked her mother if they could take their dinner as they had planned.

'Yes,' said her mother. 'You and Anne can help to make the sandwiches. You boys can go into the garden and pick some ripe plums to take with you. Julian, you can go down to the village when you've done that and buy some bottles of lemonade or ginger-beer, whichever you like.'

'Ginger-pop for me, thanks!' said Julian, and everyone else said the same. They all felt very happy. It would be marvellous to visit the strange little island. George felt happy because she would be with Tim all day.

They set off at last, the food in two kit-bags. The first thing they did was to fetch Tim. He was tied up in the fisher-boy's backyard. The boy himself was there, and grinned at George.

''Morning, Master George,' he said. It seemed so funny to the other children to hear Georgina called 'Master George'! 'Tim's been barking his head off for you. I guess he knew you were coming for him today.'

'Of course he did,' said George, untying him. He at once went completely mad, and tore round and round the children, his tail down and his ears flat.

'He'd win any race if only he was a greyhound,' said Julian, admiringly. 'You can hardly see him for dust. Tim! Hey, Tim! Come and say "Good-morning".'

Tim leapt up and licked Julian's left ear as he passed on his whirlwind way. Then he sobered down and ran lovingly by George as they all made their way to the beach. He licked George's bare legs every now and again, and she pulled at his ears gently.

They got into the boat, and George pushed off. The fisher-boy waved to them. 'You won't be very long, will you?' he called. 'There's a storm blowing up. Bad one it'll be, too.'

'I know,' shouted back George. 'But maybe we'll get back before it begins. It's pretty far off yet.'

George rowed all the way to the island. Tim stood at each end of the boat in turn, barking when the waves reared up at him. The children watched the island coming closer and closer. It looked even more exciting than it had the other day.

'George, where are you going to land?' asked Julian. 'I simply can't imagine how you know your way in and out of these awful rocks. I'm afraid every moment we'll bump into them!'

'I'm going to land at the little cove I told you about the other day,' said George. 'There's only one way to it, but I know it very well. It's hidden away on the east side of the island.'

The girl cleverly worked her boat in and out of the rocks, and suddenly, as it rounded a low wall of sharp rocks, the children saw the cove she had spoken of. It was like a natural little harbour, and was a smooth inlet of water running up to a stretch of sand, sheltered between high rocks. The boat slid into the inlet, and at once stopped rocking, for here the water was like glass, and had hardly a wrinkle.

'I say – this is fine!' said Julian, his eyes shining with delight. George looked at him and her eyes shone too, as bright as the sea itself. It was the first time she had ever taken anyone to her precious island, and she was enjoying it.

They landed on the smooth yellow sand. 'We're really on the island!' said Anne, and she capered about, Tim joining her and looking as mad as she did. The others laughed. George pulled the boat high up on the sand.

'Why so far up?' said Julian, helping her. 'The tide's almost in, isn't it? Surely it won't come as high as this.'

'I told you I thought a storm was coming,' said George. 'If one does, the waves simply tear up this inlet and we don't want to lose our boat, do we?'

'Let's explore the island, let's explore the island!'

yelled Anne, who was now at the top of the little natural harbour, climbing up the rocks there. 'Oh do come on!'

They all followed her. It really was a most exciting place. Rabbits were everywhere! They scuttled about as the children appeared, but did not go into their holes.

'Aren't they awfully tame?' said Julian, in surprise.

'Well, nobody ever comes here but me,' said George, 'and I don't frighten them. Tim! Tim, if you go after the rabbits, I'll be furious.'

Tim turned big sorrowful eyes on to George. He and George agreed about every single thing except rabbits. To Tim rabbits were made for one thing – to chase! He never could understand why George wouldn't let him do this. But he held himself in and walked solemnly by the children, his eyes watching the lolloping rabbits longingly.

'I believe they would almost eat out of my hand,' said Julian.

But George shook her head.

'No, I've tried that with them,' she said. 'They won't. Look at those baby ones. Aren't they lovely?'

'Woof!' said Tim, agreeing, and he took a few steps towards them. George made a warning noise in her throat, and Tim walked back, his tail down.

'There's the castle!' said Julian. 'Shall we explore that now? I do want to.'

'Yes, we will,' said George. 'Look – that is where the entrance used to be – through that big broken archway.'

The children gazed at the enormous old archway, now half-broken down. Behind it were ruined stone steps leading towards the centre of the castle.

'It had strong walls all round it, with two towers,' said George. 'One tower is almost gone, as you can see, but the other is not so bad. The jackdaws build in that every year. They've almost filled it up with their sticks!'

As they came near to the better tower of the two the jackdaws circled round them with loud cries of 'Chack, chack, chack!' Tim leapt into the air as if he thought he could get them, but they only called mockingly to him.

'This is the centre of the castle,' said George, as they entered through a ruined doorway into what looked like a great yard, whose stone floor was now overgrown with grass and other weeds. 'Here is where the people used to live. You can see where the rooms were – look, there's one almost whole there. Go through that little door and you'll see it.'

They trooped through a doorway and found themselves in a dark, stone-walled, stone-roofed room, with a space at one end where a fireplace must have been. Two slit-like windows lit the room. It felt very strange and mysterious.

'What a pity it's all broken down,' said Julian, wandering out again. 'That room seems to be the only one quite whole. There are some others here – but all of them seem to have either no roof, or one or other of the walls gone. That room is the only livable one. Was there an upstairs to the castle, George?'

'Of course,' said George. 'But the steps that led up are gone. Look! You can see part of an upstairs room there, by the jackdaw tower. You can't get up to it, though, because I've tried. I nearly broke my neck trying to get up. The stones crumble away so.'

'Were there any dungeons?' asked Dick.

'I don't know,' said George. 'I expect so. But nobody could find them now – everywhere is so overgrown.'

It was indeed overgrown. Big blackberry bushes grew here and there, and a few gorse bushes forced their way into gaps and corners. The coarse green grass sprang everywhere, and pink thrift grew its cushions in holes and crannies.

'Well, I think it's a perfectly lovely place,' said Anne. 'Perfectly and absolutely lovely!'

'Do you really?' said George, pleased. 'I'm so glad. Look! We're right on the other side of the island now, facing the sea. Do you see those rocks, with those peculiar big birds sitting there?'

The children looked. They saw some rocks sticking up, with great black shining birds sitting on them in strange positions.

'They are cormorants,' said George. 'They've caught plenty of fish for their dinner, and they're sitting there digesting it. Hallo – they're all flying away. I wonder why?'

She soon knew – for, from the south-west there suddenly came an ominous rumble.

'Thunder!' said George. 'That's the storm. It's coming sooner than I thought!'

6   *What the storm did*

The four children stared out to sea. They had all been so interested in exploring the exciting old castle that not one of them had noticed the sudden change in the weather.

Another rumble came. It sounded like a big dog growling in the sky. Tim heard it and growled back, sounding like a small roll of thunder himself.

'My goodness, we're in for it now,' said George, half-alarmed. 'We can't get back in time, that's certain. It's blowing up at top speed. Did ever you see such a change in the sky?'

The sky had been blue when they started. Now it was overcast, and the clouds seemed to hang very low indeed. They scudded along as if someone was chasing them – and the wind howled round in such a mournful way that Anne felt quite frightened.

'It's beginning to rain,' said Julian, feeling an enormous drop spatter on his outstretched hand. 'We had better shelter, hadn't we, George? We shall get wet through.'

'Yes, we will in a minute,' said George. 'I say, just look at these big waves coming! My word, it really *is* going to be a storm. Golly – what a flash of lightning!'

The waves were certainly beginning to run very high indeed. It was amazing to see what a change had come over them. They swelled up, turned over as soon as they came to rocks, and then rushed up the beach of the island with a great roar.

'I think we'd better pull our boat up higher still,' said George suddenly. 'It's going to be a very bad storm indeed. Sometimes these sudden summer storms are worse than a winter one.'

She and Julian ran to the other side of the island where they had left the boat. It was a good thing they went, for great waves were already racing right up to it. The two children pulled the boat up almost to the top of the low cliff and George tied it to a stout gorse bush growing there.

By now the rain was simply pelting down, and George and Julian were soaked. 'I hope the others have been sensible enough to shelter in that room that has a roof and walls,' said George.

They were there all right, looking rather cold and scared. It was very dark there, for the only light came through the two slits of windows and the small doorway.

'Could we light a fire to make things a bit more cheerful?' said Julian, looking round. 'I wonder where we can find some nice dry sticks?'

Almost as if they were answering the question a small crowd of jackdaws cried out wildly as they circled in the storm. 'Chack, chack, chack!'

'Of course! There are plenty of sticks on the ground below the tower!' cried Julian. 'You know – where the jackdaws nest. They've dropped lots of sticks there.'

He dashed out into the rain and ran to the tower. He picked up an armful of sticks and ran back.

'Good,' said George. 'We'll be able to make a nice fire with those. Anyone got any paper to start it – or matches?'

'I've got some matches,' said Julian. 'But nobody's got paper.'

'Yes,' said Anne, suddenly. 'The sandwiches are wrapped in paper. Let's undo them, and then we can use the paper for the fire.'

'Good idea,' said George. So they undid the sandwiches, and put them neatly on a broken stone, rubbing it clean first. Then they built up a fire, with the paper underneath and the sticks arranged criss-cross on top.

It was fun when they lit the paper. It flared up and the sticks at once caught fire, for they were very old and dry. Soon there was a fine cracking fire going and the little ruined room was lit by dancing flames. It was very dark outside now, for the clouds hung almost low enough to touch the top of the castle tower! And how they raced by! The wind sent them off to the north-east, roaring behind them with a noise like the sea itself.

'I've never, never heard the sea making such an awful noise,' said Anne. 'Never! It really sounds as if it's shouting at the top of its voice.'

What with the howling of the wind and the crashing of the great waves all round the little island, the children could hardly hear themselves speak! They had to shout at one another.

'Let's have our dinner!' yelled Dick, who was feeling terribly hungry as usual. 'We can't do anything much while this storm lasts.'

'Yes, let's,' said Anne, looking longingly at the ham sandwiches. 'It will be fun to have a picnic round the fire in this dark old room. I wonder how long ago other people had a meal here? I wish I could see them.'

'Well, I don't,' said Dick, looking round half-scared

as if he expected to see the old-time people walk in to share their picnic. 'It's quite a strange enough day without wanting things like that to happen.'

They all felt better when they were eating the sandwiches and drinking the ginger-beer. The fire flared up as more and more sticks caught, and gave out quite a pleasant warmth, for now that the wind had got up so strongly, the day had become cold.

'We'll take it in turns to fetch sticks,' said George. But Anne didn't want to go alone. She was trying her best not to show that she was afraid of the storm – but it was more than she could do to go out of the cosy room into the rain and thunder by herself.

Tim didn't seem to like the storm either. He sat close by George, his ears cocked, and growled whenever the thunder rumbled. The children fed him with titbits and he ate them eagerly, for he was hungry too.

All the children had four biscuits each. 'I think I shall give all mine to Tim,' said George. 'I didn't bring him any of his own biscuits, and he does seem so hungry.'

'No, don't do that,' said Julian. 'We'll each give him a biscuit – that will be four for him – and we'll still have three left each. That will be plenty for us.'

'You are really nice,' said George. 'Tim, don't you think they are nice?'

Tim did. He licked everyone and made them laugh. Then he rolled over on his back and let Julian tickle him underneath.

The children fed the fire and finished their picnic. When it came to Julian's turn to get more sticks, he disappeared out of the room into the storm. He stood and looked around, the rain wetting his bare head.

The storm seemed to be right overhead now. The lightning flashed and the thunder crashed at the same moment. Julian was not a bit afraid of storms, but he couldn't help feeling rather over-awed at this one. It was so magnificent. The lightning tore the sky in half almost every minute, and the thunder crashed so loudly that it sounded almost as if mountains were falling down all around!

The sea's voice could be heard as soon as the thunder stopped – and that was magnificent to hear too. The spray flew so high into the air that it wetted Julian as he stood in the centre of the ruined castle.

'I really must see what the waves are like,' thought the boy. 'If the spray flies right over me here, they must be simply enormous!'

He made his way out of the castle and climbed up on to part of the ruined wall that had once run all round the castle. He stood up there, looking out to the open sea. And what a sight met his eyes!

The waves were like great walls of grey-green! They dashed over the rocks that lay all around the island, and spray flew from them, gleaming white in the stormy sky. They rolled up to the island and dashed them-selves against it with such terrific force that Julian could feel the wall beneath his feet tremble with the shock.

The boy looked out to sea, marvelling at the really great sight he saw. For half a moment he wondered if the sea might come right over the island itself! Then he knew that couldn't happen, for it would have hap-pened before. He stared at the great waves coming in – and then he saw something rather strange.

There was something else out on the sea by the rocks besides the waves – something dark, something big, something that seemed to lurch out of the waves and settle down again. What could it be?

'It can't be a ship,' said Julian to himself, his heart beginning to beat fast as he strained his eyes to see through the rain and the spray. 'And yet it looks more like a ship than anything else. I hope it isn't a ship. There wouldn't be anyone saved from it on this dreadful day!'

He stood and watched for a while. The dark shape heaved into sight again and then sank away once more. Julian decided to go and tell the others. He ran back to the firelit room.

'George! Dick! There's something strange out on the rocks beyond the island!' he shouted, at the top of his voice. 'It looks like a ship – and yet it can't possibly be. Come and see!'

The others stared at him in surprise, and jumped to their feet. George hurriedly flung some more sticks on the fire to keep it going, and then she and the others quickly followed Julian out into the rain.

The storm seemed to be passing over a little now. The rain was not pelting down quite so hard. The thunder was rolling a little farther off, and the lightning did not flash so often. Julian led the way to the wall on which he had climbed to watch the sea.

Everyone climbed up to gaze out to sea. They saw a great tumbled, heaving mass of grey-green water, with waves rearing up everywhere. Their tops broke over the rocks and they rushed up to the island as if they would gobble it whole. Anne slipped her arm through Julian's. She felt rather small and scared.

'You're all right, Anne,' said Julian, loudly. 'Now just watch – you'll see something strange in a minute.'

They all watched. At first they saw nothing, for the waves reared up so high that they hid everything a

little way out. Then suddenly George saw what Julian
meant.

'Gracious!' she shouted. 'It *is* a ship! Yes, it is! Is it
being wrecked? It's a big ship – not a sailing-boat, or
fishing-smack!'

'Oh, is anyone in it?' wailed Anne.

The four children watched and Tim began to bark as
he saw the strange dark shape lurching here and there
in the enormous waves. The sea was bringing the ship
nearer to shore.

'It will be dashed on to those rocks,' said Julian,
suddenly. 'Look – there it goes!'

As he spoke there came a tremendous crashing,
splintering sound, and the dark shape of the ship
settled down on to the sharp teeth of the dangerous
rocks on the south-west side of the island. It stayed
there, shifting only slightly as the big waves ran under
it and lifted it a little.

'She's stuck there,' said Julian. 'She won't move
now. The sea will soon be going down a bit, and then
the ship will find herself held by those rocks.'

As he spoke, a ray of pale sunshine came wavering
out between a gap in the thinning clouds. It was gone
almost at once. 'Good!' said Dick, looking upwards.
'The sun will be out again soon. We can warm
ourselves then and get dry – and maybe we can find out
what that poor ship is. Oh, Julian – I do so hope there
was nobody in it. I hope they've all taken to boats and
got safely to land.'

The clouds thinned out a little more. The wind
stopped roaring and dropped to a steady breeze. The
sun shone out again for a longer time, and the children
felt its welcome warmth. They all stared at the ship on
the rocks. The sun shone on it and lighted it up.

'There's something odd about it somehow,' said Julian, slowly. 'Something awfully odd. I've never seen a ship quite like it.'

George was staring at it with a strange look in her eyes. She turned to face the three children, and they were astonished to see the bright gleam in her blue eyes. The girl looked almost too excited to speak.

'What is it?' asked Julian, catching hold of her hand.

'Julian – oh, Julian – it's my wreck!' she cried, in a high excited voice. 'Don't you see what's happened? The storm has lifted the ship up from the bottom of the sea, and has lodged it on those rocks. It's my wreck!'

The others saw at once that she was right. It was the old wrecked ship! No wonder it looked peculiar. No wonder it looked so old and dark, and such a strange shape. It was the wreck, lifted high out of its sleeping-place and put on the rocks nearby.

'George! We shall be able to row out and get into the wreck now!' shouted Julian. 'We shall be able to explore it from end to end. We may find the boxes of gold. Oh, *George*!'

7 *Back to Kirrin Cottage*

The four children were so tremendously surprised and excited that for a minute or two they didn't say a word. They just stared at the dark hulk of the old wreck, imagining what they might find. Then Julian clutched George's arm and pressed it tightly.

'Isn't this wonderful?' he said. 'Oh, George, isn't it an extraordinary thing to happen?'

Still George said nothing, but stared at the wreck, all kinds of thoughts racing through her mind. Then she turned to Julian.

'If only the wreck is still mine now it's thrown up like this!' she said. 'I don't know if wrecks belong to the queen or anyone, like lost treasure does. But after all, the ship did belong to our family. Nobody bothered much about it when it was down under the sea – but do you suppose people will still let me have it for my own now it's thrown up?'

'Well, don't let's tell anyone!' said Dick.

'Don't be silly,' said George. 'One of the fishermen is sure to see it when his ship goes slipping out of the bay. The news will soon be out.'

'Well, then, we'd better explore it thoroughly ourselves before anyone else does!' said Dick, eagerly. 'No one knows about it yet. Only us. Can't we explore it as soon as the waves go down a bit?'

'We can't wade out to the rocks, if that's what you

mean,' said George. 'We might get there by boat – but we couldn't possibly risk it now, while the waves are so big. They won't go down today, that's certain. The wind is still too strong.'

'Well, what about tomorrow morning. early?' said Julian. 'Before anyone has got to know about it? I bet if only *we* can get into the ship first, we can find anything there is to find!'

'Yes, I expect we could,' said George. 'I told you divers had been down and explored the ship as thoroughly as they could – but of course it is difficult to do that properly under water. We might find something they've missed. Oh, this is like a dream. I can't believe it's true that my old wreck has come up from the bottom of the sea like that!'

The sun was now properly out, and the children's wet clothes dried in its hot rays. They steamed in the sun, and even Tim's coat sent up a mist too. He didn't seem to like the wreck at all, and growled deeply at it.

'You are funny, Tim,' said George, patting him. 'It won't hurt you! What do you think it is?'

'He probably thinks it's a whale,' said Anne with a laugh. 'Oh, George – this is the most exciting day of my life! Oh, can't we possibly take the boat and see if we can get to the wreck?'

'No, we can't,' said George. 'I only wish we could. But it's quite impossible, Anne. For one thing, I don't think the wreck has quite settled down on the rocks yet, and maybe it won't till the tide has gone down. I can see it lifting a little still when an extra big wave comes. It would be dangerous to go into it yet. And for another thing I don't want my boat smashed to bits on the rocks, and us thrown into that wild water! That's what would happen. We must wait till tomorrow. It's a good idea to come early. I expect lots of grown-ups will think it's their business to explore it.'

The children watched the old wreck for a little time longer and then went all round the island again. It was certainly not very large, but it really was exciting, with its rocky little coast, its quiet inlet where their boat was, the ruined castle, the circling jackdaws, and the scampering rabbits everywhere.

'I do love it,' said Anne. 'I really do. It's just small enough to *feel* like an island. Most islands are too big to feel like islands. I mean, Britain is an island, but nobody living on it could possibly know it unless they were told. Now this island really *feels* like one because wherever you are you can see to the other side of it. I love it.'

George felt very happy. She had often been on her island before, but always alone except for Tim. She had always vowed that she never, never would take anyone there, because it would spoil her island for her. But it hadn't been spoilt. It had made it much nicer. For the first time George began to understand that sharing pleasures doubles their joy.

'We'll wait till the waves go down a bit then we'll go back home,' she said. 'I rather think there's some more rain coming, and we'll only get soaked through. We shan't be back till tea-time as it is, because we'll have a long pull against the out-going tide.'

All the children felt a little tired after the excitements of the morning. They said very little as they rowed home. Everyone took turns at rowing except Anne, who was not strong enough with the oars to row against the tide. They looked back at the island as they left it. They couldn't see the wreck because that was on the opposite side, facing the open sea.

'It's just as well it's there,' said Julian. 'No one can
see it yet. Only when a boat goes out to fish will it be
seen. And we shall be there as early as any boat goes
out! I vote we get up at dawn.'

'Well, that's pretty early,' said George. 'Can you
wake up? I'm often out at dawn, but you're not used to
it.'

'Of course we can wake up,' said Julian. 'Well – here
we are back at the beach again – and I'm jolly glad. My
arms are awfully tired and I'm so hungry I could eat a
whole larderful of things.'

'Woof,' said Tim, quite agreeing.

'I'll have to take Tim to Alf,' said George, jumping
out of the boat. 'You get the boat in, Julian. I'll join
you in a few minutes.'

It wasn't long before all four were sitting down to a
good tea. Aunt Fanny had baked new scones for them,
and had made a ginger cake with black treacle. It was
dark brown and sticky to eat. The children finished it
all up and said it was the nicest they had ever tasted.

'Did you have an exciting day?' asked their aunt.

'Oh yes!' said Anne, eagerly. 'The storm was grand.
It threw up . . .'

Julian and Dick both kicked her under the table.
George couldn't reach her or she would most certainly
have kicked her too. Anne stared at the boys angrily,
with tears in her eyes.

'Now what's the matter?' asked Aunt Fanny. 'Did
somebody kick you, Anne? Well, really, this kicking
under the table has got to stop. Poor Anne will be
covered with bruises. What did the sea throw up,
dear?'

'It threw up the most enormous waves,' said Anne,
looking defiantly at the others. She knew they had

thought she was going to say that the sea had thrown up the wreck – but they were wrong! They had kicked her for nothing!

'Sorry for kicking you, Anne,' said Julian. 'My foot sort of slipped.'

'So did mine,' said Dick. 'Yes, Aunt Fanny, it was a magnificent sight on the island. The waves raced up that little inlet, and we had to take our boat almost up to the top of the low cliff there.'

'I wasn't really afraid of the storm,' said Anne. 'In fact, I wasn't really as afraid of it as Ti . . .'

Everyone knew perfectly well that Anne was going to mention Timothy, and they all interrupted her at once, speaking very loudly. Julian managed to get a kick in again.

'Ooooh!' said Anne.

'The rabbits were so tame,' said Julian, loudly.

'We watched the cormorants,' said Dick and George joined in too, talking at the same time.

'The jackdaws made such a noise, they said "Chack, chack, chack," all the time.'

'Well, really, you sound like jackdaws yourselves, talking all at once like this!' said Aunt Fanny, with a laugh. 'Now, have you all finished? Very well, then, go and wash your sticky hands – yes, George, I know they're sticky, because *I* made that gingerbread, and you've had three slices! Then you had better go and play quietly in the other room, because it's raining, and you can't go out. But don't disturb your father, George. He's very busy.'

The children went to wash. 'Idiot!' said Julian to Anne. 'Nearly gave us away twice!'

'I didn't mean what you thought I meant the first time!' began Anne indignantly.

George interrupted her.

'I'd rather you gave the secret of the wreck away than my secret about Tim,' she said. 'I do think you've got a careless tongue.'

'Yes, I have,' said Anne, sorrowfully. 'I think I'd better not talk at meal-times any more. I love Tim so much I just can't seem to help wanting to talk about him.'

They all went to play in the other room. Julian turned a table upside down with a crash. 'We'll play at wrecks,' he said. 'This is the wreck. Now we're going to explore it.'

The door flew open and an angry, frowning face looked in. It was George's father!

'What was that noise?' he said. 'George! Did you overturn that table?'

'I did,' said Julian. 'I'm sorry. I quite forgot you were working.'

'Any more noise like that and I shall keep you all in tomorrow!' said his uncle Quentin. 'Georgina, keep your cousins quiet.'

The door shut and Uncle Quentin went out. The children looked at one another.

'Your father's awfully fierce, isn't he?' said Julian. 'I'm sorry I made that row. I didn't think.'

'We'd better do something really quiet,' said George. 'Or he'll keep his word – and we'll find ourselves inside tomorrow just when we want to explore the wreck.'

This was a terrible thought. Anne went to get one of her dolls to play with. She had managed to bring quite a number after all. Julian fetched a book. George took up a beautiful little boat she was carving out of a piece of wood. Dick lay back on a chair and thought of the exciting wreck. The rain poured down steadily, and everyone hoped it would have stopped by the morning.

'We'll have to be up most awfully early,' said Dick, yawning. 'What about going to bed in good time tonight? I'm tired with all that rowing.'

In the ordinary way none of the children liked going to bed early – but with such an exciting thing to look forward to, early bed seemed different that night.

'It will make the time go quickly,' said Anne, putting down her doll. 'Shall we go now?'

'Whatever do you suppose Mother would say if we went just after tea?' said George. 'She'd think we were all ill. No, let's go after supper. We'll just say we're tired with rowing – which is perfectly true – and we'll get a good night's sleep, and be ready for our adventure tomorrow morning. And it *is* an adventure, you know. It isn't many people that have the chance of exploring an old, old wreck like that, which has always been at the bottom of the sea!'

So, by eight o'clock, all the children were in bed, rather to Aunt Fanny's surprise. Anne fell asleep at once. Julian and Dick were not long – but George lay awake for some time, thinking of her island, her wreck – and, of course, her beloved dog!

'I must take Tim too,' she thought, as she fell asleep. 'We can't leave old Tim out of this. He shall share in the adventure too!'

8 Exploring the wreck

Julian woke first the next morning. He awoke just as the sun was slipping over the horizon in the east, and filling the sky with gold. Julian stared at the ceiling for a moment, and then, in a rush, he remembered all that had happened the day before. He sat up straight in bed and whispered as loudly as he could.

'Dick! Wake up! We're going to see the wreck! Do wake up!'

Dick woke and grinned at Julian. A feeling of happiness crept over him. They were going on an adventure. He leapt out of bed and ran quietly to the girls' room. He opened the door. Both the girls were fast asleep, Anne curled up like a dormouse under the sheet.

Dick shook George and then dug Anne in the back. They awoke and sat up. 'Buck up!' whispered Dick. 'The sun is just rising. We'll have to hurry.'

George's blue eyes shone as she dressed. Anne skipped about quietly, finding her few clothes – just a bathing suit, jeans and jersey – and rubber shoes for her feet. It wasn't many minutes before they were all ready.

'Now, not a creak on the stairs – not a cough or a giggle!' warned Julian, as they stood together on the landing. Anne was a dreadful giggler, and had often given secret plans away by her sudden explosive choke. But this time the little girl was as solemn as the others, and as careful. They crept down the stairs and undid the little front door. Not a sound was made. They shut the door quietly and made their way down the garden path to the gate. The gate always creaked, so they climbed over it instead of opening it.

The sun was now shining brightly, though it was still low in the eastern sky. It felt warm already. The sky was so beautifully blue that Anne couldn't help feeling it had been freshly washed! 'It looks just as if it had come back from the laundry,' she told the others.

They squealed with laughter at her. She did say odd things at times. But they knew what she meant. The day had a lovely new feeling about it – the clouds were so pink in the bright blue sky, and the sea looked so smooth and fresh. It was impossible to imagine that it had been so rough the day before.

George got her boat. Then she went to get Tim, while the boys hauled the boat down to the sea. Alf, the fisher-boy, was surprised to see George so early. He was about to go with his father, fishing. He grinned at George.

'You going fishing, too?' he said to her. 'My, wasn't that a storm yesterday! I thought you'd be caught in it.'

'We were,' said George. 'Come on, Tim! Come on!'

Tim was very pleased to see George so early. He capered round her as she ran back to the others, almost tripping her up as she went. He leapt into the boat as soon as he saw it, and stood at the stern, his red tongue out, his tail wagging violently.

'I wonder his tail keeps on,' said Anne, looking at it. 'One day, Timothy, you'll wag it right off.'

They set off to the island. It was easy to row now, because the sea was so calm. They came to the island, and rowed around it to the other side.

And there was the wreck, piled high on some sharp rocks! It had settled down now and did not stir as waves slid under it. It lay a little to one side, and the broken mast, now shorter than before, stuck out at an angle.

'There she is,' said Julian, in excitement. 'Poor old wreck! I guess she's a bit more battered now. What a noise she made when she went crashing on to those rocks yesterday!'

'How do we get to her?' asked Anne, looking at the mass of ugly, sharp rocks all around. But George was not at all dismayed. She knew almost every inch of the coast around her little island. She pulled steadily at the oars and soon came near to the rocks in which the great wreck rested.

The children looked at the wreck from their boat. It was big, much bigger than they had imagined when they had peered at it from the top of the water. It was encrusted with shellfish of some kind, and strands of brown and green seaweed hung down. It smelt funny. It had great holes in its sides, showing where it had battered against rocks. There were holes in the deck too. Altogether, it looked a sad and forlorn old ship – but to the four children it was the most exciting thing in the whole world.

They rowed to the rocks on which the wreck lay. The tide washed over them. George took a look round.

'We'll tie our boat up to the wreck itself,' she said. 'And we'll get on to the deck quite easily by climbing up the side. Look, Julian! – throw this loop of rope over that broken bit of wood there, sticking out from the side.'

Julian did as he was told. The rope tightened and the boat was held in position. Then George clambered up the side of the wreck like a monkey. She was a marvel at climbing. Julian and Dick followed her, but Anne had to be helped up. Soon all four were standing on the slanting deck. It was slippery with seaweed, and the smell was very strong indeed. Anne didn't like it.

'Well, this was the deck,' said George, 'and that's where the men got up and down.' She pointed to a large hole. They went to it and looked down. The remains of an iron ladder were still there. George looked at it.

'I think it's still strong enough to hold us,' she said. 'I'll go first. Anyone got a torch? It looks pretty dark down there.'

Julian had a torch. He handed it to George. The children became rather quiet. It was mysterious some-how to look down into the dark inside of the big ship. What would they find? George switched on the torch and then swung herself down the ladder. The others followed.

The light from the torch showed a very strange sight. The under-parts of the ship were low-ceilinged, made of thick oak. The children had to bend their heads to get about. It seemed as if there were places that might have been cabins, though it was difficult to tell now, for everything was so battered, sea-drenched and seaweedy. The smell was really horrid, though it was mostly of drying seaweed.

The children slipped about on the seaweed as they went round the inside of the ship. It didn't seem so big inside after all. There was a big hold under the cabins, which the children saw by the light of their torch.

'That's where the boxes of gold would have been kept, I expect,' said Julian. But there was nothing in the hold except water and fish! The children couldn't go down because the water was too deep. One or two barrels floated in the water, but they had burst open and were quite empty.

'I expect they were water-barrels, or barrels of pork or biscuit,' said George. 'Let's go round the other part of the ship again – where the cabins are. Isn't it strange to see bunks there that sailors have slept in? – and look at that old wooden chair. Fancy it still being here after all these years! Look at the things on those hooks too – they are all rusty now, and covered with seaweedy stuff – but they must have been the cook's pans and dishes!'

It was a very weird trip round the old wreck. The children were all on the look-out for boxes which might contain bars of gold – but there didn't seem to be one single box of any kind anywhere!

They came to a rather bigger cabin than the others. It had a bunk in one corner, in which a large crab rested. An old bit of furniture looking rather like a table with two legs, all encrusted with greyish shells, lay against the bunk. Wooden shelves, festooned with grey-green seaweed, hung crookedly on the walls of the cabin.

'This must have been the captain's own cabin,' said Julian. 'It's the biggest one. Look, what's that in the corner?'

'An old cup!' said Anne, picking it up. 'And here's half of a saucer. I expect the captain was sitting here having a cup of tea when the ship went down.'

This made the children feel rather uneasy. It was

dark and smelly in the little cabin, and the floor was
wet and slippery to their feet. George began to feel that
her wreck was really more pleasant sunk under the
water than raised above it!

'Let's go,' she said, with a shiver. 'I don't like it
much. It *is* exciting, I know – but it's a bit frightening
too.'

They turned to go. Julian flashed his torch round the
little cabin for the last time. He was about to switch it
off and follow the others up to the deck above when he
caught sight of something that made him stop. He
flashed his torch on to it, and then called to the others.

'I say! Wait a bit. There's a cupboard here in the
wall. Let's see if there's anything in it!'

The others turned back and looked. They saw what
looked like a small cupboard set in level with the wall
of the cabin. What had caught Julian's eye was the
keyhole. There was no key there, though.

'There just *might* be something inside,' said Julian.
He tried to prise open the wooden door with his
fingers, but it wouldn't move. 'It's locked,' he said.
'Of course it would be!'

'I expect the lock is rotten by now,' said George, and
she tried too. Then she took out her big strong pocket-
knife and inserted it between the cupboard door and
the cabin-wall. She forced back the blade – and the lock
of the cupboard suddenly snapped! As she had said, it
was quite rotten. The door swung open, and the
children saw a shelf inside with a few curious things on
it.

There was a wooden box, swollen with the wet
sea-water in which it had lain for years. There were
two or three things that looked like old, pulpy books.
There was some sort of glass drinking-vessel, cracked

in half – and two or three funny objects so spoilt by sea-water that no one could possibly say what they were.

'Nothing very interesting – except the box,' said Julian, and he picked it up. 'Anyway, I expect that whatever is inside is ruined. But we may as well try and open it.'

He and George tried their best to force the lock of the old wooden box. On the top of it were stamped initials – H. J. K.

'I expect those were the captain's initials,' said Dick.

'No, they were the initials of my great-great-great-grandfather!' said George, her eyes shining suddenly. 'I've heard all about him. His name was Henry John Kirrin. This was his ship, you know. This must have been his very private box in which he kept his old papers or diaries. Oh – we simply *must* open it!'

But it was quite impossible to force the lid up with the tools they had there. They soon gave it up, and Julian picked up the box to carry it to the boat.

'We'll open it at home,' he said, his voice sounding rather excited. 'We'll get a hammer or something, and get it open somehow. Oh, George – this really is a find!'

They all of them felt that they really had something mysterious in their possession. Was there anything inside the box – and if so, what would it be? They longed to get home and open it!

They went up on deck, climbing the old iron ladder. As soon as they got there they saw that others besides themselves had discovered that the wreck had been thrown up from the bottom of the sea!

'Golly! Half the fishing-smacks of the bay have discovered it!' cried Julian, looking round at the fishing-boats that had come as near as they dared to the wreck. The fishermen were looking at the wreck in wonder. When they saw the children on board they halloo-ed loudly.

'Ahoy there! What's that ship?'

'It's the old wreck!' yelled back Julian. 'She was thrown up yesterday in the storm!'

'Don't say any more,' said George, frowning. 'It's *my* wreck. I don't want sightseers on it!'

So no more was said, and the four children got into their boat and rowed home as fast as they could. It was past their breakfast-time. They might get a good scolding. They might even be sent to bed by George's fierce father – but what did they care? They had explored the wreck – and had come away with a box which *might* contain – well, if not bars of gold, one *small* bar, perhaps!

They did get a scolding. They had to go without half their breakfast, too, because Uncle Quentin said that children who came in so late didn't deserve hot bacon and eggs – only toast and marmalade. It was very sad.

They hid the box under the bed in the boys' room. Tim had been left with the fisher-boy – or rather, had been tied up in his back yard, for Alf had gone out fishing, and was even now gazing from his father's boat at the strange wreck.

'We can make a bit of money taking sightseers out to this wreck,' said Alf. And before the day was out scores of interested people had seen the old wreck from the decks of motor-boats and fishing-smacks.

George was furious about it. But she couldn't do anything. After all, as Julian said, anybody could have a look!

9 The box from the wreck

The first thing that the children did after breakfast was to fetch the precious box and take it out to the tool-shed in the garden. They were simply longing to force it open. All of them secretly felt certain that it would hold treasure of some sort.

Julian looked round for a tool. He found a chisel and decided that would be just the thing to force the box open. He tried, but the tool slipped and jabbed his fingers. Then he tried other things, but the box obstinately refused to open. The children stared at it crossly.

'I know what to do,' said Anne at last. 'Let's take it to the top of the house and throw it down to the ground. It would burst open then, I expect.'

The others thought over the idea. 'It might be worth trying,' said Julian. 'The only thing is it might break or spoil anything inside the box.'

But there didn't seem any other way to open the box, so Julian carried it up to the top of the house. He went to the attic and opened the window there. The others were down below, waiting. Julian hurled the box out of the window as violently as he could. It flew through the air and landed with a terrific crash on the crazy paving below.

At once the french window there opened and their

Uncle Quentin came out like a bullet from a gun.

'Whatever are you doing?' he cried. 'Surely you aren't throwing things at each other out of the window? What's this on the ground?'

The children looked at the box. It had burst open, and lay on the ground, showing a tin lining that was waterproof. Whatever was in the box would not be spoilt! It would be quite dry!

Dick ran to pick it up.

'I said, what's this on the ground?' shouted his uncle and moved towards him.

'It's – it's something that belongs to us,' said Dick, going red.

'Well, I shall take it away from you,' said his uncle. 'Disturbing me like this! Give it to me. Where did you get it?'

Nobody answered. Uncle Quentin frowned till his glasses nearly fell off. 'Where did you get it?' he barked, glaring at poor Anne, who was nearest.

'Out of the wreck,' stammered the little girl, scared.

'Out of the *wreck*!' said her uncle, in surprise. 'The old wreck that was thrown up yesterday? I heard about that. Do you mean to say you've been in it?'

'Yes,' said Dick. Julian joined them at that moment, looking worried. It would be too awful if his uncle took the box just as they got it open. But that was exactly what he did do!

'Well, this box may contain something important,' he said, and he took it from Dick's hands. 'You've no right to go prying about in that old wreck. You might take something that mattered.'

'Well, it's my wreck,' said George, in a defiant tone. 'Please, Father, let us have the box. We'd just got it opened. We thought it might hold – a gold bar – or something like that!'

'A gold bar!' said her father, with a snort. 'What a baby you are! This small box would never hold a thing like that! It's much more likely to contain particulars of what happened to the bars! I have always thought that the gold was safely delivered somewhere – and that the ship, empty of its valuable cargo, got wrecked as it left the bay!'

'Oh, Father – please, please let us have our box,' begged George, almost in tears. She suddenly felt certain that it did contain papers that might tell them what had happened to the gold. But without another word her father turned and went into the house, carrying the box, burst open and cracked, its tin lining showing through under his arm.

Anne burst into tears. 'Don't blame me for telling him we got it from the wreck,' she sobbed. 'Please don't. He glared at me so. I just had to tell him.'

'All right, Baby,' said Julian, putting his arm round Anne. He looked furious. He thought it was very unfair of his uncle to take the box like that. 'Listen – I'm not going to stand this. We'll get hold of that box somehow and look into it. I'm sure your father won't bother himself with it, George – he'll start writing his book again and forget all about it. I'll wait my chance and slip into his study and get it, even if it means a telling off if I'm discovered!'

'Good!' said George. 'We'll all keep a watch and see if Father goes out.'

So they took it in turns to keep watch, but most annoyingly their Uncle Quentin remained in his study all the morning. Aunt Fanny was surprised to see one or two children always about the garden that day, instead of down on the beach.

'Why don't you all keep together and bathe or do something?' she said. 'Have you quarrelled with one another?'

'No,' said Dick. 'Of course not.' But he didn't say why they were in the garden!

'Doesn't your father *ever* go out?' he said to George, when it was her turn to keep watch. 'I don't think he leads a very healthy life.'

'Scientists never do,' said George, as if she knew all about them. 'But I tell you what – he may go to sleep this afternoon! He sometimes does!'

Julian was left behind in the garden that afternoon. He sat down under a tree and opened a book. Soon he heard a curious noise that made him look up. He knew at once what it was!

'That's Uncle Quentin snoring!' he said in excitement. 'It is! Oh – I wonder if I could possibly creep in at the french window and get our box!'

He stole to the windows and looked in. One was a little way open and Julian opened it a little more. He saw his uncle lying back in a comfortable armchair, his mouth a little open, his eyes closed, fast asleep! Every time he took a breath, he snored.

'Well, he really does look sound asleep,' thought the boy. 'And there's the box, just behind him, on that table. I'll risk it. I bet I'll get an awful telling off if I'm caught, but I can't help that!'

He stole in. His uncle still snored. He tiptoed by him to the table behind his uncle's chair. He took hold of the box.

And then a bit of the broken wood of the box fell to the floor with a thud! His uncle stirred in his chair and opened his eyes. Quick as lightning the boy crouched down behind his uncle's chair, hardly breathing.

'What's that?' he heard his uncle say. Julian didn't move. Then his uncle settled down again and shut his eyes. Soon there was the sound of his rhythmic snoring!

'Hurrah!' thought Julian. 'He's off again!'

Quietly he stood up, holding the box. On tiptoe he crept to the french window. He slipped out and ran softly down the garden path. He didn't think of hiding the box. All he wanted to do was to get to the other children and show them what he had done!

He ran to the beach where the others were lying in the sun. 'Hi!' he yelled. 'Hi! I've got it! I've got it!'

They all sat up with a jerk, thrilled to see the box in Julian's arms. They forgot all about the other people on the beach. Julian dropped down on the sand and grinned.

'Your father went to sleep,' he said to George. 'Tim, don't lick me like that! And George, I went in – and a bit of the box dropped on the floor – and it woke him up!'

'Golly!' said George. 'What happened?'

'I crouched down behind his chair till he went to sleep again,' said Julian. 'Then I fled. Now – let's see what's in here. I don't believe your father's even tried to see!'

He hadn't. The tin lining was intact. It had rusted with the years of lying in the wet, and the lid was so tightly fitted down that it was almost impossible to move it.

But once George began to work at it with her pocket-knife, scraping away the rust, it began to loosen – and in about a quarter of an hour it came off!

The children bent eagerly over it. Inside lay some

old papers and a book of some kind with a black cover. Nothing else at all. No bar of gold. No treasure. Everyone felt a little bit disappointed.

'It's all quite dry,' said Julian, surprised. 'Not a bit damp. The tin lining kept everything perfect.'

He picked up the book and opened it. 'It's a diary your great-great-great-grandfather kept of the ship's voyages,' he said. 'I can hardly read the writing. It's so small and funny.'

George picked up one of the papers. It was made of thick parchment, quite yellow with age. She spread it out on the sand and looked at it. The others glanced at it too, but they couldn't make out what it was at all. It seemed to be a kind of map.

'Perhaps it's a map of some place he had to go to,' said Julian. But suddenly George's hands began to shake as she held the map, and her eyes gleamed brilliantly as she looked up at the others. She opened her mouth but didn't speak.

'What's the matter?' said Julian, curiously. 'What's up? Have you lost your tongue?'

George shook her head and then began to speak with a rush. 'Julian! Do you know what this is? It's a map of my old castle – of Kirrin Castle – when it wasn't a ruin. And it shows the dungeons! And look – just look what's written in this corner of the dungeons!'

She put a trembling finger on one part of the map. The others leaned over to see what it was – and, printed in old-fashioned letters was a curious word.

INGOTS

'Ingots!' said Anne, puzzled. 'What does that mean? I've never heard that word before.'

But the two boys had. 'Ingots!' cried Dick. 'Why – that must be the bars of gold. They were called ingots.'

'Most bars of metal are called ingots,' said Julian, going red with excitement. 'But as we know there is gold missing from that ship, then it really looks as if ingots here meant bars of gold. Oh golly! To think they may still be hidden somewhere under Kirrin Castle. George! George! Isn't it terribly, awfully exciting?'

George nodded. She was trembling all over with excitement. 'If only we could find it!' she whispered. 'If only we could!'

'We'll have a jolly good hunt for it,' said Julian. 'It will be awfully difficult because the castle is in ruins now, and so overgrown. But somehow or other we'll find those ingots. What a lovely word. Ingots! Ingots! Ingots!'

It sounded somehow more exciting than the word gold. Nobody spoke about gold any more. They talked about the ingots. Tim couldn't make out what the excitement was at all. He wagged his tail and tried hard to lick first one and then another of the children, but for once not one of them paid any attention to him! He simply couldn't understand it, and after a while he went and sat down by himself with his back to the children, and his ears down.

'Oh, do look at poor Timothy!' said George. 'He can't understand your excitement. Tim! Tim, darling, it's all right, you're not in disgrace or anything. Oh, Tim, we've got the most wonderful secret in the whole world.'

Tim bounded up, his tail wagging, pleased to be taken notice of once more. He put his big paw on the precious map, and the four children shouted at him at once.

'Golly! We can't have that torn!' said Julian. Then he looked at the others and frowned. 'What are we going to do about the box?' he said. 'I mean – George's father will be sure to miss it, won't he? We'll have to give it back.'

'Well, can't we take out the map and keep it?' said Dick. 'He won't know it was there if he hasn't looked in the box. And it's pretty certain he hasn't. The other things don't matter much – they are only that old diary and a few letters.'

'To be on the safe side, let's take a copy of the map,' said Julian. 'Then we can put the real map back and replace the box.'

They all voted that a very good idea. They went back to Kirrin Cottage and traced out the map carefully. They did it in the tool-shed because they didn't want anyone to see them. It was a strange map. It was in three parts.

'This part shows the dungeons under the castle,' said Julian. 'And this shows a plan of the ground floor of the castle – and this shows the top part. My word, it was a fine place in those days! The dungeons run all under the castle. I bet they were pretty awful places. I wonder how people got down to them.'

'We'll have to study the map a bit more and see,' said George. 'It all looks rather muddled to us at present – but once we take the map over to the castle and study it there, we may be able to make out how to get down to the hidden dungeons. Ooooh! I don't expect any children ever had such an adventure as this.'

Julian put the traced map carefully into his jeans pocket. He didn't mean it to leave him. It was very

precious. Then he put the real map back into the box
and looked towards the house. 'What about putting it
back now?' he said. 'Maybe your father is still asleep,
George.'

But he wasn't. He was awake. Luckily he hadn't
missed the box! He came into the dining-room to have
tea with the family, and Julian took his chance. He
muttered an excuse, slipped away from the table, and
replaced the box on the table behind his uncle's chair!

He winked at the others when he came back. They
felt relieved. They were all scared of Uncle Quentin,
and were not at all anxious to be in his bad books.
Anne didn't say one word during the whole of the
meal. She was so terribly afraid she might give something away, either about Tim or the box. The others
spoke very little too. While they were at tea the
telephone rang and Aunt Fanny went to answer it.

She soon came back. 'It's for you, Quentin,' she
said. 'Apparently the old wreck has caused quite a lot
of excitement, and there are men from a London paper
who want to ask you questions about it.'

'Tell them I'll see them at six,' said Uncle Quentin.
The children looked at one another in alarm. They
hoped that their uncle wouldn't show the box to the
newspaper men. Then the secret of the hidden gold
might come out!

'What a mercy we took a tracing of the map!' said
Julian, after tea. 'But I'm jolly sorry now we left the
real map in the box. Someone else may guess our
secret!'

10   An astonishing offer

The next morning the papers were full of the extraordinary way in which the old wreck had been thrown
up out of the sea. The newspaper men had got out of
the children's uncle the tale of the wreck and the lost
gold, and some of them even managed to land on
Kirrin Island and take pictures of the old ruined castle.

George was furious. 'It's *my* castle!' she stormed to
her mother. 'It's *my* island. You said it could be mine.
You did, you did!'

'I know, George dear,' said her mother. 'But you
really must be sensible. It can't hurt the island to be
landed on, and it can't hurt the castle to be photo-
graphed.'

'But I don't want it to be,' said George, her face dark
and sulky. 'It's mine. And the wreck is mine. You said
so.'

'Well, I didn't know it was going to be thrown up
like that,' said her mother. 'Do be sensible, George.
What can it possibly matter if people go to look at the
wreck? You can't stop them.'

George couldn't stop them, but that didn't make her
any the less angry about it. The children were astonished at the interest that the cast-up wreck caused, and
because of that, Kirrin Island became an object of great
interest too. Sightseers from the places all around came
to see it, and the fishermen managed to find the little

inlet and land the people there. George sobbed with rage, and Julian tried to comfort her.

'Listen, George! No one knows our secret yet. We'll wait till this excitement has died down, and then we'll go to Kirrin Castle and find the ingots.'

'If someone doesn't find them first,' said George, drying her eyes. She was furious with herself for crying, but she really couldn't help it.

'How could they?' said Julian. 'No one has seen inside the box yet! I'm going to wait my chance and get that map out before anyone sees it!'

But he didn't have a chance, because something dreadful happened. Uncle Quentin sold the old box to a man who bought antique things! He came out from his study, beaming, a day or two after the excitement began, and told Aunt Fanny and the children.

'I've struck a very good bargain with that man,' he said to his wife. 'You know that old tin-lined box from the wreck? Well, this fellow collects curious things like that, and he gave me a very good price for it. Very good indeed. More even that I could expect for the writing of my book! As soon as he saw the old map there and the old diary he said at once that he would buy the whole collection.'

The children stared at him in horror. The box was sold! Now someone would study that map and perhaps jump to what 'ingots' meant. The story of the lost gold had been put into all the newspapers now. Nobody could fail to know what the map showed if they studied it carefully.

The children did not dare to tell Uncle Quentin what they knew. It was true he was all smiles now, and was promising to buy them new shrimping-nets, and a raft for themselves – but he was such a changeable

person. He might fly into a furious temper if he heard
that Julian had taken the box and opened it himself,
while his uncle was sleeping.

When they were alone the children discussed the
whole matter. It seemed very serious indeed to them.
They half-wondered if they should let Aunt Fanny
into the secret – but it was such a precious secret, and
so marvellous, that they felt they didn't want to give it
away to anyone at all.

'Now listen!' said Julian, at last. 'We'll ask Aunt
Fanny if we can go to Kirrin Island and spend a day or
two there – sleep there at night too, I mean. That will
give us a little time to poke round and see what we can
find. The sightseers won't come after a day or two, I'm
sure. Maybe we'll get in before anyone tumbles to our
secret. After all, the man who bought the box may not
even guess that the map shows Kirrin Castle.'

They felt more cheerful. It was so awful to do
nothing. As soon as they had planned to act, they felt
better. They decided to ask their aunt the next day if
they might go and spend the weekend at the castle.
The weather was gloriously fine, and it would be great
fun. They could take plenty of food with them.

When they went to ask Aunt Fanny, Uncle Quentin
was with her. He was all smiles again, and even
clapped Julian on the back. 'Well!' he said. 'What's this
deputation for?'

'We just wanted to ask Aunt Fanny something,' said
Julian, politely. 'Aunt Fanny, as the weather is so fine,
do you think you would let us go for the weekend to
Kirrin Castle, please, and spend a day or two there on
the island? You can't think how we would love to!'

'Well – what do you think, Quentin?' asked their
aunt, turning to her husband.

'If they want to, they can,' said Uncle Quentin. 'They won't have a chance to, soon. My dears, we have had a marvellous offer for Kirrin Island! A man wants to buy it, rebuild the castle as a hotel, and make it into a proper holiday place! What do you think of that?'

All four children stared at the smiling man, shocked and horrified. Somebody was going to buy the island! Had their secret been discovered? Did the man want to buy the castle because he had read the map, and knew there was plenty of gold hidden there?

George gave a curious choke. Her eyes burned as if they were on fire. 'Mother! You can't sell my island! You can't sell my castle! I won't let them be sold.'

Her father frowned. 'Don't be silly, Georgina,' he said. 'It isn't really yours. You know that. It belongs to your mother, and naturally she would like to sell it if she could. We need the money very badly. You will be able to have a great many nice things once we sell the island.'

'I don't want nice things!' cried poor George. 'My castle and my island are the nicest things I could ever have. Mother! Mother! You know you said I could have them. You know you did! I believed you.'

'George dear, I did mean you to have them to play on, when I thought they couldn't possibly be worth anything,' said her mother, looking distressed. 'But now things are different. Your father has been offered quite a good sum, far more than we ever thought of getting – and we really can't afford to turn it down.'

'So you only gave me the island when you thought it wasn't worth anything,' said George, her face white and angry. 'As soon as it is worth money you take it away again. I think that's horrid. It – it isn't honourable.'

'That's enough, Georgina,' said her father, angrily. 'Your mother is guided by me. You're only a child. Your mother didn't really mean what she said – it was only to please you. But you know well enough you will share in the money we get and have anything you want.'

'I won't touch a penny!' said George, in a low, choking voice. 'You'll be sorry you sold it.'

The girl turned and stumbled out of the room. The others felt very sorry for her. They knew what she was feeling. She took things so very seriously. Julian thought she didn't understand grown-ups very well. It wasn't a bit of good fighting grown-ups. They could do exactly as they liked. If they wanted to take away George's island and castle, they could. If they wanted to sell it, they could! But what Uncle Quentin didn't know was the fact that there might be a store of gold ingots there! Julian stared at his uncle and wondered whether to warn him. Then he decided not to. There was just a chance that the four children could find the gold first!

'When are you selling the island, Uncle?' he asked quietly.

'The deeds will be signed in about a week's time,' was the answer. 'So if you really want to spend a day or two there, you'd better do so quickly, for after that you may not get permission from the new owners.'

'Was it the man who bought the old box who wants to buy the island?' asked Julian.

'Yes,' said his uncle. 'I was a little surprised myself, for I thought he was just a buyer of old things. It was astonishing to me that he should get the idea of buying the island to rebuild the castle as a hotel. Still, I dare say there will be big money in running an hotel there – very romantic, staying on a little island like that – people will like it. I'm no businessman myself, and I certainly shouldn't care to invest my money in a place like Kirrin Island. But I should think he knows what he is doing all right.'

'Yes, he certainly does,' thought Julian to himself, as he went out of the room with Dick and Anne. 'He's read that map – and has jumped to the same idea that we did – the store of hidden ingots is somewhere on that island – and he's going to get it! He doesn't want to build an hotel! He's after the treasure! I expect he's offered Uncle Quentin some silly low price that poor old uncle thinks is marvellous! Oh dear – this is a horrible thing to happen.'

He went to find George. She was in the tool-shed, looking quite green. She said she felt sick.

'It's only because you're so upset,' said Julian. He slipped his arm round her. For once George didn't push it away. She felt comforted. Tears came into her eyes, and she angrily tried to blink them away.

'Listen, George!' said Julian. 'We mustn't give up hope. We'll go to Kirrin Island tomorrow, and we'll do our very, very best to get down into the dungeons somehow and find the ingots. We'll jolly well stay there till we do. See? Now cheer up, because we'll want your help in planning everything. Thank goodness we took a tracing of the map.'

George cheered up a little. She still felt angry with her father and mother, but the thought of going to Kirrin Island for a day or two, and taking Timothy too, certainly seemed rather good.

'I do think my father and mother are unkind,' she said.

'Well, they're not really,' said Julian, wisely. 'After all, if they need money badly, they would be silly not to part with something they think is quite useless. And you know, your father did say you could have anything you want. I know what I would ask for, if I were you!'

'What?' asked George.

'Timothy, of course!' said Julian. And that made George smile and cheer up tremendously!

11 Off to Kirrin Island

Julian and George went to find Dick and Anne. They were waiting for them in the garden, looking rather upset. They were glad to see Julian and George and ran to meet them.

Anne took George's hands. 'I'm awfully sorry about your island, George,' she said.

'So am I,' said Dick. 'Bad luck, old girl – I mean, old boy!'

George managed to smile. 'I've been behaving like a girl,' she said, half-ashamed. 'But I did get an awful shock.'

Julian told the others what they had planned. 'We'll go tomorrow morning,' he said. 'We'll make out a list of all the things we shall need. Let's begin now.'

He took out a pencil and notebook. The others looked at him.

'Things to eat,' said Dick at once. 'Plenty because we'll be hungry.'

'Something to drink,' said George. 'There's no water on the island – though I believe there was a well or something, years ago, that went right down below the level of the sea, and was fresh water. Anyway, I've never found it.'

'Food,' wrote down Julian, 'and drink.' He looked at the others.

'Spades,' he said solemnly, and scribbled the word down.

Anne stared in surprise.

'What for?' she asked.

'Well, we'll want to dig about when we're hunting for a way down to the dungeons,' said Julian.

'Ropes,' said Dick. 'We may want those too.'

'And torches,' said George. 'It'll be dark in the dungeons.'

'Oooh!' said Anne, feeling a pleasant shiver go down her back at the thought. She had no idea what dungeons were like, but they sounded thrilling.

'Rugs,' said Dick. 'We'll be cold at night if we sleep in that little old room.'

Julian wrote them down. 'Mugs to drink from,' he said. 'And we'll take a few tools too – we may perhaps need them. You never know.'

At the end of half an hour they had quite a nice long list, and everyone felt pleased and excited. George was beginning to recover from her rage and disappointment. If she had been alone, and had brooded over everything, she would have been in an even worse sulk and temper – but somehow the others were so calm and sensible and cheerful. It was impossible to sulk for long if she was with them.

'I think I'd have been much nicer if I hadn't been on my own so much,' thought George to herself, as she looked at Julian's bent head. 'Talking about things to other people does help a lot. They don't seem so dreadful then; they seem more bearable and ordinary. I like my three cousins awfully. I like them because they talk and laugh and are always cheerful and kind. I wish I was like them. I'm sulky and bad-tempered and fierce, and no wonder Father doesn't like me and scolds me so often. Mother's a dear, but I understand now why she says I am difficult. I'm different from my cousins – they're easy to understand, and everyone likes them. I'm glad they came. They are making me more like I ought to be.'

This was a long thought to think, and George looked very serious while she was thinking it. Julian looked up and caught her blue eyes fixed on him. He smiled.

'Penny for your thoughts!' he said.

'They're not worth a penny,' said George, going red. 'I was just thinking how nice you all are – and how I wished I could be like you.'

'You're an awfully nice person,' said Julian, surprisingly. 'You can't help being an only child. They're always a bit odd, you know, unless they're mighty careful. You're a most interesting person, I think.'

George flushed red again, and felt pleased. 'Let's go and take Timothy for a walk,' she said. 'He'll be wondering what's happened to us today.'

They all went off together, and Timothy greeted them at the top of his voice. They told him all about their plans for the next day, and he wagged his tail and looked up at them out of his soft brown eyes as if he understood every single word they said!

'He must feel pleased to think he's going to be with us for two or three days,' said Anne.

It was very exciting the next morning, setting off in the boat with all their things packed neatly at one end. Julian checked them all by reading out aloud from his list. It didn't seem as if they had forgotten anything.

'Got the map?' said Dick, suddenly.

Julian nodded.

'I put on clean jeans this morning,' he said, 'but you

may be sure I remembered to pop the map into my pocket. Here it is!'

He took it out – and the wind at once blew it right out of his hands! It fell into the sea and bobbed there in the wind. All four children gave a cry of utter dismay. Their precious map!

'Quick! Row after it!' cried George, and swung the boat round. But someone was quicker than she was! Tim had seen the paper fly from Julian's hand, and had heard and understood the cries of dismay. With an enormous splash he leapt into the water and swam valiantly after the map.

He could swim well for a dog, for he was strong and powerful. He soon had the map in his mouth and was swimming back to the boat. The children thought he was simply marvellous!

George hauled him into the boat and took the map from his mouth. There was hardly the mark of his teeth on it he had carried it so carefully! It was wet, and the children looked anxiously at it to see if the tracing had been spoilt. But Julian had traced it very strongly, and it was quite all right. He placed it on a seat to dry, and told Dick to hold it there in the sun.

'That was a narrow squeak!' he said, and the others agreed.

George took the oars again, and they set off once more to the island, getting a perfect shower-bath from Timothy when he stood up and shook his wet coat. He was given a big biscuit as a reward, and crunched it up with great enjoyment.

George made her way through the reefs of rocks with a sure hand. It was marvellous to the others how she could slide the boat in between the dangerous rocks and never get a scratch. They thought she was really wonderful. She brought them safely to the little inlet, and they jumped out on to the sand. They pulled the boat high up, in case the tide came far up the tiny cove, and then began to unload their goods.

'We'll carry all the things to that little stone room,' said Julian. 'They will be safe there and won't get wet if it rains. I hope nobody comes to the island while we are here, George.'

'I shouldn't think they would,' said George. 'Father said it would be about a week before the deeds were signed, making over the island to that man. It won't be his till then. We've got a week, anyhow.'

'Well, we don't need to keep a watch in case anyone else arrives then,' said Julian, who had half thought that it would be a good idea to make someone stay on guard at the inlet, to give a warning to the others in case anyone else arrived. 'Come on! You take the spades, Dick. I'll take the food and drink with George. And Anne can take the little things.'

The food and drink were in a big box, for the children did not mean to starve while they were on the island! They had brought loaves of bread, butter, biscuits, jam, tins of fruit, ripe plums, bottles of ginger-beer, a kettle to make tea, and anything else they could think of! George and Julian staggered up the cliff with the heavy box. They had to put it down once or twice to give themselves a rest!

They put everything into the little room. Then they went back to get the collection of blankets and rugs from the boat. They arranged them in the corners of the little room, and thought that it would be most exciting to spend the night there.

'The two girls can sleep together on this pile of

rugs,' said Julian. 'And we two boys will have this pile.'

George looked as if she didn't want to be put with Anne, and classed as a girl. But Anne didn't wish to sleep alone in her corner, and she looked so beseechingly at George that the bigger girl smiled at her and made no objection. Anne thought that George was getting nicer and nicer!

'Well, now we'll get down to business,' said Julian, and he pulled out his map. 'We must study this really carefully, and find out exactly under what spot the entrances to the dungeons are. Now – come around and let's do our best to find out! It's up to us to use our brains – and beat that man who's bought the island!'

They all bent over the traced map. It was quite dry now, and the children looked at it earnestly. It was plain that in the old days the castle had been a very fine place.

'Now look,' said Julian, putting his finger on the plan of the dungeons. 'These seem to run all along under the castle – and here – and – here – are the marks that seem to be meant to represent steps or stairs.'

'Yes,' said George. 'I should think they are. Well, if so, there appear to be two ways of getting down into the dungeons. One lot of steps seems to begin somewhere near this little room – and the other seems to start under the tower there. And what do you suppose this thing is here, Julian?'

She put her finger on a round hole that was shown not only in the plan of the dungeons, but also in the plan of the ground floor of the castle.

'I can't imagine what that is,' said Julian, puzzled. 'Oh yes, I know what it might be! You said there was an old well somewhere, do you remember? Well, that may be it, I should think. It would have to be very deep to get fresh water right under the sea – so it probably goes down through the dungeons too. Isn't this thrilling?'

Everyone thought it was. They felt happy and excited. There was something to discover – something they could and must discover within the next day or two.

They looked at one another. 'Well,' said Dick, 'what are we going to start on? Shall we try to find the entrance to the dungeons – the one that seems to start round about this little room? For all we know there may be a big stone we can lift that opens above the dungeon steps!'

This was a thrilling thought, and the children jumped up at once. Julian folded up the precious map and put it into his pocket. He looked round. The stone floor of the little room was overgrown with creeping weeds. They must be cleared away before it was possible to see if there were any stones that looked as if they might be moved.

'We'd better set to work,' said Julian, and he picked up a spade. 'Let's clear away these weeds with our spades – scrape them off, look, like this – and then examine every single stone!'

They all picked up spades and soon the little stone room was full of a scraping sound as the four of them chiselled away at the close-growing weeds with their spades. It wasn't very difficult to get the stones clear of them, and the children worked with a will.

Tim got most excited about everything. He hadn't any idea at all what they were doing, but he joined in valiantly. He scraped away at the floor with his four paws, sending earth and plants flying high into the air!

'Hi, Tim!' said Julian, shaking a clod of earth out of his hair. 'You're being a bit too vigorous. My word, you'll send the stones flying into the air too, in a minute. George, isn't Tim marvellous the way he joins in everything?'

How they all worked! How they all longed to find the entrance to the underground dungeons! What a thrill that would be.

12   *Exciting discoveries*

Soon the stones of the little room were clear of earth, sand and weeds. The children saw that they were all the same size – big and square, fitted well together. They went over them carefully with their torches, trying to find one that might move or lift.

'We should probably find one with an iron ring handle sunk into it,' said Julian. But they didn't. All the stones looked exactly the same. It was most disappointing.

Julian tried inserting his spade into the cracks between the various stones, to see if by any chance he could move one. But they couldn't be moved. It seemed as if they were all set in the solid ground. After about three hours' hard work the children sat down to eat a meal.

They were very hungry indeed, and felt glad to think there were so many things to eat. As they ate they discussed the problem they were trying to solve.

'It looks as if the entrance to the dungeons was not under this little room after all,' said Julian. 'It's disappointing – but somehow I don't think now that the steps down to the dungeon started from here. Let's measure the map and see if we can make out exactly where the steps do start. It may be, of course, that the measurements aren't correct and won't be any help to us at all. But we can try.'

So they measured as best they could, to try and find out in exactly what place the dungeon steps seemed to begin. It was impossible to tell, for the plans of the three floors seemed to be done to different scales. Julian stared at the map, puzzled. It seemed rather hopeless. Surely they wouldn't have to hunt all over the ground floor of the castle! It would take ages.

'Look,' said George, suddenly, putting her finger on the hole that they all thought must be meant to represent the well. 'The entrance to the dungeons seems to be not very far off the well. If only we could find the well, we could hunt around a bit for the beginning of the dungeon steps. The well is shown in both maps. It seems to be somewhere about the middle of the castle.'

'That's a good idea of yours,' said Julian, pleased. 'Let's go out into the middle of the castle – we can more or less guess where the old well ought to be, because it definitely seems to be about the middle of the old yard out there.'

Out they all went into the sunshine. They felt very important and serious. It was marvellous to be looking for lost ingots of gold. They all felt perfectly certain that they really were somewhere beneath their feet. It didn't occur to any of the children that the treasure might not be there.

They stood in the ruined courtyard that had once been the centre of the castle. They paced out the middle of the yard and then stood there, looking around in vain for anything that might perhaps have been the opening of an old well. It was all so overgrown. Sand had blown in from the shore, and weeds and bushes of all kinds grew there. The stones that had once formed the floor of the big courtyard were now cracked and were no longer lying flat. Most of them were covered with sand or weeds.

'Look! There's a rabbit!' cried Dick, as a big sandy rabbit lollopped slowly across the yard. It disappeared into a hole on the other side. Then another rabbit appeared, sat up and looked at the children, and then vanished too. The children were thrilled. They had never seen such tame rabbits before.

A third rabbit appeared. It was a small one with absurdly big ears, and the tiniest white bob of a tail. It didn't even look at the children. It bounded about in a playful way, and then, to the children's enormous delight, it sat up on its hind legs, and began to wash its big ears, pulling down first one and then the other.

But this was too much for Timothy. He had watched the other two bound across the yard and then disappear without so much as barking at them. But to see this youngster actually sitting there washing its ears under his very nose was really too much for any dog. He gave an excited yelp and rushed full-tilt at the surprised rabbit.

For a moment the little thing didn't move. It had never been frightened or chased before, and it stared with big eyes at the rushing dog. Then it turned itself about and tore off at top speed, its white bobtail going up and down as it bounded away. It disappeared under a gorse bush near the children. Timothy went after it, vanishing under the big bush too.

Then a shower of sand and earth was thrown up as Tim tried to go down the hole after the rabbit and scraped and scrabbled with his strong front paws as fast as he could. He yelped and whined in excitement, not seeming to hear George's voice calling to him. He meant to get that rabbit! He went almost mad as he scraped at the hole, making it bigger and bigger.

'Tim! Do you hear me! Come out of there!' shouted George. 'You're not to chase the rabbits here. You know you mustn't. You're very naughty. Come out!'

But Tim didn't come out. He just went on and on scraping away madly. George went to fetch him. Just as she got up to the gorse bush the scraping suddenly stopped. There came a scared yelp – and no more noise was heard. George peered under the prickly bush in astonishment.

Tim had disappeared! He just simply wasn't there any more. There was the big rabbit-hole, made enormous by Tim – but there was no Tim.

'I say, Julian – Tim's gone,' said George in a scared voice. 'He surely can't have gone down the rabbit's hole, can he? I mean – he's such a big dog!'

The children crowded round the big gorse bush. There came the sound of a muffled whine from somewhere below it. Julian looked astonished.

'He *is* down the hole!' he said. 'How funny! I never heard of a dog really going down a rabbit-hole before. How ever are we going to get him out?'

'We'll have to dig up the gorse bush, to begin with,' said George, in a determined voice. She would have dug up the whole of Kirrin Castle to get Tim back, that was certain! 'I can't have poor old Tim whining for help down there and not do what we can to help him.'

The bush was far too big and prickly to creep underneath. Julian was glad they had brought tools of all kinds. He went to fetch an axe. They had brought a small one with them and it would do to chop away the prickly branches and trunk of the gorse bush. The children slashed at it and soon the poor bush began to look a sorry sight.

It took a long time to destroy it, for it was prickly,

sturdy and stout. Every child's hands were scratched by the time the bush had been reduced to a mere stump. Then they could see the hole quite well. Julian shone his torch down it.

He gave a shout of surprise. 'I know what's happened! The old well is here! The rabbits had a hole at the side of it – and Tim scraped away to make it bigger and uncovered a bit of the well-hole – and he's fallen down the well!'

'Oh no, oh no,' cried George, in panic. 'Oh Tim, Tim, are you all right?'

A distant whine came to their ears. Evidently Tim was there somewhere. The children looked at one another.

'Well, there's only one thing to do,' said Julian. 'We must get out spades now and dig out the hole of the well. Then maybe we can let a rope down or something and get Tim.'

They set to work with their spades. It was not really difficult to uncover the hole, which had been blocked only by the spreading roots of the big gorse bush, some fallen masonry, earth, sand and small stones. Apparently a big slab had fallen from part of the tower across the well-hole, and partly closed it. The weather and the growing gorse bush had done the rest.

It took all the children together to move the slab. Underneath was a very rotten wooden cover, which had plainly been used in the old days to protect the well. It had rotted so much that when Tim's weight had been pressed on it, it had given just there and made a hole for Tim to fall through.

Julian removed the old wooden cover and then the children could see down the well-hole. It was very deep and very dark. They could not possibly see the bottom. Julian took a stone and dropped it down. They all listened for the splash. But there was no splash. Either there was no longer any water there, or the well was too deep even to hear the splash!

'I think it's too deep for us to hear anything,' said Julian. 'Now – where's Tim?'

He shone his torch down – and there was Tim! Many years before a big slab had fallen down the well itself and had stuck a little way down, across the well-hole – and on this old cracked slab sat Tim, his big eyes staring up in fright. He simply could not imagine what had happened to him.

There was an old iron ladder fastened to the side of the well. George was on it before anyone else could get there! Down she went, not caring if the ladder held or not, and reached Tim. Somehow she got him on to her shoulder and, holding him there with one hand, she climbed slowly up again. The other three hauled her out and Tim jumped round her, barking and licking for all he was worth!

'Well, Tim!' said Dick. 'You shouldn't chase rabbits – but you've certainly done us a good turn, because you've found the well for us! Now we've only got to look around a little to find the dungeon entrance!'

They set to work again to hunt for the dungeon entrance. They dug about with their spades under all the bushes. They pulled up crooked stones and dug their spades into the earth below, hoping that they might suddenly find them going through into space! It was really very thrilling.

And then Anne found the entrance! It was quite by accident. She was tired and sat down to rest. She lay on her front and scrabbled about in the sand. Suddenly her fingers touched something hard and cold in the sand. She uncovered it – and lo and behold, it was an iron ring! She gave a shout and the others looked up.

'There's a stone with an iron ring in it here!' yelled Anne, excitedly. They all rushed over to her. Julian dug about with his spade and uncovered the whole stone. Sure enough, it did have a ring in it – and rings are only set into stones that need to be moved! Surely this stone must be the one that covered the dungeon entrance!

All the children took turns at pulling on the iron ring, but the stone did not move. Then Julian tied two or three turns of rope through it and the four children put out their full strength and pulled for all they were worth.

The stone moved. The children distinctly felt it stir. 'All together again!' cried Julian. And all together they pulled. The stone stirred again and then suddenly gave way. It moved upwards – and the children fell over on top of one another like a row of dominoes suddenly pushed down! Tim darted to the hole and barked madly down it as if all the rabbits of the world lived there!

Julian and George shot to their feet and rushed to the opening that the moved stone had disclosed. They stood there, looking downwards, their faces shining with delight. They *had* found the entrance to the dungeons! A steep flight of steps, cut out of the rock itself, led downwards into deep darkness.

'Come on!' cried Julian, snapping on his torch. 'We've found what we wanted! Now for the dungeons!'

The steps down were slippery. Tim darted down first, lost his foot-hold and rolled down five or six steps, yelping with fright. Julian went after him, then

George, then Dick and then Anne. They were all tremendously thrilled. Indeed, they quite expected to see piles of gold and all kinds of treasure everywhere around them!

It was dark down the steep flight of steps, and smelt very musty. Anne choked a little.

'I hope the air down here is all right,' said Julian. 'Sometimes it isn't good in these underground places. If anyone feels a bit funny they'd better say so and we'll go up into the open air again.'

But however funny they might feel, nobody would have said so. It was all far too exciting to worry about feeling strange.

The steps went down a long way. Then they came to an end. Julian stepped down from the last rock-stair and flashed his torch around. It was a weird sight that met his eyes.

The dungeons of Kirrin Castle were made out of the rock itself. Whether there were natural caves there, or whether they had been hollowed out by man the children could not tell. But certainly they were very mysterious, dark and full of echoing sounds. When Julian gave a sigh of excitement it fled into the rocky hollows and swelled out and echoed around as if it were a live thing. It gave all the children a very peculiar feeling.

'Isn't it strange?' said George, in a low voice. At once the echoes took up her words, and multiplied them and made them louder – and all the dungeon caves gave back the girl's words over and over again. 'Isn't it strange, ISN'T IT STRANGE, ISN'T IT STRANGE.'

Anne slipped her hand into Dick's. She felt scared. She didn't like the echoes at all. She knew they *were* only echoes – but they did sound exactly like the voices of scores of people hidden in the caves!

'Where do you suppose the ingots are?' said Dick. And at once the caves threw him back his words. 'INGOTS! INGOTS are! INGOTS ARE! ARE! ARE!'

Julian laughed – and his laugh was split up into dozens of different laughs that came out of the dungeons and spun round the listening children. It really was the strangest thing.

'Come on,' said Julian. 'Maybe the echoes won't be so bad a little farther in.'

'FARTHER IN,' said the echoes at once. 'FARTHER IN!'

They moved away from the end of the rocky steps and explored the nearby dungeons. They were really only rocky cellars stretching under the castle. Maybe wretched prisoners had been kept there many, many years before, but mostly they had been used for storing things.

'I wonder which dungeon was used for storing the ingots,' said Julian. He stopped and took the map out of his pocket. He flashed his torch on to it. But although it showed him quite plainly the dungeon where INGOTS were marked, he had no idea at all of the right direction.

'I say – look – there's a door here, shutting off the next dungeon!' suddenly cried Dick. 'I bet this is the dungeon we're looking for! I bet there are ingots in here!'

13   Down in the dungeons

Four torches were flashed on to the wooden door. It
was big and stout, studded with great iron nails. Julian
gave a whoop of delight and rushed to it. He felt
certain that behind it was the dungeon used for storing
things.

But the door was fast shut. No amount of pushing
or pulling would open it. It had a great keyhole – but
no key there! The four children stared in exasperation
at the door. Bother it! Just as they really thought they
were near the ingots, this door wouldn't open!

'We'll fetch the axe,' said Julian, suddenly. 'We may
be able to chop round the keyhole and smash the
lock.'

'That's a good idea!' said George, delighted. 'Come
on back!'

They left the big door, and tried to get back the way
they had come. But the dungeons were so big and so
rambling that they lost their way. They stumbled over
old broken barrels, rotting wood, empty bottles and
many other things as they tried to find their way back
to the big flight of rock-steps.

'This is sickening!' said Julian, at last. 'I simply
haven't any idea at all where the entrance is. We keep
on going into one dungeon after another, and one
passage after another, and they all seem to be exactly
the same – dark and smelly and mysterious.'

'Suppose we have to stay here all the rest of our lives!' said Anne, gloomily.

'Idiot!' said Dick, taking her hand. 'We shall soon find the way out. Hallo! – what's this? –'

They all stopped. They had come to what looked like a chimney shaft of brick, stretching down from the roof of the dungeon to the floor. Julian flashed his torch on to it. He was puzzled.

'I know what it is!' said George, suddenly. 'It's the well, of course! You remember it was shown in the plan of the dungeons, as well as in the plan of the ground floor. Well, that's the shaft of the well going down and down. I wonder if there's any opening in it just here – so that water could be taken into the dungeons as well as up to the ground floor.'

They went to see. On the other side of the well-shaft was a small opening big enough for one child at a time to put his head and shoulders through and look down. They shone their torches down and up. The well was so deep that it was still impossible to see the bottom of it. Julian dropped a stone down again, but there was no sound of either a thud or a splash. He looked upwards, and could see the faint gleam of daylight that slid round the broken slab of stone lying a little way down the shaft – the slab on which Tim had sat, waiting to be rescued.

'Yes,' he said, 'this is the well all right. Isn't it weird? Well – now we've found the well we know that the entrance to the dungeons isn't very far off!'

That cheered them all up tremendously. They took hands and hunted around in the dark, their torches making bright beams of light here and there.

Anne gave a screech of excitement. 'Here's the

entrance! It must be, because I can see faint daylight coming down!'

The children rounded a corner and sure enough, there was the steep, rocky flight of steps leading upwards. Julian took a quick look round so that he might know the way to go when they came down again. He didn't feel at all certain that he would find the wooden door!

They all went up into the sunshine. It was delicious to feel the warmth on their heads and shoulders after the cold air down in the dungeons. Julian looked at his watch and gave a loud exclamation.

'It's half-past six! *Half-past six!* No wonder I feel hungry. We haven't had any tea. We've been working, and wandering about those dungeons for hours.'

'Well, let's have a kind of tea-supper before we do anything else,' said Dick. 'I don't feel as if I've had anything to eat for about twelve months.'

'Well, considering you ate about twice as much as anyone else at dinner-time,' began Julian, indignantly. Then he grinned. 'I feel the same as you,' he said. 'Come on! – let's get a really good meal. George, what about boiling a kettle and making some cocoa, or something? I feel cold after all that time underground.'

It was fun boiling the kettle on a fire of dry sticks. It was lovely to lie about in the warmth of the evening sun and munch bread and cheese and enjoy cake and biscuits. They all enjoyed themselves thoroughly. Tim had a good meal too. He hadn't very much liked being underground, and had followed the others very closely indeed, his tail well down. He had been very frightened, too, of the curious echoes here and there.

Once he had barked, and it had seemed to Tim as if the whole of the dungeons were full of other dogs, all

barking far more loudly than he could. He hadn't even
dared to whine after that! But now he was happy
again, eating the tit-bits that the children gave him,
and licking George whenever he was near her.

It was past eight o'clock by the time that the children
had finished their meal and tidied up. Julian looked at
the others. The sun was sinking, and the day was no
longer so warm.

'Well,' he said, 'I don't know what you feel. But I
don't somehow want to go down into those dungeons
again today, not even for the sake of smashing in that
door with the axe and opening it! I'm tired – and I don't
like the thought of losing my way in those dungeons at
night.'

The others heartily agreed with him, especially
Anne, who had secretly been dreading going down
again with the night coming on. The little girl was
almost asleep; she was so tired out with hard work and
excitement.

'Come on, Anne!' said George, pulling her to her
feet. 'Bed for you. We'll cuddle up together in the rugs
on the floor of that little room – and in the morning
when we wake we'll be simply thrilled to think of
opening that big wooden door.'

All four children, with Tim close behind, went off
to the little stone room. They curled up on their piles
of rugs, and Tim crept in with George and Anne. He
lay down on them, and felt so heavy that Anne had to
push him off her legs.

He sat himself down on her again, and she groaned,
half-asleep. Tim wagged his tail and thumped it hard
against her ankles. Then George pulled him on to her
own legs and lay there, feeling him breathe. She was
very happy. She was spending the night on her island.

They had almost found the ingots, she was sure. She had Tim with her, actually sleeping on her rugs. Perhaps everything would come right after all – somehow.

She fell asleep. The children felt perfectly safe with Tim on guard. They slept peacefully until the morning, when Tim saw a rabbit through the broken archway leading to the little room, and sped away to chase it. He awoke George as he got up from the rugs, and she sat up and rubbed her eyes.

'Wake up!' she cried to the others. 'Wake up, all of you! It's morning! And we're on the island!'

They all awoke. It was really thrilling to sit up and remember everything. Julian thought of the big wooden door at once. He would soon smash it in with his axe, he felt sure. And then what would they find?

They had breakfast, and ate just as much as ever. Then Julian picked up the axe they had brought and took everyone to the flight of steps. Tim went too, wagging his tail, but not really feeling very pleased at the thought of going down into the strange places where other dogs seemed to bark, and yet were not to be found. Poor Tim would never understand echoes!

They all went down underground again. And then, of course, they couldn't find the way to the wooden door! It was most tiresome.

'We shall lose our way all over again,' said George, desperately. 'These dungeons are about the most rambling spread-out maze of underground caves I've ever known! We shall lose the entrance again too!'

Julian had a bright idea. He had a piece of white chalk in his pocket, and he took it out. He went back to the steps, and marked the wall there. Then he began to put chalk-marks along the passages as they walked in the musty darkness. They came to the well, and Julian was pleased.

'Now,' he said, 'whenever we come to the well we shall at least be able to find the way back to the steps, because we can follow my chalk-marks. Now the thing is – which is the way next? We'll try and find it and I'll put chalk-marks along the walls here and there – but if we go the wrong way and have to come back, we'll rub out the marks, and start again from the well another way.'

This was really a very good idea. They did go the wrong way, and had to come back, rubbing out Julian's marks. They reached the well, and set off in the opposite direction. And this time they did find the wooden door!

There it was, stout and sturdy, its old iron nails rusty and red. The children stared at it in delight. Julian lifted his axe.

Crash! He drove it into the wood and round about the keyhole. But the wood was still strong, and the axe only went in an inch or two. Julian drove it in once more. The axe hit one of the big nails and slipped a little to one side. A big splinter of wood flew out – and struck poor Dick on the cheek!

He gave a yell of pain. Julian jumped in alarm, and turned to look at him. Dick's cheek was pouring with blood!

'Something flew out of the door and hit me,' said poor Dick. 'It's a splinter, or something.'

'Golly!' said Julian, and he shone his torch on to Dick. 'Can you bear it a moment if I pull the splinter out? It's a big one, and it's still sticking into your poor cheek.'

But Dick pulled it out himself. He made a face with

the pain, and then turned very white.

'You'd better get up into the open air for a bit,' said Julian. 'And we'll have to bathe your cheek and stop it bleeding somehow. Anne's got a clean hanky. We'll bathe it and dab it with that. We brought some water with us, luckily.'

'I'll go with Dick,' said Anne. 'You stay here with George. There's no need for us all to go.'

But Julian thought he would like to see Dick safely up into the open air first, and then he could leave him with Anne while he went back to George and went on with the smashing down of the door. He handed the axe to George.

'You can do a bit of chopping while I'm gone,' he said. 'It will take some time to smash that big door in. You get on with it – and I'll be down in a few minutes again. We can easily find the way to the entrance because we've only got to follow my chalk-marks.'

'Right!' said George, and she took the axe. 'Poor old Dick – you do look a sight.'

Leaving George behind with Tim, valiantly attacking the big door, Julian took Dick and Anne up to the open air. Anne dipped her hanky into the kettle of water and dabbed Dick's cheek gently. It was bleeding very much, as cheeks do, but the wound was not really very bad. Dick's colour soon came back, and he wanted to go down into the dungeons again.

'No, you'd better lie down on your back for a little,' said Julian. 'I know that's good for nose-bleeding – and maybe it's good for cheek-bleeding too. What about Anne and you going out on the rocks over there, where you can see the wreck, and staying there for half an hour or so? Come on – I'll take you both there, and leave you for a bit. You'd better not get up till your cheek's stopped bleeding, old boy.'

Julian took the two out of the castle yard and out on to the rocks on the side of the island that faced the open sea. The dark hulk of the old wreck was still there on the rocks. Dick lay down on his back and stared up into the sky, hoping that his cheek would soon stop bleeding. He didn't want to miss any of the fun!

Anne took his hand. She was very upset at the little accident, and although she didn't want to miss the fun either, she meant to stay with Dick till he felt better. Julian sat down beside them for a minute or two. Then he went back to the rocky steps and disappeared down them. He followed his chalk-marks, and soon came to where George was attacking the door.

She had smashed it well round the lock – but it simply would *not* give way. Julian took the axe from her and drove it hard into the wood.

After a blow or two something seemed to happen to the lock. It became loose, and hung a little sideways. Julian put down his axe.

'I think somehow that we can open the door now,' he said, in an excited voice. 'Get out of the way, Tim, old fellow. Now then, push, George!'

They both pushed – and the lock gave way with a grating noise. The big door opened creakingly, and the two children went inside, flashing their torches in excitement.

The room was not much more than a cave, hollowed out of the rock – but in it was something quite different from the old barrels and boxes the children had found before. At the back, in untidy piles, were curious, brick-shaped things of dull yellow-brown metal. Julian picked one up.

'George!' he cried. 'The ingots!' These are real gold!

Oh, I know they don't look like it – but they are, all the same. George, oh George, there's a small fortune here in this cellar – and it's yours! We've found it at last!'

14 Prisoners!

George couldn't say a word. She just stood there, staring at the pile of ingots, holding one in her hand. She could hardly believe that these strange brick-shaped things were really gold. Her heart thumped fast. What a wonderful, marvellous find!

Suddenly Tim began to bark loudly. He stood with his back to the children, his nose towards the door – and how he barked!

'Shut up, Tim!' said Julian. 'What can you hear? Is it the others coming back?'

He went to the door and yelled down the passage outside. 'Dick! Anne! Is it you? Come quickly, because we've found the ingots! We've found them! Hurry! Hurry!'

Tim stopped barking and began to growl. George looked puzzled. 'Whatever *can* be the matter with Tim?' she said. 'He surely can't be growling at Dick and Anne.'

Then both children got a most tremendous shock – for a man's voice came booming down the dark passage, making strange echoes all around.

'Who is here? Who is down here?'

George clutched Julian in fright. Tim went on growling, all the hairs on his neck standing up straight. 'Do be quiet, Tim!' whispered George, snapping off her torch. But Tim simply would *not* be quiet. He went on growling as if he were a small thunderstorm.

The children saw the beam of a powerful torchlight coming round the corner of the dungeon passage. Then the light picked them out, and the holder of the torch came to a surprised stop.

'Well, well, well!' said a voice. 'Look who's here! Two children in the dungeons of my castle.'

'What do you mean, *your* castle!' cried George.

'Well, my dear little girl, it *is* my castle, because I'm in the process of buying it,' said the voice. Then another voice spoke, more gruffly.

'What are you doing down here? What did you mean when you shouted out "Dick" and "Anne", and said you had found the ingots? What ingots?'

'Don't answer,' whispered Julian to George. But the echoes took his words and made them very loud in the passage. 'DON'T ANSWER! DON'T ANSWER!'

'Oh, so you won't answer,' said the second man, and he stepped towards the children. Tim bared his teeth, but the man didn't seem at all frightened of him. The man went to the door and flashed his torch inside the dungeon. He gave a long whistle of surprise.

'Jake! Look here!' he said. 'You were right. The gold's here all right. And how easy to take away! All in ingots – my word, this is the most amazing thing we've ever struck.'

'This gold is mine,' said George, in a fury. 'This island and the castle belong to my mother – and so does anything found here. This gold was brought here and stored by my great-great-great-grandfather before his ship got wrecked. It's not yours, and never will be. As soon as I get back home I shall tell my father and mother what we've found – and then you may be sure you won't be able to buy the castle or the island! You were very clever, finding out from the map in the old box about the gold – but just not clever enough for us. We found it first!'

The men listened in silence to George's clear and angry voice. One of them laughed. 'You're only a child,' he said. 'You surely don't think you can keep us from getting our way? We're going to buy this island – and everything in it – and we shall take the gold when the deeds are signed. And if by any chance we couldn't buy the island, we'd take the gold just the same. It would be easy enough to bring a ship here and transfer the ingots from here by boat to the ship. Don't worry – we shall get what we want all right.'

'You will not!' said George, and she stepped out of the door. 'I'm going straight home now – and I'll tell my father all you've said.'

'My dear little girl, you are not going home,' said the first man, putting his hands on George and forcing her back into the dungeon. 'And, by the way, unless you want me to shoot this unpleasant dog of yours, call him off, will you?'

George saw, to her dismay, that the man had a shining revolver in his hand. In fright she caught hold of Tim's collar and pulled him to her. 'Be quiet, Tim,' she said. 'It's all right.'

But Tim knew quite well that it wasn't all right. Something was very wrong. He went on growling fiercely.

'Now listen to me,' said the man, after he had had a hurried talk with his companion. 'If you are going to be sensible, nothing unpleasant will happen to you. But if you want to be obstinate, you'll be very sorry. What we are going to do is this – we're going off in our motor-boat, leaving you nicely locked up here – and we're going to get a ship and come back for the gold. We don't think it's worthwhile buying the island now we know where the ingots are.'

'And you are going to write a note to your companions above, telling them you've found the gold and they are to come down and look for it,' said the other man. 'Then we shall lock up all of you in this dungeon, with the ingots to play with, leaving you food and drink till we come back. Now then – here is a pencil. Write a note to Dick and Anne, whoever they are, and send your dog up with it. Come on.'

'I won't,' said George, her face furious. 'I won't. You can't make me do a thing like that. I won't get poor Dick and Anne down here to be made prisoners. And I won't let you have my gold, just when I've discovered it.'

'We shall shoot your dog if you don't do as you're told,' said the first man, suddenly. George's heart sank down and she felt cold and terrified.

'No, no,' she said in a low, desperate voice.

'Well, write the note then,' said the man, offering her a pencil and paper. 'Go on. I'll tell you what to say.'

'I can't!' sobbed George. 'I don't want to get Dick and Anne down here to be made prisoners.'

'All right – I'll shoot the dog then,' said the man, in a cold voice and he levelled his revolver at poor Tim. George threw her arms round her dog and gave a scream.

'No, no! I'll write the note. Don't shoot Tim, don't shoot him!'

The girl took the paper and pencil in a shaking hand and looked at the man. 'Write this,' he ordered. '"Dear Dick and Anne. We've found the gold. Come on down at once and see it." Then sign your name, whatever it is.'

George wrote what the man had said. Then she signed her name. But instead of writing 'George' she put 'Georgina'. She knew that the others would feel certain she would never sign herself that – and she hoped it would warn them that something odd was up. The man took the note and fastened it to Tim's collar. The dog growled all the time, but George kept telling him not to bite.

'Now tell him to go and find your friends,' said the man.

'Find Dick and Anne,' commanded George. 'Go on, Tim. Find Dick and Anne. Give them the note.'

Tim did not want to leave George, but there was something very urgent in her voice. He took one last look at his mistress, gave her hand a lick and sped off down the passage. He knew the way now. Up the rocky steps he bounded and into the open air. He stopped in the old yard, sniffing. Where were Dick and Anne?

He smelt their footsteps and ran off, his nose to the ground. He soon found the two children out on the rocks. Dick was feeling better now and was sitting up. His cheek had almost stopped bleeding.

'Hallo,' he said in surprise, when he saw Tim. 'Here's Timothy! Why, Tim, old chap, why have you come to see us? Did you get tired of being under-ground in the dark?'

'Look, Dick – he's got something twisted into his collar,' said Anne, her sharp eyes seeing the paper there. 'It's a note. I expect it's from the others, telling us to go down. Isn't Tim clever to bring it?'

Dick took the paper from Tim's collar. He undid it and read it.

'"Dear Dick and Anne,"' he read out aloud. '"We've found the gold. Come on down at once and see it. Georgina."'

'Oooh!' said Anne, her eyes shining. 'They've found it. Oh, Dick – are you well enough to come now? Let's hurry.'

But Dick did not get up from the rocks. He sat and stared at the note, puzzled.

'What's the matter?' said Anne, impatiently.

'Well, don't you think it's funny that George should suddenly sign herself "Georgina"?' said Dick, slowly. 'You know how she hates being a girl, and having a girl's name. You know how she will never answer if anyone calls her Georgina. And yet in this note she signs herself by the name she hates. It does seem a bit funny to me. Almost as if it's a kind of warning that there's something wrong.'

'Oh, don't be so silly, Dick,' said Anne. 'What could be wrong? Do come on.'

'Anne, I'd like to pop over to that inlet of ours to make sure there's no one else come to the island,' said Dick. 'You stay here.'

But Anne didn't want to stay there alone. She ran round the coast with Dick, telling him all the time that she thought he was very silly.

But when they came to the little harbour, they saw that there was another boat there, as well as their own. It was a motor-boat! Someone else *was* on the island!

'Look,' said Dick, in a whisper. 'There *is* someone else here. And I bet it's the men who want to buy the island. I bet they've read that old map and know there's gold here. And they've found George and

Julian and want to get us all together down in the dungeons so that they can keep us safe till they've stolen the gold. That's why they made George send us that note – but she signed it with a name she never uses – to warn us! Now – we must think hard. What are we going to do?'

15 Dick to the rescue!

Dick caught hold of Anne's hand and pulled her quickly away from the cove. He was afraid that whoever had come to the island might be somewhere about and see them. The boy took Anne to the little stone room where their things were and they sat down in a corner.

'Whoever has come has discovered Julian and George smashing in that door, I should think,' said Dick, in a whisper. 'I simply can't think what to do. We mustn't go down into the dungeons or we'll most certainly be caught. Hallo – where's Tim off to?'

The dog had kept with them for a while but now he ran off to the entrance of the dungeons. He disappeared down the steps. He meant to get back to George, for he knew she was in danger. Dick and Anne stared after him. They had felt comforted while he was there, and now they were sorry he had gone.

They really didn't know what to do. Then Anne had an idea. 'I know!' she said. 'We'll row back to the land in our boat and get help.'

'I'd thought of that,' said Dick, gloomily. 'But you know perfectly well we'd never know the way in and out of those awful rocks. We'd wreck the boat. I'm sure we're not strong enough either to row all the way back. Oh, dear – I do wish we could think what to do.'

They didn't need to puzzle their brains long. The

men came up out of the dungeons and began to hunt
for the two children! They had seen Tim when he came
back and had found the note gone. So they knew the
two children had taken it – and they couldn't imagine
why they had not obeyed what George had said in the
note, and come down to the dungeons!

Dick heard their voices. He clutched hold of Anne to
make her keep quiet. He saw through the broken
archway that the men were going in the opposite
direction.

'Anne! I know where we can hide!' said the boy,
excitedly. 'Down the old well! We can climb down the
ladder a little way and hide there. I'm sure no one
would ever look there!'

Anne didn't at all want to climb down the well even
a little way. But Dick pulled her to her feet and hurried
her off to the middle of the old courtyard. The men
were hunting around the other side of the castle. There
was just time to climb in. Dick slipped aside the old
wooden cover of the well and helped Anne down the
ladder. She was very scared. Then the boy climbed
down himself and slipped the wooden cover back
again over his head, as best he could.

The old stone slab that Tim had sat on when he fell
down the well was still there. Dick climbed down to it
and tested it. It was immovable.

'It's safe for you to sit on, Anne, if you don't want to
keep clinging to the ladder,' he whispered. So Anne sat
shivering on the stone slab across the well-shaft, waiting to see if they were discovered or not. They kept
hearing the voices of the men, now near at hand and
now far-off. Then the men began to shout for them.

'Dick! Anne! The others want you! Where are you?
We've exciting news for you.'

'Well, why don't they let Julian and George come up and tell us then?' whispered Dick. 'There's something wrong, I know there is. I do wish we could get to Julian and George and find out what has happened.'

The two men came into the courtyard. They were angry. 'Where have those kids got to?' said Jake. 'Their boat is still in the cove, so they haven't got away. They must be hiding somewhere. We can't wait all day for them.'

'Well, let's take some food and drink down to the two we've locked up,' said the other man. 'There's plenty in that little stone room. I suppose it's a store the children brought over. We'll leave half in the room so that the other two kids can have it. And we'll take their boat with us so that they can't escape.'

'Right,' said Jake. 'The thing to do is to get the gold away as quickly as possible, and make sure the children are prisoners here until we've made a safe getaway. We won't bother any more about trying to buy the island. After all, it was only the idea of getting the ingots that put us up to the idea of getting Kirrin Castle and the island.'

'Well – come on,' said his companion. 'We will take the food down now, and not bother about the other kids. You stay here and see if you can spot them while I go down.'

Dick and Anne hardly dared to breathe when they heard all this. How they hoped that the men wouldn't think of looking down the well! They heard one man walk to the little stone room. It was plain that he was getting food and drink to take down to the two prisoners in the dungeons below. The other man stayed in the courtyard, whistling softly.

After what seemed a very long time to the hidden

children, the first man came back. Then the two talked together, and at last went off to the cove. Dick heard the motor-boat being started up.

'It's safe to get out now, Anne,' he said. 'Isn't it cold down here? I'll be glad to get out into the sunshine.'

They climbed out and stood warming themselves in the hot summer sunshine. They could see the motor-boat streaking towards the mainland.

'Well, they're gone for the moment,' said Dick. 'And they've not taken our boat, as they said. If only we could rescue Julian and George, we could get help, because George could row us back.'

'Why *can't* we rescue them?' cried Anne, her eyes shining. 'We can go down the steps and unbolt the door, can't we?'

'No – we can't,' said Dick. 'Look!'

Anne looked to where he pointed. She saw that the two men had piled big, heavy slabs of broken stone over the dungeon entrance. It had taken all their strength to put the big stones there. Neither Dick nor Anne could hope to move them.

'It's quite impossible to get down the steps,' said Dick. 'They've made sure we shan't do that! And you know we haven't any idea where the second entrance is. We only know it was somewhere near the tower.'

'Let's see if we can find it,' said Anne eagerly. They set off to the tower on the right of the castle – but it was quite clear that whatever entrance there might have been once, it was gone now! The castle had fallen in very much just there, and there were piles of old broken stones everywhere, quite impossible to move. The children soon gave up the search.

'Blow!' said Dick. 'How I do hate to think of poor old Julian and George prisoners down below, and we

can't even help them! Oh, Anne – can't *you* think of
something to do?'

Anne sat down on a stone and thought hard. She
was very worried. Then she brightened up a little and
turned to Dick.

'Dick! I suppose – I suppose we couldn't *possibly*
climb down the well, could we?' she asked. 'You
know it goes past the dungeons – and there's an
opening on the dungeon floor from the well-shaft,
because don't you remember we were able to put in
our heads and shoulders and look right up the well to
the top? Could we get past that slab, do you think – the
one that I sat on just now, that has fallen across the
well?'

Dick thought it all over. He went to the well and
peered down it. 'You know, I believe you are right,
Anne,' he said at last. 'We might be able to squeeze past
that slab. There's just about room. I don't know how
far the iron ladder goes down though.'

'Oh, Dick – do let's try,' said Anne. 'It's our only
chance of rescuing the others!'

'Well,' said Dick, 'I'll try it – but not you, Anne. I'm
not going to have you falling down that well. The
ladder might be broken half-way down – anything
might happen. You must stay up here and I'll see what
I can do.'

'You will be careful, won't you?' said Anne,
anxiously. 'Take a rope with you, Dick, so that if you
need one you won't have to climb all the way up
again.'

'Good idea,' said Dick. He went to the little stone
room and got one of the ropes they had put there. He
wound it round and round his waist. Then he went
back to Anne.

'Well, here goes!' he said, in a cheerful voice. 'Don't worry about me. I'll be all right.'

Anne was rather white. She was terribly afraid that Dick might fall right down to the bottom of the well. She watched him climb down the iron ladder to the slab of stone. He tried his best to squeeze by it, but it was very difficult. At last he managed it and after that Anne could see him no more. But she could hear him, for he kept calling up to her.

'Ladder's still going strong, Anne! I'm all right. Can you hear me?'

'Yes,' shouted Anne down the well, hearing her voice echo in a funny hollow manner. 'Take care, Dick. I do hope the ladder goes all the way down.'

'I think it does!' yelled back Dick. Then he gave a loud exclamation. 'Blow! It's broken just here. Broken right off. Or else it ends. I'll have to use my rope.'

There was a silence as Dick unwound the rope from his waist. He tied it firmly to the last but one rung of the ladder, which seemed quite strong.

'I'm going down the rope now!' he shouted to Anne. 'Don't worry. I'm all right. Here I go!'

Anne couldn't hear what Dick said after that, for the well-shaft made his words go crooked and she couldn't make out what they were. But she was glad to hear him shouting even though she didn't know what he said. She yelled down to him too, hoping he could hear her.

Dick slid down the rope, holding on to it with hands, knees and feet, glad that he was so good at gym at school. He wondered if he was anywhere near the dungeons. He seemed to have gone down a long way. He managed to get out his torch. He put it between his teeth after he had switched it on, so that he might have both hands free for the rope. The light from the torch showed him the walls of the well around him. He couldn't make out if he was above or below the dungeons. He didn't want to go right down to the bottom of the well!

He decided that he must have just passed the opening into the dungeon-caves. He climbed back up the rope a little way and to his delight saw that he was right. The opening on to the dungeons was just by his head. He climbed up till he was level with it and then swung himself to the side of the well where the small opening was. He managed to get hold of the bricked edge, and then tried to scramble through the opening into the dungeon.

It was difficult, but luckily Dick was not very big. He managed it at last and stood up straight with a sigh of relief. He was in the dungeons! He could now follow the chalk-marks to the room or cave where the ingots were – and where he felt sure that George and Julian were imprisoned!

He shone his torch on the wall. Yes – there were the chalk-marks. Good! He put his head into the well-opening and yelled at the top of his voice.

'Anne! I'm in the dungeons! Watch out that the men don't come back!'

Then he began to follow the white chalk-marks, his heart beating fast. After a while he came to the door of the store-room. As he had expected, it was fastened so that George and Julian couldn't get out. Big bolts had been driven home at the top and bottom, and the children inside could not possibly get out. They had tried their hardest to batter down the door, but it was no good at all.

They were sitting inside the store-cave, feeling

angry and exhausted. The man had brought them food and drink, but they had not touched it. Tim was with them, lying down with his head on his paws, half-angry with George because she hadn't let him fly at the men as he had so badly wanted to. But George felt certain that Tim would be shot if he tried biting or snapping.

'Anyway, the other two had sense enough not to come down and be made prisoners too,' said George. 'They must have known there was something funny about that note when they saw I had signed myself Georgina instead of George. I wonder what they are doing. They must be hiding.'

Tim suddenly gave a growl. He leapt to his feet and went to the closed door, his head on one side. He had heard something, that was certain.

'I hope it's not those men back again already,' said George. Then she looked at Tim in surprise, flashing her torch on to him. He was wagging his tail!

A great bang at the door made them all jump out of their skins! Then came Dick's cheerful voice. 'Hi, Julian! Hi, George! Are you here?'

'Wuffffff!' barked Tim joyfully, and scratched at the door.

'Dick! Open the door!' yelled Julian in delight. 'Quick, open the door!'

16 A plan – and a narrow escape

Dick unbolted the door at the top and bottom and flung it open. He rushed in and thumped George and Julian happily on the back.

'Hallo!' he said. 'How does it feel to be rescued?'

'Fine!' cried Julian, and Tim barked madly round them.

George grinned at Dick.

'Good work!' she said. 'What happened?'

Dick told them in a few words all that had happened. When he related how he had climbed down the old well, George and Julian could hardly believe their ears. Julian slipped his arm through his younger brother's.

'You're a brick!' he said. 'A real brick! Now quick – what are we going to do?'

'Well, if they've left us our boat I'm going to take us all back to the mainland as quickly as possible,' said George. 'I'm not playing about with men who brandish revolvers all the time. Come on! Up the well we go and find the boat.'

They ran to the well-shaft and squeezed through the small opening one by one. Up the rope they went and soon found the iron ladder. Julian made them go up one by one in case the ladder wouldn't bear the weight of all three at once.

It really wasn't very long before they were all up in

the open air once more, giving Anne hugs, and hearing
her exclaim gladly, with tears in her eyes, how pleased
she was to see them all again.

'Now come on!' said George after a minute. 'Off to
the boat. Quick! Those men may be back at any time.'

They rushed to the cove. There was their boat, lying
where they had pulled it, out of reach of the waves.
But what a shock for them!

'They've taken the oars!' said George, in dismay.
'The beasts! They know we can't row the boat away
without oars. They were afraid you and Anne might
row off, Dick – so instead of bothering to tow the boat
behind them, they just grabbed the oars. Now we're
stuck. We can't possibly get away.'

It was a great disappointment. The children were
almost ready to cry. After Dick's marvellous rescue of
George and Julian, it had seemed as if everything was
going right – and now suddenly things were going
wrong again.

'We must think this out,' said Julian, sitting down
where he could see at once if any boat came in sight.
'The men have gone off – probably to get a ship from
somewhere in which they can put the ingots and sail
away. They won't be back for some time, I should
think, because you can't charter a ship all in a hurry –
unless, of course, they've got one of their own.'

'And in the meantime we can't get off the island to
get help, because they've got our oars,' said George.
'We can't even signal to any passing fishing-boat
because they won't be out just now. The tide's wrong.
It seems as if all we've got to do is wait here patiently
till the men come back and take my gold! And we can't
stop them.'

'You know – I've got a sort of plan coming into my

head,' said Julian, slowly. 'Wait a bit – don't interrupt me. I'm thinking.'

The others waited in silence while Julian sat and frowned, thinking of his plan. Then he looked at the others with a smile.

'I believe it will work,' he said. 'Listen! We'll wait here in patience till the men come back. What will they do? They'll drag away those stones at the top of the dungeon entrance, and go down the steps. They'll go to the store-room, where they left us – thinking we are still there – and they will go into the room. Well, what about one of us being hidden down there ready to bolt *them* into the room? Then we can either go off in their motor-boat or our own boat if they bring back our oars – and get help.'

Anne thought it was a marvellous idea. But Dick and George did not look so certain. 'We'd have to go down and bolt that door again to make it seem as if we are still prisoners there,' said George. 'And suppose the one who hides down there doesn't manage to bolt the men in? It might be very difficult to do that quickly enough. They will simply catch whoever we plan to leave down there – and come up to look for the rest of us.'

'That's true,' said Julian, thoughtfully. 'Well – we'll suppose that Dick, or whoever goes down, doesn't manage to bolt them in and make them prisoners – and the men come up here again. All right – while they are down below we'll pile big stones over the entrance, just as they did. Then they won't be able to get out.'

'What about Dick down below?' said Anne, at once.

'I could climb up the well again!' said Dick, eagerly. 'I'll be the one to go down and hide. I'll do my best to bolt the men into the room. And if I have to escape I'll

climb up the well-shaft again. The men don't know
about that. So even if they are not prisoners in the
dungeon room, they'll be prisoners underground!'

The children talked over this plan, and decided that
it was the best they could think of. Then George said
she thought it would be a good thing to have a meal.
They were all half-starved and, now that the worry
and excitement of being rescued was over, they were
feeling very hungry!

They fetched some food from the little room and ate
it in the cove, keeping a sharp look-out for the return
of the men. After about two hours they saw a big
fishing-smack appear in the distance, and heard the
chug–chug–chug of a motor-boat too.

'There they are!' said Julian, in excitement, and he
jumped to his feet. 'That's the ship they mean to load
with the ingots, and sail away in safety – and there's the
motor-boat bringing the men back! Quick, Dick,
down the well you go, and hide until you hear them in
the dungeons!'

Dick shot off. Julian turned to the others. 'We'll
have to hide,' he said. 'Now that the tide is out we'll
hide over there, behind those uncovered rocks. I
don't somehow think the men will do any hunting for
Dick and Anne – but they might. Come on! Quick!'

They all hid themselves behind the rocks, and heard
the motor-boat come chugging into the tiny harbour.
They could hear men calling to one another. There
sounded to be more than two men this time. Then the
men left the inlet and went up the low cliff towards the
ruined castle.

Julian crept behind the rocks and peeped to see what
the men were doing. He felt certain they were pulling
away the slabs of stone that had been piled on top of the

entrance to prevent Dick and Anne going down to
rescue the others.

'George! Come on!' called Julian in a low tone. 'I
think the men have gone down the steps into the
dungeons now. We must go and try to put those big
stones back. Quick!'

George, Julian and Anne ran softly and swiftly to the
old courtyard of the castle. They saw that the stones
had been pulled away from the entrance to the dungeons. The men had disappeared. They had plainly
gone down the steps.

The three children did their best to tug at the heavy
stones to drag them back. But their strength was not
the same as that of the men, and they could not manage
to get any very big stones across. They put three
smaller ones, and Julian hoped the men would find
them too difficult to move from below. 'If only Dick
has managed to bolt them into that room!' he said to
the others. 'Come on, back to the well now. Dick will
have to come up there, because he won't be able to get
out of the entrance.'

They all went to the well. Dick had removed the old
wooden cover, and it was lying on the ground. The
children leaned over the hole of the well and waited
anxiously. What was Dick doing? They could hear
nothing from the well and they longed to know what
was happening.

There was plenty happening down below! The two
men, and another, had gone down into the dungeons,
expecting, of course, to find Julian, George and the
dog still locked up in the store-room with the ingots.
They passed the well-shaft not guessing that an excited
small boy was hidden there, ready to slip out of the
opening as soon as they had passed.

Dick heard them pass. He slipped out of the well-opening and followed behind quietly, his feet making no sound. He could see the beams made by the men's powerful torches, and with his heart thumping loudly he crept along the smelly old passages, between great caves, until the men turned into the wide passage where the store-cave lay.

'Here it is,' Dick heard one of the men say, as he flashed his torch on to the great door. 'The gold's in there – so are the kids!'

The men unbolted the door at top and bottom. Dick was glad that he had slipped along to bolt the door, for if he hadn't done that before the men had come they would have known that Julian and George had escaped, and would have been on their guard.

The man opened the door and stepped inside. The second man followed him. Dick crept as close as he dared, waiting for the third man to go in too. Then he meant to slam the door and bolt it!

The first man swung his torch round and gave a loud exclamation. 'The children are gone! How strange! Where are they?'

Two of the men were now in the cave – and the third stepped in at that moment. Dick darted forward and slammed the door. It made a crash that went echoing round and round the caves and passages. Dick fumbled with the bolts, his hand trembling. They were stiff and rusty. The boy found it hard to shoot them home in their sockets. And meanwhile the men were not idle!

As soon as they heard the door slam they spun round. The third man put his shoulder to the door at once and heaved hard. Dick had just got one of the bolts almost into its socket. Then all three men forced their strength against the door, and the bolt gave way!

Dick stared in horror. The door was opening! He turned and fled down the dark passage. The men flashed their torches on and saw him. They went after the boy at top speed.

Dick fled to the well-shaft. Fortunately the opening was on the opposite side, and he could clamber into it without being seen in the light of the torches. The boy only just had time to squeeze through into the shaft before the three men came running by. Not one of them guessed that the runaway was squeezed into the well-shaft they passed! Indeed, the men did not even know that there was a well there.

Trembling from head to foot, Dick began to climb the rope he had left dangling from the rungs of the iron ladder. He undid it when he reached the ladder itself, for he thought that perhaps the men might discover the old well and try to climb up later. They would not be able to do that if there was no rope dangling down.

The boy climbed up the ladder quickly, and squeezed round the stone slab near the top. The other children were there, waiting for him.

They knew at once by the look on Dick's face that he had failed in what he had tried to do. They pulled him out quickly. 'It was no good,' said Dick, panting with his climb. 'I couldn't do it. They burst the door open just as I was bolting it, and chased me. I got into the shaft just in time.'

'They're trying to get out of the entrance now!' cried Anne, suddenly. 'Quick! What shall we do? They'll catch us all!'

'To the boat!' shouted Julian, and he took Anne's hand to help her along. 'Come along! It's our only chance. The men will perhaps be able to move those stones.'

The four children fled down the courtyard. George
darted into the little stone room as they passed it, and
caught up an axe. Dick wondered why she bothered to
do that. Tim dashed along with them, barking madly.

They came to the cove. Their own boat lay there
without oars. The motor-boat was there too. George
jumped into it and gave a yell of delight.

'Here are our oars!' she shouted. 'Take them, Julian,
I've got a job to do here! Get the boat down to the
water, quick!'

Julian and Dick took the oars. Then they dragged
their boat down to the water, wondering what George
was doing. All kinds of crashing sounds came from the
motor-boat!

'George! George! Buck up. The men are out!' suddenly yelled Julian. He had seen the three men running
to the cliff that led down to the cove. George leapt out
of the motor-boat and joined the others. They pushed
their boat out on to the water, and George took the
oars at once, pulling for all she was worth.

The three men ran to their motor-boat. Then they
paused in the greatest dismay – for George had completely ruined it! She had chopped wildly with her axe
at all the machinery she could see – and now the boat
could not possibly be started! It was damaged beyond
any repair the men could make with the few tools they
had.

'You wicked girl!' yelled Jake, shaking his fist at
George. 'Wait till I get you!'

'I'll wait!' shouted back George, her blue eyes shining dangerously. 'And you can wait too! You won't be
able to leave my island now!'

17 The end of the great adventure

The three men stood at the edge of the sea, watching George pull away strongly from the shore. They could do nothing. Their boat was quite useless.

'The fishing-smack they've got waiting out there is too big to use in that little inlet,' said George, as she pulled hard at her oars. 'They'll have to stay there till someone goes in with a boat. I guess they're as wild as can be!'

Their boat had to pass fairly near to the big fishing-boat. A man hailed them as they came by.

'Ahoy there! Have you come from Kirrin Island?'

'Don't answer,' said George. 'Don't say a word.' So no one said anything at all, but looked the other way as if they hadn't heard.

'AHOY THERE!' yelled the man, angrily. 'Are you deaf? Have you come from the island?'

Still the children said nothing at all, but looked away while George rowed steadily. The man on the ship gave it up, and looked in a worried manner towards the island. He felt sure the children had come from there – and he knew enough of his comrades' adventures to wonder if everything was right on the island.

'He may put out a boat from the smack and go and see what's happening,' said George. 'Well, he can't do much except take the men off – with a few ingots! I hardly think they'll dare to take any of the gold though, now that we've escaped to tell our tale!'

Julian looked behind at the ship. He saw after a time that the little boat it carried was being lowered into the sea. 'You're right,' he said to George. 'They're afraid something is up. They're going to rescue those three men. What a pity!'

Their little boat reached land. The children leapt out into the shallow water and dragged it up to the beach. Tim pulled at the rope too, wagging his tail. He loved to join in anything that the children were doing.

'Shall you take Tim to Alf?' asked Dick.

George shook her head. 'No,' she said, 'we haven't any time to waste. We must go and tell everything that has happened. I'll tie Tim up to the fence in the front garden.'

They made their way to Kirrin Cottage at top speed. Aunt Fanny was gardening there. She stared in surprise to see the hurrying children.

'Why,' she said, 'I thought you were not coming back till tomorrow or the next day! Has anything happened? What's the matter with Dick's cheek?'

'Nothing much,' said Dick.

The others chimed in.

'Aunt Fanny, where's Uncle Quentin? We have something important to tell him!'

'Mother, we've had such an adventure!'

'Aunt Fanny, we've an awful lot to tell you! We really have!'

Aunt Fanny looked at the untidy children in amazement. 'Whatever has happened?' she said. Then she turned towards the house and called 'Quentin! Quentin! The children have something to tell us!'

Uncle Quentin came out, looking rather cross, for

he was in the middle of his work. 'What's the matter?' he asked.

'Uncle, it's about Kirrin Island,' said Julian, eagerly. 'Those men haven't bought it yet, have they?'

'Well, it's practically sold,' said his uncle. 'I've signed my part, and they are to sign their part tomorrow. Why? What's that to do with you?'

'Uncle, those men won't sign tomorrow,' said Julian. 'Do you know why they wanted to buy the island and the castle? Not because they really wanted to build an hotel or anything like that – but because they knew the lost gold was hidden there!'

'What nonsense are you talking?' said his uncle.

'It isn't nonsense, Father!' cried George indignantly. 'It's all true. The map of the old castle was in that box you sold – and in the map was shown where the ingots were hidden by my great-great-great-grandfather!'

George's father looked amazed and annoyed. He simply didn't believe a word! But his wife saw by the solemn and serious faces of the four children that something important really had happened. And then Anne suddenly burst into loud sobs! The excitement had been too much for her and she couldn't bear to think that her uncle wouldn't believe that everything was true.

'Aunt Fanny, Aunt Fanny, it's all true!' she sobbed. 'Uncle Quentin is horrid not to believe us. Oh, Aunt Fanny, the man had a revolver – and oh, he made Julian and George prisoners in the dungeons – and Dick had to climb down the well to rescue them. And George has smashed up their motor-boat to stop them escaping!'

Her aunt and uncle couldn't make head or tail of this, but Uncle Quentin suddenly seemed to think that the matter was serious and worth looking into. 'Smashed up a motor-boat!' he said. 'Whatever for? Come indoors. I shall have to hear the story from beginning to end. It seems quite unbelievable to me.'

They all trooped indoors. Anne sat on her aunt's knee and listened to George and Julian telling the whole story. They told it well and left nothing out. Aunt Fanny grew quite pale as she listened, especially when she heard about Dick climbing down the well.

'You might have been killed,' she said. 'Oh, Dick! What a brave thing to do!'

Uncle Quentin listened in the utmost amazement. He had never had much liking or admiration for any children – he always thought they were noisy, tiresome, and silly. But now, as he listened to Julian's tale, he changed his mind about these four children at once!

'You've been very clever,' he said. 'And very brave too. I'm proud of you. Yes, I'm very proud of you all. No wonder you didn't want me to sell the island, George, when you knew about the ingots! But why didn't you tell me?'

The four children stared at him and didn't answer. They couldn't very well say, 'Well, firstly, you wouldn't have believed us. Secondly, you are bad-tempered and unjust and we are frightened of you. Thirdly, we didn't trust you enough to do the right thing.'

'Why don't you answer?' said their uncle. His wife answered for them, in a gentle voice.

'Quentin, you scare the children, you know, and I don't expect they liked to go to you. But now that they have, you will be able to take matters into your own hands. The children cannot do any more. You must ring up the police and see what they have to say about all this.'

'Right,' said Uncle Quentin, and he got up at once. He patted Julian on the back. 'You have all done well,' he said. Then he ruffled George's short curly hair. 'And I'm proud of you, too, George,' he said.

'Oh, Father!' said George, going red with surprise and pleasure. She smiled at him and he smiled back. The children noticed that he had a very nice face when he smiled. He and George were really very alike to look at. Both looked ugly when they sulked and frowned – and both were good to look at when they laughed or smiled!

George's father went off to telephone the police and his lawyer too. The children sat and ate biscuits and plums, telling their aunt a great many little details they had forgotten when telling the story before.

As they sat there, there came a loud and angry bark from the front garden. George looked up. 'That's Tim,' she said, with an anxious look at her mother. 'I hadn't time to take him to Alf, who keeps him for me. Mother, Tim was such a comfort to us on the island, you know. I'm sorry he's barking now – but I expect he's hungry.'

'Well, fetch him in,' said her mother, unexpectedly. 'He's quite a hero, too – we must give him a good dinner.'

George smiled in delight. She sped out of the door and went to Tim. She set him free and he came bounding indoors, wagging his long tail. He licked George's mother and cocked his ears at her.

'Good dog,' she said, and actually patted him. 'I'll get you some dinner!'

Tim trotted out to the kitchen with her. Julian

grinned at George. 'Well, look at that,' he said. 'Your mother's a brick, isn't she?'

'Yes – but I don't know what Father will say when he sees Tim in the house again,' said George, doubtfully.

Her father came back at that minute, his face grave. 'The police take a serious view of all this,' he said, 'and so does my lawyer. They all agree in thinking that you children have been remarkably clever and brave. And George – my lawyer says that the ingots definitely belong to us. Are there really a lot?'

'Father! There are hundreds!' cried George. 'Simply hundreds – all in a big pile in the dungeon. Oh, Father – shall we be rich now?'

'Yes,' said her father. 'We shall. Rich enough to give you and your mother all the things I've longed to give you for so many years and couldn't. I've worked hard enough for you – but it's not the kind of work that brings in a lot of money, and so I've become irritable and bad-tempered. But now you shall have everything you want!'

'I don't really want anything I haven't already got,' said George. 'But Father, there is one thing I'd like more than anything else in the world – and it won't cost you a penny!'

'You shall have it, my dear!' said her father, slipping his arm around George, much to her surprise. 'Just say what it is – and even if it costs a hundred pounds you shall have it!'

Just then there came the pattering of big feet down the passage to the room they were in. A big hairy head pushed itself through the door and looked inquiringly at everyone there. It was Tim, of course!

Uncle Quentin stared at him in surprise. 'Why, isn't

that Tim?' he asked. 'Hallo, Tim!'

'Father! Tim is the thing I want most in all the world,' said George, squeezing her father's arm. 'You can't think what a friend he was to us on the island – and he wanted to fly at those men and fight them. Oh, Father, I don't want any other present – I only want to keep Tim and have him here for my very own. We could afford to give him a proper kennel to sleep in now, and I'd see that he didn't disturb you, I really would.'

'Well, of course you can have him!' said her father – and Tim came right into the room at once, wagging his tail, looking for all the world as if he had understood every word that had been said. He actually licked Uncle Quentin's hand! Anne thought that was very brave of him.

But Uncle Quentin was quite different now. It seemed as if a great weight had been lifted off his shoulders. They were rich now – George could go to a good school – and his wife could have the things he had so much wanted her to have – and he would be able to go on with the work he loved without feeling that he was not earning enough to keep his family in comfort. He beamed round at everyone, looking as jolly a person as anyone could wish!

George was overjoyed about Tim. She flung her arms round her father's neck and hugged him, a thing she had not done for a long time. He looked astonished but very pleased. 'Well, well,' he said, 'this is all very pleasant. Hallo – is this the police already?'

It was. They came up to the door and had a few words with Uncle Quentin. Then one stayed behind to take down the children's story in his notebook and the others went off to get a boat to the island.

The men had gone from there! The boat from the fishing-smack had fetched them away! – and now both ship and boat had disappeared! The motor-boat was still there, quite unusable. The inspector looked at it with a grin.

'Fierce young lady, isn't she, that Miss Georgina?' he said. 'Done this job pretty well – no one could get away in this boat. We'll have to get it towed into harbour.'

The police brought back with them some of the ingots of gold to show Uncle Quentin. They had sealed up the door of the dungeon so that no one else could get in until the children's uncle was ready to go and fetch the gold. Everything was being done thoroughly and properly – though far too slowly for the children! They had hoped that the men would have been caught and taken to prison – and that the police would bring back the whole of the gold at once!

They were all very tired that night and didn't make any fuss at all when their aunt said that they must go to bed early. They undressed and then the boys went to eat their supper in the girls' bedroom. Tim was there, ready to lick up any fallen crumbs.

'Well, I must say we've had a wonderful adventure,' said Julian, sleepily. 'In a way I'm sorry it's ended – though at times I didn't enjoy it very much – especially when you and I, George, were prisoners in that dungeon. That was awful.'

George was looking very happy as she nibbled her gingerbread biscuits. She grinned at Julian.

'And to think I hated the idea of you all coming here to stay!' she said. 'I was going to be such a beast to you! I was going to make you wish you were all home again! And now the only thing that makes me sad is the idea of you going away – which you will do, of course, when the holidays end. And then, after having three friends with me, enjoying adventures like this, I'll be all on my own again. I've never been lonely before – but I know I shall be now.'

'No, you won't,' said Anne, suddenly. 'You can do something that will stop you being lonely ever again.'

'What?' said George in surprise.

'You can ask to go to the same boarding-school as I go to,' said Anne. 'It's such a lovely one – and we are allowed to keep our pets, so Tim could come too!'

'Gracious! Could he really?' said George, her eyes shining. 'Well, I'll go then. I always said I wouldn't – but I will because I see now how much better and happier it is to be with others than all by myself. And if I can have Tim, well that's simply wonderful!'

'You'd better go back to your own bedroom now, boys,' said Aunt Fanny, appearing at the doorway. 'Look at Dick, almost dropping with sleep! Well, you should all have pleasant dreams tonight, for you've had an adventure to be proud of. George – is that Tim under your bed?'

'Well, yes it is, Mother,' said George, pretending to be surprised. 'Dear me! Tim, what are you doing here?'

Tim crawled out and went over to George's mother. He lay flat on his tummy and looked up at her most appealingly out of his soft brown eyes.

'Do you want to sleep in the girls' room tonight?' said George's mother, with a laugh. 'All right – just for once!'

'*Mother!*' yelled George, overjoyed. 'Oh, thank you, thank you, thank you! How did you guess that I just didn't want to be parted from Tim tonight? Oh,

Mother! Tim, you can sleep on the rug over there.'

Four happy children snuggled down into their beds. Their wonderful adventure had come to a happy end. They had plenty of holidays still in front of them – and now that Uncle Quentin was no longer poor, he would give them the little presents he wanted to. George was going to school with Anne – and she had Tim for her own again! The island and castle still belonged to George – everything was marvellous!

'I'm so glad Kirrin Island wasn't sold, George,' said Anne, sleepily. 'I'm so glad it still belongs to you.'

'It belongs to three other people too,' said George. 'It belongs to me – and to you and Julian and Dick. I've discovered that it's fun to share things. So tomorrow I am going to draw up a deed, or whatever it's called, and put in it that I give you and the others a quarter-share each. Kirrin Island and Castle shall belong to us all!'

'Oh, George – how lovely!' said Anne, delighted. 'Won't the boys be pleased? I do feel so ha . . .'

But before she could finish, the little girl was asleep. So was George. In the other room the two boys slept, too, dreaming of ingots and dungeons and all kinds of exciting things.

Only one person was awake – and that was Tim. He had one ear up and was listening to the children's breathing. As soon as he knew they were asleep he got up quietly from his rug. He crept softly over to George's bed. He put his front paws up and sniffed at the sleeping girl.

Then, with a bound he was on the bed, and snuggled himself down into the crook of her legs. He gave a sigh, and shut his eyes. The four children might be happy – but Tim was happiest of all.

'Oh, Tim,' murmured George, half waking up as she felt him against her. 'Oh, Tim, you mustn't – but you do feel so nice. Tim – we'll have other adventures together, the five of us – won't we?'

They will – but that's another story!

ENID BLYTON

FIVE GO ADVENTURING AGAIN

Illustrated by Betty Maxey

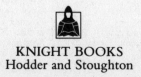

KNIGHT BOOKS
Hodder and Stoughton

Five go Adventuring Again
First published in a single volume by
Hodder and Stoughton, 1942

First Knight Book single volume
edition 1967

Printed and bound in Great Britain for Hodder and Stoughton Children's Books, a division of Hodder and Stoughton Ltd., Mill Road, Dunton Green, Sevenoaks, Kent TN13 2YA. Editorial Office: 47 Bedford Square, London WC1B 3DP) by Cox & Wyman Ltd., Reading, Berks. Photoset by Rowland Phototypesetting Ltd., Bury St Edmunds, Suffolk.

British Library C.I.P.

Blyton, Enid
   Five go adventuring again. –
   (Blyton, Enid. Famous Five).
   I. Title
   823'.912[J]   PZ7

FIVE GO ADVENTURING
AGAIN

Contents

1 Christmas holidays   165
2 All together again   173
3 The new tutor   181
4 An exciting discovery   191
5 An unpleasant walk   199
6 Lessons with Mr Roland   207
7 Directions for the Secret Way   217
8 What happened on Christmas night   225
9 A hunt for the Secret Way   233
10 A shock for George and Tim   241
11 Stolen papers   249
12 George in trouble   257
13 Julian has a surprise   267
14 The Secret Way at last!   279
15 An exciting journey and hunt   287
16 The children are discovered   297
17 Good old Tim!   305

1 Christmas holidays

It was the last week of the Christmas term, and all the girls at Gaylands School were looking forward to the Christmas Holidays. Anne sat down at the breakfast-table and picked up a letter addressed to her. .

'Hallo, look at this!' she said to her cousin Georgina, who was sitting beside her. 'A letter from Daddy – and I only had one from him and Mummy yesterday.'

'I hope it's not bad news,' said George. She would not allow anyone to call her Georgina, and now even the mistresses called her George. She really was very like a boy with her short curly hair, and her boyish ways. She looked anxiously at Anne as her cousin read the letter.

'Oh, George – we can't go home for the holidays!' said Anne, with tears in her eyes. 'Mummy's got scarlet fever – and Daddy is in quarantine for it – so they can't have us back. Isn't it just too bad?'

'Oh, I *am* sorry,' said George. She was just as disappointed for herself as for Anne, because Anne's mother had invited George, and her dog Timothy, to stay for the Christmas holidays with them. She had been promised many things she had never seen before – the pantomime, and the circus – and a big party with a fine Christmas tree! Now it wouldn't happen.

'Whatever will the two boys say?' said Anne, think-ing of Julian and Dick, her two brothers. 'They won't be able to go home either.'

'Well – what Are you going to do for the holidays then?' asked George. 'Won't you come and stay at Kirrin Cottage with *me*? I'm sure my mother would love to have you again. We had such fun when you came to stay for the summer hols.'

'Wait a minute – let me finish the letter and see what Daddy says,' said Anne, picking up the note again. 'Poor Mummy – I do hope she isn't feeling very ill.'

She read a few more lines and then gave such a delighted exclamation that George and the other girls waited impatiently for her to explain.

'George! We *are* to come to you again – but oh blow, blow, blow! – we've got to have a tutor for the hols, partly to look after us so that your mother doesn't have too much bother with us, and partly because both Julian and Dick have been ill with 'flu twice this term, and have got behind in their work.'

'A tutor! How sickening! That means I'll have to do lessons too, I'll bet!' said George, in dismay. 'When my mother and father see my report I guess they'll find out how little I know. After all, this is the first time I've ever been to a proper school, and there are heaps of things I don't know.'

'What horrid hols they'll be, if we have a tutor running after us all the time,' said Anne, gloomily. 'I expect I'll have quite a good report, because I've done well in the exams – but it won't be any fun for me not doing lessons with you three in the hols. Though, of course, I could go off with Timothy, I suppose. *He* won't be doing lessons!'

'Yes, he will,' said George, at once. She could not bear the idea of her beloved dog Timothy going off each morning with Anne, while she, George, sat and worked hard with Julian and Dick.

'Timothy can't do lessons, don't be silly, George,' said Anne.

'He can sit under my feet while *I'm* doing them,' said George. 'It will be a great help to feel him there. For goodness' sake eat up your sausages, Anne. We've all nearly finished. The bell will be going in a minute and you won't have had any breakfast.'

'I am glad Mummy isn't very bad,' said Anne, hurriedly finishing her letter. 'Daddy says he's written to Dick and Julian – and to your father to ask him to engage a tutor for us. Oh dash – this is an awful disappointment, isn't it? I don't mean I shan't enjoy going to Kirrin Cottage again – and seeing Kirrin Island – but after all there are no pantomimes or circuses or parties to look forward to at Kirrin.'

The end of the term came quickly. Anne and George packed up their trunks, and put on the labels, enjoying the noise and excitement of the last two days. The big school coaches rolled up to the door, and the girls clambered in.

'Off to Kirrin again!' said Anne. 'Come on, Timothy darling, you can sit between me and George.'

Gaylands School allowed the children to keep their own pets, and Timothy, George's big mongrel dog, had been a great success. Except for the time when he had run after the dustman, and dragged the dustbin away from him, all the way up the school grounds and into George's classroom, he had really behaved extremely well.

'I'm sure *you'll* have a good report, Tim,' said George, giving the dog a hug. 'We're going home again. Will you like that?'

'Woof,' said Tim, in his deep voice. He stood up, wagging his tail, and there was a squeal from the seat behind.

'George! Make Tim sit down. He's wagging my hat off!'

It was not very long before the two girls and Timothy were in London, being put into the train for Kirrin.

'I do wish the boys broke up today too,' sighed Anne. 'Then we could all have gone down to Kirrin together. That would have been fun.'

Julian and Dick broke up the next day and were to join the girls then at Kirrin Cottage. Anne was very much looking forward to seeing them again. A term was a long time to be away from one another. She had been glad to have her cousin George with her. The three of them had stayed with George in the summer, and had had some exciting adventures together on the little island off the coast. An old castle stood on the island and in the dungeons the children had made all kinds of wonderful discoveries.

'It will be lovely to go across to Kirrin Island again, George,' said Anne, as the train sped off towards the west.

'We shan't be able to,' said George. 'The sea is terribly rough round the island in the winter. It would be too dangerous to try and row there.'

'Oh, what a pity,' said Anne disappointed. 'I was looking forward to some more adventures there.'

'There won't be any adventures at Kirrin in the winter,' said George. 'It's cold down there – and when it snows we sometimes get frozen up completely – can't even walk to the village because the sea-wind blows the snow-drifts so high.'

'Oooh – that sounds rather exciting!' said Anne.

'Well, it isn't really,' said George. 'It's awfully boring – nothing to do but sit at home all day, or turn out with a spade and dig the snow away.'

It was a long time before the train reached the little station that served Kirrin. But at last it was there pulling in slowly and stopping at the tiny platform. The two girls jumped out eagerly, and looked to see if anyone had met them. Yes – there was George's mother!

'Hallo, George darling – hallo, Anne!' said George's mother, and gave both children a hug. 'Anne, I'm so sorry about your mother, but she's getting on all right, you'll be glad to know.'

'Oh, good!' said Anne. 'It's nice of you to have us, Aunt Fanny. We'll try and be good! What about Uncle Quentin? Will he mind having four children in the house in the winter-time? We won't be able to go out and leave him in peace as often as we did in the summer!'

George's father was a scientist, a very clever man, but rather frightening. He had little patience with children, and the four of them had felt very much afraid of him at times in the summer.

'Oh, your uncle is still working very hard at his book,' said Aunt Fanny. 'You know, he has been working out a secret theory – a secret idea – and putting it all into his book. He says that once it is all explained and finished, he is to take it to some high authority, and then his idea will be used for the good of the country.'

'Oh, Aunt Fanny – it does sound exciting,' said Anne. 'What's the secret?'

'I can't tell you that, silly,' said her aunt, laughing. 'Why, even I myself don't know it. Come along, now – it's cold standing here. Timothy looks very fat and well, George dear.'

'Oh Mother, he's had a marvellous time at school,'

said George. 'He really has. He chewed up the cook's
old slippers . . .'

'And he chased the cat that lives in the stables every
time he saw her,' said Anne.

'And he once got into the larder and ate a whole
steak pie,' said George; 'and once . . .'

'Good gracious, George, I should think the school
will refuse to have Timothy next term,' said her
mother, in horror. 'Wasn't he well punished? I hope he
was.'

'No – he wasn't,' said George, going rather red.
'You see, Mother, we are responsible for our pets and
their behaviour ourselves – so if ever Timothy does
anything bad *I'm* punished for it, because I haven't
shut him up properly, or something like that.'

'Well, you must have had quite a lot of punishments
then,' said her mother, as she drove the little pony-trap
along the frosty roads. 'I really think that's rather a
good idea!' There was a twinkle in her eyes as she
spoke. 'I think I'll keep on with the same idea – punish
you every time Timothy misbehaves himself!'

The girls laughed. They felt happy and excited.
Holidays were fun. Going back to Kirrin was lovely.
Tomorrow the boys would come – and then
Christmas would be there!

'Good old Kirrin Cottage!' said Anne, as they came
in sight of the pretty old house. 'Oh – look, there's
Kirrin Island!' The two looked out to sea, where the
old ruined castle stood on the little island of Kirrin –
what adventures they had had there in the summer!

The girls went into the house. 'Quentin!' called
George's mother. 'Quentin! The girls are here.'

Uncle Quentin came out of his study at the other
side of the house. Anne thought he looked taller and
darker than ever. 'And frownier!' she said to herself.

Uncle Quentin might be very clever, but Anne pre-
ferred someone jolly and smiling like her own father.
She shook hands with her uncle politely, and watched
George kiss him.

'Well!' said Uncle Quentin to Anne. 'I hear I've got
to get a tutor for you! At least, for the two boys. My
word, you *will* have to behave yourself with a tutor, I
can tell you!'

This was meant to be a joke, but it didn't sound very
nice to Anne and George. People you had to behave
well with were usually very strict and tiresome. Both
girls were glad when George's father had gone back
into his study.

'Your father has been working far too hard lately,'
said George's mother to her. 'He is tired out. Thank
goodness his book is nearly finished. He had hoped to
finish it by Christmas so that he could join in the fun
and games – but now he says he can't.'

'What a pity,' said Anne, politely, though secretly
she thought it was a good thing. It wouldn't be much
fun having Uncle Quentin to play charades and things
like that! 'Oh, Aunt Fanny, I'm so looking forward to
seeing Julian and Dick – and won't they be pleased to
see Tim and George? Aunt Fanny, nobody calls
George Georgina at school, not even our form mistress. I was rather hoping they would, because I
wanted to see what would happen when she refused to
answer to Georgina! George, you liked school, didn't
you?'

'Yes,' said George, 'I did. I thought I'd hate being
with a lot of others, but it's fun, after all. But Mother,
you won't find my report very good, I'm afraid. There
were such a lot of things I was bad at because I'd never
done them before.'

'Well, you'd never been to school before!' said her

mother. 'I'll explain it to your father if he gets upset. Now go along and get ready for a late tea. You must be very hungry.'

The girls went upstairs to their little room. 'I'm glad I'm not spending my hols by myself,' said George. 'I've had much more fun since I've known you and the boys. Hey, Timothy, where have you gone?'

'He's gone to smell all around the house to make sure it's his proper home!' said Anne, with a giggle. 'He wants to know if the kitchen smells the same – and the bathroom – and his basket. It must be just as exciting for him to come home for the holidays as it is for us!'

Anne was right. Timothy was thrilled to be back again. He ran round George's mother, sniffing at her legs in friendliness, pleased to see her again. He ran into the kitchen but soon came out again because someone new was there – Joanna the cook – a fat, panting person who eyed him with suspicion.

'You can come into this kitchen once a day for your dinner,' said Joanna. 'And that's all. I'm not having meat and sausages and chicken disappearing under my nose if I can help it. I know what dogs are, I do!'

Timothy ran into the scullery and sniffed round there. He ran into the dining-room and the sitting-room, and was pleased to find they had the same old smell. He put his nose to the door of the study where George's father worked, and sniffed very cautiously. He didn't mean to go in. Timothy was just as wary of George's father as the others were!

He ran upstairs to the girl's bedroom again. Where was his basket? Ah, there it was by the window-seat. Good! That meant he was to sleep in the girls' bedroom once more. He curled himself up in his basket, and thumped loudly with his tail.

'Glad to be back,' said his tail, 'glad – to – be – back!'

2 All together again

The next day the boys came back. Anne and George went to meet them with Timothy. George drove the pony-trap, and Tim sat beside her. Anne could hardly wait for the train to stop at the station. She ran along the platform, looking for Julian and Dick in the carriages that passed.

Then she saw them. They were looking out of a window at the back of the train, waving and yelling.

'Anne! Anne! Here we are! Hallo, George! Oh, there's Timothy!'

'Julian! Dick!' yelled Anne. Timothy began to bark and leap about. It was most exciting.

'Oh, Julian! It's lovely to see you both again!' cried Anne, giving her two brothers a hug each. Timothy leapt up and licked them both. He was beside himself with joy. Now he had all the children around him that he loved.

The three children and the dog stood happily together, all talking at once while the porter got the luggage out of the train. Anne suddenly remembered George. She looked round her. She was nowhere to be seen, although she had come on the station platform with Anne.

'Where's old George?' said Julian. 'I saw her here when I waved out of the window.'

'She must have gone back to the pony-trap,' said Anne. 'Tell the porter to bring your trunks out to the trap, Julian. Come along! We'll go and find George.'

George was standing by the pony, holding his head. She looked rather gloomy, Anne thought. The boys went up to her.

'Hallo, George, old thing!' cried Julian, and gave her a hug. Dick did the same.

'What's up?' asked Anne, wondering at George's sudden silence.

'I believe George felt left-out!' said Julian with a grin. 'Funny old Georgina!'

'*Don't* call me Georgina!' said the little girl fiercely. The boys laughed.

'Ah, it's the same fierce old George, all right,' said Dick, and gave the girl a friendly slap on the shoulder. 'Oh, George – it's good to see you again. Do you remember our marvellous adventures in the summer?'

George felt her awkwardness slipping away from her. She *had* felt left-out when she had seen the great welcome that the two boys gave to their small sister – but no one could sulk for long with Julian and Dick. They just wouldn't let anyone feel left-out or awkward or sulky.

The four children climbed into the trap. The porter heaved in the two trunks. There was only just room for them. Timothy sat on top of the trunks, his tail wagging nineteen to the dozen, and his tongue hanging out because he was panting with delight.

'You two girls were lucky to be able to take Tim to school with you,' said Dick, patting the big dog lovingly. 'No pets are allowed at our school. Awfully hard on those fellows who like live things.'

'Thompson Minor kept white mice,' said Julian. 'And one day they escaped and met Matron round a corner of the passage. She squealed the place down.'

The girls laughed. The boys always had funny tales to tell when they got home.

'And Kennedy keeps snails,' said Dick. 'You know, snails sleep for the winter – but Kennedy kept his in far too warm a place, and they all crawled out of their box and went up the walls. You should have heard how we laughed when the geography master asked Thompson to point out Cape Town on the map – and there was one of the snails in the very place!'

Everyone laughed again. It was so good to be all together once more. They were very much of an age – Julian was twelve. George and Dick were eleven, and Anne was ten. Holidays and Christmas time were in front of them. No wonder they laughed at everything, even the silliest little joke!

'It's good that Mummy is getting on all right, isn't it?' said Dick, as the pony went along the road at a great pace. 'I was disappointed not to go home. I must say – I did want to go to see Aladdin and the Lamp, and the circus – but still, it's good to be back at Kirrin Cottage again. I wish we could have some more exciting adventures. Not a hope of that this time, though.'

'There's one snag about these hols,' said Julian. 'And that's the tutor. I hear we've got to have one because Dick and I missed so much school this term, and we've got to take important exams next summer.'

'Yes,' said Anne. 'I wonder what he'll be like. I do hope he will be a sport. Uncle Quentin is going to choose one today.'

Julian and Dick made faces at one another. They felt sure that any tutor chosen by Uncle Quentin would be anything but a sport. Uncle Quentin's idea of a tutor would be somebody strict and gloomy and forbidding.

Never mind! He wouldn't come for a day or two. And he *might* be fun. The boys cheered up and pulled Timothy's thick coat. The dog pretended to growl and bite. *He* wasn't worried about tutors. Lucky Timothy!

They all arrived at Kirrin Cottage. The boys were really pleased to see their aunt, and rather relieved when she said that their uncle had not yet come back.

'He's gone to see two or three men who have answered the advertisement for a tutor,' she said. 'It won't be long before he's back.'

'Mother, I haven't got to do lessons in the hols too, have I?' asked George. Nothing had yet been said to her about this, and she longed to know.

'Oh yes, George,' said her mother. 'Your father has seen your report, and although it isn't really a bad one, and we certainly didn't expect a marvellous one, still it does show that you are behind your age in some things. A little extra coaching will soon help you along.'

George looked gloomy. She had expected this but it was tiresome all the same. 'Anne's the only one who won't have to do lessons,' she said.

'I'll do some too,' promised Anne. 'Perhaps not always, George, if it's a very fine day, for instance – but sometimes, just to keep you company.'

'Thanks,' said George. 'But you needn't. I shall have Timmy.'

George's mother looked doubtful about this. 'We'll have to see what the tutor says about that,' she said.

'Mother! If the tutor says I can't have Timothy in the room, I jolly well won't do holiday lessons!' began George, fiercely.

Her mother laughed. 'Well, well – here's our fierce, hot-tempered George again!' she said. 'Go along, you two boys, and wash your hands and do your hair.

You seem to have collected all the grime on the railway.'

The children and Timothy went upstairs. It was such fun to be five again. They always counted Tim as one of themselves. He went everywhere with them, and really seemed to understand every single word they said.

'I wonder what sort of a tutor Uncle Quentin will choose,' said Dick, as he scrubbed his nails. 'If only he would choose the right kind – someone jolly and full of fun, who knows that holiday lessons are sickening to have, and tries to make up for them by being a sport out of lesson-time. I suppose we'll have to work every morning.'

'Hurry up. I want my tea,' said Julian. 'Come on down, Dick. We'll know about the tutor soon enough!'

They all went down together, and sat round the table. Joanna the cook had made a lovely lot of buns and a great big cake. There was not much left of either by the time the four children had finished!

Uncle Quentin returned just as they were finishing. He seemed rather pleased with himself. He shook hands with the two boys and asked them if they had had a good term.

'Did you get a tutor, Uncle Quentin?' asked Anne, who could see that everyone was simply bursting to know this.

'Ah – yes, I did,' said her uncle. He sat down, while Aunt Fanny poured him out a cup of tea. 'I interviewed three applicants, and had almost chosen the last one, when another fellow came in, all in a hurry. Said he had only just seen the advertisement, and hoped he wasn't too late.'

'Did you choose him?' asked Dick.

'I did,' said his uncle. 'He seemed a most intelligent fellow. Even knew about me and my work! And he had the most wonderful letters of recommendation.'

'I don't think the children need to know all these details,' murmured Aunt Fanny. 'Anyway – you asked him to come?'

'Oh yes,' said Uncle Quentin. 'He's a good bit older than the others – they were rather young fellows – this one seems very responsible and intelligent. I'm sure you'll like him, Fanny. He'll fit in here very well. I feel I would like to have him to talk to me sometimes in the evening.'

The children couldn't help feeling that the new tutor sounded rather alarming. Their uncle smiled at the gloomy faces.

'You'll like Mr Roland,' he said. 'He knows how to handle youngsters – knows he's got to be very firm, and to see that you know a good bit more at the end of the holidays than you did at the beginning.'

This sounded even more alarming. All four children wished heartily that Aunt Fanny had been to choose the tutor, and not Uncle Quentin.

'When is he coming?' asked George.

'Tomorrow,' said her father. 'You can all go to meet him at the station. That will make a nice welcome for him.'

'We *had* thought of taking the bus and going to do a bit of Christmas shopping,' said Julian, seeing Anne looked very disappointed.

'Oh, no, you must certainly go and meet Mr Roland,' said his uncle. 'I told him you would. And mind you, you four – no nonsense with him! You've to do as you're told, and you must work hard with him, because your father is paying very high fees for his coaching. I'm paying a third, because I want him to coach George a little too – so George, you must do your best.'

'I'll try,' said George. 'If he's nice, I'll do my very best.'

'You'll do your best whether you think him nice or not!' said her father, frowning. 'He will arrive by the ten-thirty train. Be sure to be there in time.'

'I do hope he won't be too strict,' said Dick, that evening, when the five of them were alone for a minute or two. 'It's going to spoil the hols, if we have someone down on us all the time. And I do hope he'll like Timothy.'

George looked up at once. 'Like Timothy!' she said. 'Of course he'll like Timothy! How couldn't he?'

'Well – your father didn't like Timothy very much last summer,' said Dick. 'I don't see how anyone could *dislike* darling Tim – but there are people who don't like dogs, you know, George.'

'If Mr Roland doesn't like Timothy, I'll not do a single thing for him,' said George. 'Not one single thing!'

'She's gone all fierce again!' said Dick, with a laugh. 'My word – the sparks will fly if Mr Roland dares to dislike our Timothy!'

3 *The new tutor*

Next morning the sun was out, all the sea-mist that had hung about for the last two days had disappeared, and Kirrin Island showed plainly at the mouth of Kirrin Bay. The children stared longingly at the ruined castle on it.

'I do wish we could get over to the castle,' said Dick. 'It looks quite calm enough, George.'

'It's very rough by the island,' said George. 'It always is at this time of year. I know Mother wouldn't let us go.'

'It's a lovely island, and it's all our own!' said Anne. 'You said you would share it with us for ever and ever, didn't you, George?'

'Yes, I did,' said George. 'And so I will, dungeons and all. Come on – we must get the trap out. We shall be late meeting the train if we stand here all day looking at the island.'

They got the pony and trap and set off down the hard lanes. Kirrin Island disappeared behind the cliffs as they turned inland to the station.

'Did all this land round about belong to your family once upon a time?' asked Julian.

'Yes, all of it,' said George. 'Now we don't own anything except Kirrin Island, our own house and that farm away over there – Kirrin Farm.'

She pointed with her whip. The children saw a fine

old farmhouse standing on a hill a good way off, over the heather-clad common.

'Who lives there?' asked Julian.

'Oh, an old farmer and his wife,' said George. 'They were nice to me when I was smaller. We'll go over there one day, if you like. Mother says they don't make the farm pay any more, and in the summertime they take in people who want a holiday.'

'Listen! That's the train whistling in the tunnel!' said Julian, suddenly. 'Buck up, for goodness' sake, George. We shan't be there in time!'

The four children and Timothy looked at the train coming out of the tunnel and drawing in at the station. The pony cantered along swiftly. They would be just in time.

'Who's going on to the platform to meet him?' asked George, as they drew into the little station yard. 'I'm not. I must look after Tim and the pony.'

'I don't want to,' said Anne. 'I'll stay with George.'

'Well, we'd better go, then,' said Julian, and he and Dick leapt out of the trap. They ran on to the platform just as the train pulled up.

Not many people got out. A woman clambered out with a basket. A young man leapt out, whistling, the son of the baker in the village. An old man climbed down with difficulty. The tutor could be none of those!

Then, right at the front of the train, rather an odd-looking man got out. He was short and burly, and he had a beard rather like a sailor. His eyes were piercingly blue, and his thick hair was sprinkled with grey. He glanced up and down the platform, and then beckoned to the porter.

'That must be Mr Roland,' said Julian to Dick.

'Come on – let's ask him. There's no one else it could be.'

The boys went up to the bearded man. 'Are you Mr Roland, sir?' he asked.

'I am,' said the man. 'I suppose you are Julian and Dick?'

'Yes, sir,' answered the boys together. 'We brought the pony-trap for your luggage.'

'Oh, fine,' said Mr Roland. His bright blue eyes looked the boys up and down, and he smiled. Julian and Dick liked him. He seemed sensible and jolly.

'Are the other two here as well?' said Mr Roland, walking down the platform, with the porter trailing behind with his luggage.

'Yes – George and Anne are outside with the trap,' said Julian.

'George and Anne,' said Mr Roland, in a puzzled voice. 'I thought the others were girls. I didn't know there was a third boy.'

'Oh, George is a girl,' said Dick, with a laugh. 'Her real name is Georgina.'

'And a very nice name, too,' said Mr Roland.

'George doesn't think so,' said Julian. 'She won't answer if she's called Georgina. You'd better call her George, sir!'

'Really?' said Mr Roland, in rather a chilly tone. Julian took a glance at him.

'Not quite so jolly as he looks!' thought the boy.

'Tim's out there too,' said Dick.

'Oh – and is Tim a boy or a girl?' inquired Mr Roland, cautiously.

'A dog, sir!' said Dick, with a grin.

Mr Roland seemed rather taken aback. 'A dog?' he said. 'I didn't know there was a dog in the household. Your uncle said nothing to me about a dog.'

'Don't you like dogs?' asked Julian, in surprise.

'No,' said Mr Roland, shortly. 'But I dare say your dog won't worry me much. Hallo, hallo – so here are the little girls! How do you do?'

George was not very pleased at being called a little girl. For one thing she hated to be spoken of as little, and for another thing she always tried to be a boy. She held out her hand to Mr Roland and said nothing. Anne smiled at him, and Mr Roland thought she was much the nicer of the two.

'Tim! Shake hands with Mr Roland!' said Julian to Timothy. This was one of Tim's really good tricks. He could hold out his right paw in a very polite manner. Mr Roland looked down at the big dog, and Tim looked back at him.

Then, very slowly and deliberately, Timothy turned his back on Mr Roland and climbed up into the pony-trap! Usually he put out his paw at once when told to, and the children stared at him in amazement.

'Timothy! What's come over you?' cried Dick. Tim put his ears down and did not move.

'He doesn't like you,' said George, looking at Mr Roland. 'That's very strange. He usually likes people. But perhaps you don't like dogs?'

'No, I don't, as a matter of fact,' said Mr Roland. 'I was once very badly bitten as a boy, and somehow or other I've never managed to like dogs since. But I dare say your Tim will take to me sooner or later.'

They all got into the trap. It was a tight squeeze. Timothy looked at Mr Roland's ankles as if he would rather like to nibble them. Anne laughed.

'Tim *is* behaving strangely!' she said. 'It's a good thing you haven't come to teach him, Mr Roland!' She smiled up at the tutor, and he smiled back, showing very white teeth. His eyes were as brilliant a blue as George's.

Anne liked him. He joked with the boys as they drove him, and both of them began to feel that their Uncle Quentin hadn't made such a bad choice after all.

Only George said nothing. She sensed that the tutor disliked Timothy, and George was not prepared to like anyone who didn't take to Timothy at first sight. She thought it was very peculiar too, that Tim would not shake paws with the tutor. 'He's a clever dog,' she thought. 'He knows Mr Roland doesn't like him, so he won't shake hands. I don't blame you, Tim darling, I wouldn't shake hands with anyone who didn't like *me*!'

Mr Roland was shown up to his room when he arrived. Aunt Fanny came down and spoke to the children. 'Well! He seems very nice, youngish and jolly.'

'Youngish!' exclaimed Julian. 'Why, he's awfully old! Must be forty at the very least!'

Aunt Fanny laughed. 'Does he seem so old to you?' she said. 'Well, old or not, he'll be quite nice to you, I'm sure.'

'Aunt Fanny, we shan't begin lessons until after Christmas, shall we?' asked Julian, anxiously.

'Of course you will!' said his aunt. 'It is almost a week till Christmas – you don't suppose we have asked Mr Roland to come and do nothing till Christmas is over, do you?'

The children groaned. 'We wanted to do some Christmas shopping,' said Anne.

'Well, you can do that in the afternoon,' said her aunt. 'You will only do lessons in the morning, for three hours. That won't hurt any of you!'

The new tutor came downstairs at that moment,

and Aunt Fanny took him to see Uncle Quentin. She
came out after a while, looking very pleased.

'Mr Roland will be nice company for your uncle,'
she said to Julian. 'I think they wil! get on very well
together. Mr Roland seems to understand quite a bit
about your uncle's work.'

'Let's hope he spends most of his time with him
then!' said George, in a low voice.

'Come on out for a walk,' said Dick. 'It's so fine
today. We shan't have lessons this morning, shall we,
Aunt Fanny?'

'Oh, no,' said his aunt. 'You'll begin tomorrow. Go
for a walk now, all of you – we shan't often get sunny
days like this!'

'Let's go over to Kirrin Farm,' said Julian. 'It looks
such a nice place. Show us the way, George.'

'Right!' said George. She whistled to Timothy, and
he came bounding up. The five of them set off
together, going down the lane, and then on to a rough
road over the common that led to the farm on the
distant hill.

It was lovely walking in the December sun. Their
feet rang on the frosty path, and Tim's blunt claws
made quite a noise as he pattered up and down,
overjoyed at being with his four friends again.

After a good long walk across the common the
children came to the farmhouse. It was built of white
stone, and stood strong and lovely on the hillside.
George opened the farm-gate and went into the farmyard. She kept her hand on Tim's collar for there were
two farm-dogs somewhere about.

Someone clattered round the barn near-by. It was an
old man, and George hailed him loudly.

'Hallo, Mr Sanders! How are you?'

'Why, if it isn't Master George!' said the old fellow

with a grin. George grinned too. She loved being
called Master instead of Miss.

'These are my cousins,' shouted George. She turned
to the others. 'He's deaf,' she said. 'You'll have to
shout to make him hear.'

'I'm Julian,' said Julian in a loud voice and the others
said their names too. The farmer beamed at them.

'You come along in and see the Missis,' he said.
'She'll be rare pleased to see you all. We've known
Master George since she was a baby, and we knew her
mother when *she* was a baby too, and we knew her
granny as well.'

'You must be very, very old,' said Anne.

The farmer smiled down at her.

'As old as my tongue and a little older than my
teeth!' he said, chuckling. 'Come away in now.'

They all went into the big, warm farmhouse kitchen, where a little old woman, as lively as a bantam
hen, was bustling about. She was just as pleased to see
the four children as her husband was.

'Well, there now!' she said. 'I haven't seen you for
months, Master George. I did hear that you'd gone
away to school.'

'Yes, I did,' said George. 'But I'm home for the
holidays now. Does it matter if I let Timothy loose,
Mrs Sanders? I think he'll be friendly if your dogs are,
too.'

'Yes, you let him loose,' said the old lady. 'He'll
have a fine time in the farmyard with Ben and Rikky.
Now what would you like to drink? Hot milk? Cocoa?
Coffee? And I've some new shortbread baked yesterday. You shall have some of that.'

'Ah, my wife's very busy this week, cooking up all
sorts of things,' said the old farmer, as his wife bustled
off to the larder. 'We've company this Christmas!'

'Have you?' said George, surprised, for she knew that the old pair had never had any children of their own. 'Who is coming? Anyone I know?'

'Two artists from London Town!' said the old farmer. 'Wrote and asked us to take them for three weeks over Christmas – and offered us good money too. So my old wife's as busy as a bee.'

'Are they going to paint pictures?' asked Julian, who rather fancied himself as an artist, too. 'I wonder if I could come and talk to them some day. I'm rather good at pictures myself. They might give me a few hints.'

'You come along whenever you like,' said old Mrs Sanders, making cocoa in a big jug. She set out a plate of most delicious-looking shortbreads, and the children ate them hungrily.

'I should think the two artists will be rather lonely down here, in the depths of the country at Christmas-time,' said George. 'Do they know anyone?'

'They say they don't know a soul,' said Mrs Sanders. 'But there – artists can be peculiar folk. I've had some here before. They seemed to like mooning about all alone. These two will be happy enough, I'll be bound.'

'They should be, with all the good things you're cooking up for them,' said her old husband. 'Well, I must be out after the sheep. Good-day to you, young-sters. Come again and see us sometime.'

He went out. Old Mrs Sanders chattered on to the children as she bustled about the big kitchen. Timothy ran in and settled down on the rug by the fire.

He suddenly saw a tabby cat slinking along by the wall, all her hairs on end with fear of the strange dog. He gave a delighted wuff and sprang at the cat. She fled out of the kitchen into the old panelled hall. Tim flew after her, taking no notice at all of George's stern shout.

The cat tried to leap on top of an old grandfather clock in the hall. With a joyous bark Tim sprang too. He flung himself against a polished panel – and then a most extraordinary thing happened!

The panel disappeared – and a dark hole showed in the old wall! George, who had followed Tim out into the hall, gave a loud cry of surprise. 'Look! Mrs Sanders, come and look!'

4 An exciting discovery

Old Mrs Sanders and the other three children rushed out into the hall when they heard George's shout.

'What's up?' cried Julian. 'What's happened?'

'Tim sprang at the cat, missed her, and fell hard against the panelled wall,' said George, 'and the panel moved, and look – there's a hole in the wall!'

'It's a secret panel!' cried Dick, in excitement, peering into the hole. 'Golly! Did you know there was one here, Mrs Sanders?'

'Oh yes,' said the old lady. 'This house is full of funny things like that. I'm very careful when I polish that panel, because if I rub too hard in the top corner, it always slides back.'

'What's behind the panel?' asked Julian. The hole was only about the width of his head, and when he stuck his head inside, he could see only darkness. The wall itself was about eight inches behind the panelling, and was of stone.

'Get a candle, do get a candle!' said Anne, thrilled. 'You haven't got a torch, have you, Mrs Sanders?'

'No,' said the old woman. 'But you can get a candle if you like. There's one on the kitchen mantelpiece.'

Anne shot off to get it. Julian lit it and put it into the hole behind the panel. The others pushed against him to try and peep inside.

'Don't,' said Julian, impatiently. 'Wait your turn, sillies! Let me have a look.'

He had a good look, but there didn't really seem anything to see. It was all darkness behind, and stone wall. He gave the candle to Dick, and then each of the children had a turn at peeping. Old Mrs Sanders had gone back to the kitchen. She was used to the sliding panel!

'She said this house was full of strange things like that,' said Anne. 'What other things are there, do you think? Let's ask her.'

They slid the panel back into place and went to find Mrs Sanders. 'Mrs Sanders, what other funny things are there in Kirrin Farmhouse?' asked Julian.

'There's a cupboard upstairs with a false back,' said Mrs Sanders. 'Don't look so excited! There's nothing in it at all! And there's a big stone over there by the fireplace that pulls up to show a hidey-hole. I suppose in the old days people wanted good hiding-places for things.'

The children ran to the stone she pointed out. It had an iron ring in it, and was easily pulled up. Below was a hollowed-out place, big enough to take a small box. It was empty now, but all the same it looked exciting.

'Where's the cupboard?' asked Julian.

'My old legs are too tired to go traipsing upstairs this morning,' said the farmer's wife. 'But you can go yourselves. Up the stairs, turn to the right, and go into the second door you see. The cupboard is at the farther end. Open the door and feel about at the bottom till you come across a dent in the wood. Press it hard, and the false back slides to the side.'

The four children and Timothy ran upstairs as fast as they could, munching shortbread as they went. This really was a very exciting morning!

They found the cupboard and opened the door. All four went down on hands and knees to press round the bottom of the cupboard to find the dented place. Anne found it.

'I've got it!' she cried. She pressed hard, but her little fingers were not strong enough to work the mechanism of the sliding back. Julian had to help her.

There was a creaking noise, and the children saw the false back of the cupboard sliding sideways. A big space showed behind, large enough to take a fairly thin man.

'A jolly good hiding-place,' said Julian. 'Anyone could hide there and no one would ever know!'

'I'll get in and you shut me up,' said Dick. 'It would be exciting.'

He got into the space. Julian slid the back across, and Dick could no longer be seen!

'Bit of a tight fit!' he called. 'And awfully dark! Let me out again.'

The children all took turns at going into the space behind the back of the cupboard and being shut up. Anne didn't like it very much.

They went down to the warm kitchen again. 'It's a most exciting cupboard, Mrs Sanders,' said Julian. 'I do wish we lived in a house like this, full of secrets!'

'Can we come and play in that cupboard again?' asked George.

'No, I'm afraid you can't, George,' said Mrs Sanders. 'That room where the cupboard is, is one the two gentlemen are going to have.'

'Oh!' said Julian, disappointed. 'Shall you tell them about the sliding back, Mrs Sanders?'

'I don't expect so,' said the old lady. 'It's only you children that get excited about things like that, bless you. Two gentlemen wouldn't think twice about it.'

'How funny grown-ups are!' said Anne, puzzled. 'I'm quite certain I shall be thrilled to see a sliding panel or a trapdoor even when I'm a hundred.'

'Same here,' said Dick. 'Could I just go and look into the sliding panel in the hall once more, Mrs Sanders? I'll take the candle.'

Dick never knew why he suddenly wanted to have another look. It was just an idea he had. The others didn't bother to go with him, for there really was nothing to see behind the panelling except the old stone wall.

Dick took the candle and went into the hall. He pressed on the panel at the top and it slid back. He put the candle inside and had another good look. There was nothing at all to be seen. Dick took out his head and put in his arm, stretching along the wall as far as his hand would reach. He was just about to take it back when his fingers found a hole in the wall.

'Funny!' said Dick. 'Why should there be a hole in the stone wall just there?'

He stuck in his finger and thumb and worked them about. He felt a little ridge inside the wall, rather like a bird's perch, and was able to get hold of it. He wriggled his fingers about the perch, but nothing happened. Then he got a good hold and pulled.

The stone came right out! Dick was so surprised that he let go the heavy stone and it fell to the ground behind the panelling with a crash!

The noise brought the others out into the hall. 'Whatever are you doing, Dick?' said Julian. 'Have you broken something?'

'No,' said Dick, his face reddening with excitement. 'I say – I put my hand in here – and found a hole in one of the stones the wall is made of – and I got hold of a sort of ridge with my finger and thumb and pulled. The stone came right out, and I got such a surprise I let go. It fell, and that's what you heard!'

'Golly!' said Julian, trying to push Dick away from the open panel. 'Let me see.'

'No, Julian,' said Dick, pushing him away. 'This is *my* discovery. Wait till I see if I can feel anything in the hole. It's difficult to get at!'

The others waited impatiently. Julian could hardly prevent himself from pushing Dick right away. Dick put his arm in as far as he could, and curved his hand round to get into the space behind where the stone had been. His fingers felt about and he closed them round something that felt like a book. Cautiously and carefully he brought it out.

'An old book!' he said.

'What's in it?' cried Anne.

They turned the pages carefully. They were so dry and brittle that some of them fell into dust.

'I think it's a book of recipes,' said Anne, as her sharp eyes read a few words in the old brown, faded handwriting. 'Let's take it to Mrs Sanders.'

The children carried the book to the old lady. She laughed at their beaming faces. She took the book and looked at it, not at all excited.

'Yes,' she said. 'It's a book of recipes, that's all it is. See the name in the front – Alice Mary Sanders – that must have been my husband's great-grandmother. She was famous for her medicines, I know. It was said she could cure any ill in man or animal, no matter what it was.'

'It's a pity it's so hard to read her writing,' said Julian, disappointed. 'The whole book is falling to pieces too. It must be very old.'

'Do you think there's anything else in that hidy-hole?' asked Anne. 'Julian, you go and put *your* arm in, it's longer than Dick's.'

'There didn't seem to be anything else at all,' said

Dick. 'It's a very small place – just a few inches of hollow space behind that brick or stone that fell down.'

'Well, I'll just put my hand in and see,' said Julian. They all went back into the hall. Julian put his arm into the open panel, and slid it along the wall to where the stone had fallen out. His hand went into the space there, and his long fingers groped about, feeling for anything else that might be there.

There was something else, something soft and flat that felt like leather. Eagerly the boy's fingers closed over it and he drew it out carefully, half afraid that it might fall to pieces with age.

'I've got something!' he said, his eyes gleaming brightly. 'Look – what is it?'

The others crowded round. 'It's rather like Daddy's tobacco pouch,' said Anne, feeling it. 'The same shape. Is there anything inside?'

It was a tobacco pouch, very dark brown, made of soft leather and very much worn. Carefully Julian undid the flap, and unrolled the leather.

A few bits of black tobacco were still in the pouch – but there was something else, too! Tightly rolled up in the last bit of pouch was a piece of linen. Julian took it out and unrolled it. He put it flat on the hall-table.

The children stared at it. There were marks and signs on the linen, done in black ink that had hardly faded. But the four of them could not make head or tail of the marks.

'It's not a map,' said Julian. 'It seems a sort of code, or something. I do wonder what it means. I wish we could make it out. It must be some sort of secret.'

The children stared at the piece of linen, very thrilled. It was so old – and contained some kind of secret. Whatever could it be?

They ran to show it to Mrs Sanders. She was studying the old recipe book, and her face glowed with pleasure as she raised it to look at the excited children.

'This book's a wonder!' she said. 'I can hardly read the writing, but here's a recipe for backache. I shall try it myself. My back aches so much at the end of the day. Now, you listen . . .'

But the children didn't want to listen to recipes for backache. They pushed the piece of linen on to Mrs Sanders's lap.

'Look! What's this about, Mrs Sanders? Do you know? We found it in a kind of tobacco pouch in that place behind the panel.'

Mrs Sanders took off her glasses, polished them, and put them on again. She looked carefully at the piece of linen with its strange marks.

She shook her head. 'No – this doesn't make any sense to me. And what's this now? – it looks like an old tobacco pouch. Ah, my John would like that, I guess. He's got such an old one that it won't hold his tobacco any more! This is old too – but there's a lot of wear in it yet.'

'Mrs Sanders, do you want this piece of linen too?' asked Julian, anxiously. He was longing to take it home and study it. He felt certain there was some kind of exciting secret hidden there, and he could not bear the thought of leaving it with Mrs Sanders.

'You take it, Julian, if you want it,' said Mrs Sanders, with a laugh. 'I'll keep the recipes for myself, and John shall have the pouch. You can have the old rag if you want it, though it beats me why you think it's so fascinating! Ah, here's John!'

She raised her voice and shouted to the deaf old man. 'Hey, John, here's a tobacco pouch for you. The children found it somewhere behind that panel that opens in the hall.'

John took it and fingered it. 'It's a strange one,' he said, 'but better than mine. Well, youngsters, I don't want to hurry you, but it's one o'clock now, and you'd better be going if it's near your dinner-time!'

'Gracious!' said Julian. 'We shall be late! Goodbye, Mrs Sanders, and thanks awfully for the shortbread and this old rag. We'll try our best to make out what's on it and tell you. Hurry, everyone! Where's Tim? Come on, Timothy, we're late!'

The five of them ran off quickly. They really were late, and had to run most of the way, which meant that it was difficult to talk. But they were so excited about their morning that they panted remarks to one another as they went.

'I wonder what this old rag says!' panted Julian. 'I mean to find out. I'm sure it's something mysterious.'

'Shall we tell anyone?' asked Dick.

'No!' said George. 'Let's keep it a secret.'

'If Anne starts to give away anything, kick her under the table, like we did last summer,' said Julian, with a grin. Poor Anne always found it difficult to keep a secret, and often had to be nudged or kicked when she began to give things away.

'I won't say a word,' said Anne, indignantly. 'And don't you dare to kick me. It only makes me cry out and then the grown-ups want to know why.'

'We'll have a good old puzzle over this piece of linen after dinner,' said Julian. 'I bet we'll find out what it says, if we really make up our minds to!'

'Here we are,' said George. 'Not too late. Hallo, Mother! We won't be a minute washing our hands! We've had a lovely time.'

5   An unpleasant walk

After dinner the four children went upstairs to the boys' bedroom and spread out the bit of linen on a table there. There were words here and there, scrawled in rough printing. There was the sign of a compass, with E marked clearly for East. There were eight rough squares, and in one of them, right in the middle, was a cross. It was all very mysterious.

'You know, I believe these words are Latin,' said Julian, trying to make them out. 'But I can't read them properly. And I expect if I *could* read them, I wouldn't know what they meant. I wish we knew someone who could read Latin like this.'

'Could your father, George?' asked Anne.

'I expect so,' said George. But nobody wanted to ask George's father. He might take the curious old rag away. He might forget all about it, he might even burn it. Scientists were such peculiar people.

'What about Mr Roland?' said Dick. 'He's a tutor. He knows Latin.'

'We won't ask him till we know a bit more about him,' said Julian, cautiously. 'He *seems* jolly and nice – but you never know. Oh, blow – I wish we could make this out, I really do.'

'There are two words at the top,' said Dick, and he tried to spell them out. 'VIA OCCULTA.' 'What do you think they could mean, Julian?'

'Well – the only thing I can think of that they can

mean is – Secret Way, or something like that,' said
Julian, screwing up his forehead into a frown.

'Secret Way!' said Anne, her eyes shining. 'Oh, I
hope it's that! Secret Way! How exciting. What sort of
secret way would it be, Julian?'

'How do I know, Anne, silly?' said Julian. 'I don't
even know that the words are meant to mean "Secret
Way". It's really a guess on my part.'

'If they did mean that – the linen might have direc-
tions to find the Secret Way, whatever it is,' said Dick.
'Oh Julian, isn't it exasperating that we can't read it?
Do, do try. You know more Latin than I do.'

'It's so hard to read the funny old letters,' said Julian,
trying again. 'No – it's no good at all. I can't make
them out.'

Steps came up the stairs, and the door opened. Mr
Roland looked in.

'Hallo, hallo!' he said. 'I wondered where you all
were. What about a walk over the cliffs?'

'We'll come,' said Julian, rolling up the old rag.

'What have you got there? Anything interesting?'
asked Mr Roland.

'It's a –' began Anne, and at once all the others began
to talk, afraid that Anne was going to give the secret
away.

'It's a wonderful afternoon for a walk.'

'Come on, let's get our things on!'

'Tim, Tim, where are you?' George gave a piercing
whistle. Tim was under the bed and came bounding
out. Anne went red as she guessed why all the others
had interrupted her so quickly.

'Idiot,' said Julian, under his breath. 'Baby.'

Fortunately Mr Roland said no more about the piece
of linen he had seen Julian rolling up. He was looking
at Tim.

'I suppose he must come,' he said. George stared at him in indignation.

'Of course he must!' she said. 'We never never go anywhere without Timothy.'

Mr Roland went downstairs, and the children got ready to go out. George was scowling. The very idea of leaving Tim behind made her angry.

'You nearly gave our secret away, you silly,' said Dick to Anne.

'I didn't think,' said the little girl, looking ashamed of herself. 'Anyway, Mr Roland seems very nice. I think we might ask him if he could help us to understand those funny words.'

'You leave that to me to decide,' said Julian, crossly. 'Now don't you dare to say a word.'

They all set out, Timothy too. Mr Roland need not have worried about the dog, for Timothy would not go near him. It was very strange, really. He kept away from the tutor, and took not the slightest notice of him even when Mr Roland spoke to him.

'He's not usually like that,' said Dick. 'He's a most friendly dog, really.'

'Well, as I've got to live in the same house with him, I must try and make him friends with me,' said the tutor. 'Hi, Timothy! Come here! I've got a biscuit in my pocket.'

Timothy pricked up his ears at the word 'biscuit', but did not even look towards Mr Roland. He put his tail down and went to George. She patted him.

'If he doesn't like anyone, not even a biscuit or a bone will make him go to them when he is called,' she said.

Mr Roland gave it up. He put the biscuit back into his pocket. 'He's a peculiar-looking dog, isn't he?' he said. 'A terrible mongrel! I must say I prefer well-bred dogs.'

George went purple in the face. 'He's *not* peculiar-looking!' she spluttered. 'He's not nearly so peculiar-looking as you! He's not a terrible mongrel. He's the best dog in the world!'

'I think you are being a little rude,' said Mr Roland, stiffly. 'I don't allow my pupils to be cheeky, Georgina.'

Calling her Georgina made George still more furious. She lagged behind with Tim, looking as black as a thundercloud. The others felt uncomfortable. They knew what tempers George got into, and how difficult she could be. She had been so much better and happier since the summer, when they had come to stay for the first time. They did hope she wasn't going to be silly and get into rows. It would spoil the Christmas holidays.

Mr Roland took no more notice of George. He did not speak to her, but strode on ahead with the others, doing his best to be jolly. He could really be very funny, and the boys began to laugh at him. He took Anne's hand, and the little girl jumped along beside him, enjoying the walk.

Julian felt sorry for George. It wasn't nice to be left out of things, and he knew how George hated anything like that. He wondered if he dared to put in a good word for her. It might make things easier.

'Mr Roland, sir,' he began. 'Could you call my cousin by the name she likes – George – she simply hates Georgina. And she's very fond of Tim. She can't bear anyone to say horrid things about him.'

Mr Roland looked surprised. 'My dear boy, I am sure you mean well,' he said, in rather a dry sort of voice, 'but I hardly think I want your advice about any of my pupils. I shall follow my own wishes in my treatment of Georgina, not yours. I want to be friends with you all, and I am sure we shall be – but Georgina has got to be sensible, as you three are.'

Julian felt rather squashed. He went red and looked at Dick. Dick gave him a squeeze on his arm. The boys knew George could be silly and difficult, especially if anyone didn't like her beloved dog – but they thought Mr Roland might try to be a bit more understanding too. Dick slipped behind and walked with George.

'You needn't walk with me,' said George at once, her blue eyes glinting. 'Walk with your friend Mr Roland.'

'He isn't my friend,' said Dick. 'Don't be silly.'

'I'm not silly,' said George, in a tight sort of voice. 'I heard you all laughing and joking with him. You go on and have a good laugh again. I've got Timothy.'

'George, it's Christmas holidays,' said Dick. 'Do let's all be friends. Do. Don't let's spoil Christmas.'

'I can't like anyone who doesn't like Tim,' said George, obstinately.

'Well, after all, Mr Roland did offer him a biscuit,' said Dick, trying to make peace as hard as he could.

George said nothing. Her small face looked fierce. Dick tried again.

'George! Promise to try and be nice till Christmas is over, anyway. Don't let's spoil Christmas, for goodness' sake! Come on, George.'

'All right,' said George, at last. 'I'll try.'

'Come and walk with us then,' said Dick. So George caught up the others, and tried not to look too sulky. Mr Roland guessed that Dick had been trying to make George behave, and he included her in his talk. He could not make her laugh, but she did at least answer politely.

'Is that Kirrin Farmhouse?' asked Mr Roland, as they came in sight of the farm.

'Yes. Do you know it?' asked Julian, in surprise.

'No, no,' said Mr Roland, at once, 'I've heard of it, and wondered if that was the place.'

'We went there this morning,' said Anne. 'It's an exciting place.' She looked at the others, wondering if they would mind if she said anything about the things they had seen that morning. Julian thought for a moment. After all, it couldn't matter telling him about the stone in the kitchen and the false back to the cupboard. Mrs Sanders would tell anyone that. He could speak about the sliding panel in the hall too, and say they had found an old recipe book there. He did not need to say anything about the old bit of marked linen.

So he told their tutor about the exciting things there had been at the old farmhouse, but said nothing at all about the linen and its strange markings. Mr Roland listened with the greatest interest.

'This is all very remarkable,' he said. 'Very remarkable indeed. Most interesting. You say the old couple live there quite alone?'

'Well, they are having two people to stay over Christmas,' said Dick. 'Artists. Julian thought he would go over and talk to them. He can paint awfully well, you know.'

'Can he really?' said Mr Roland. 'Well, he must show me some of his pictures. But I don't think he'd better go and worry the artists at the farmhouse. They might not like it.'

This remark made Julian feel obstinate. He made up his mind at once that he *would* go and talk to the two artists when he got the chance!

It was quite a pleasant walk on the whole except that

George was quiet, and Timothy would not go anywhere near Mr Roland. When they came to a frozen
pond Dick threw sticks on it for Tim to fetch. It was so
funny to see him go slithering about on his long legs,
trying to run properly!

Everyone threw sticks for the dog, and Tim fetched
all the sticks except Mr Roland's. When the tutor
threw a stick the dog looked at it and took no more
notice. It was almost as if he had said, 'What, *your*
stick! No, thank you!'

'Now, home we go,' said Mr Roland, trying not to
look annoyed with Tim. 'We shall just be in time for
tea!'

6   *Lessons with Mr Roland*

Next morning the children felt a little gloomy.
Lessons! How horrid in the holidays! Still, Mr Roland
wasn't so bad. The children had not had him with
them in the sitting-room the night before, because he
had gone to talk to their uncle. So they were able to get
out the mysterious bit of linen again and pore over it.

But it wasn't a bit of good. Nobody could make
anything of it at all. Secret Way! What did it mean?
Was it really directions for a Secret Way? And where
was the way, and why was it secret? It was most
exasperating not to be able to find out.

'I really feel we'll have to ask someone soon,' Julian
had said with a sigh. 'I can't bear this mystery much
longer. I keep on and on thinking of it.'

He had dreamt of it too that night, and now it was
morning, with lessons ahead. He wondered what
lesson Mr Roland would take – Latin perhaps. Then he
could ask him what the words 'VIA OCCULTA' meant.

Mr Roland had seen all their reports and had noted
the subjects they were weak in. One was Latin, and
another was French. Maths were very weak in both
Dick's report and George's. Both children must be
helped on in those. Geometry was Julian's weakest
spot.

Anne was not supposed to need any coaching. 'But
if you like to come along and join us, I'll give you
some painting to do,' said Mr Roland, his blue eyes

twinkling at her. He liked Anne. She was not difficult and sulky like George.

Anne loved painting. 'Oh, yes,' she said, happily, 'I'd love to do some painting. I can paint flowers, Mr Roland. I'll paint you some red poppies and blue cornflowers out of my head.'

'We will start at half-past nine,' said Mr Roland. 'We are to work in the sitting-room. Take your school-books there, and be ready punctually.'

. So all the children were there, sitting round a table, their books in front of them, at half-past nine. Anne had some painting water and her painting-box. The others looked at her enviously. Lucky Anne, to be doing painting while they worked hard at difficult things like Latin and Maths!

'Where's Timothy?' asked Julian in a low voice, as they waited for their tutor to come in.

'Under the table,' said George, defiantly. 'I'm sure he'll lie still. Don't any of you say anything about him. I want him there. I'm not going to do lessons without Tim here.'

'I don't see why he shouldn't be here with us,' said Dick. 'He's very very good. Sh! Here comes Mr Roland.'

The tutor came in, his black beard bristling round his mouth and chin. His eyes looked very piercing in the pale winter sunlight that filtered into the room. He told the children to sit down.

'I'll have a look at your exercise books first,' he said, 'and see what you were doing last term. You come first, Julian.'

Soon the little class were working quietly together. Anne was very busy painting a bright picture of poppies and cornflowers. Mr Roland admired it very much. Anne thought he really was very nice.

Suddenly there was a huge sigh from under the table. It was Tim, tired of lying so still. Mr Roland looked up, surprised. George at once sighed heavily, hoping that Mr Roland would think it was she who had sighed before.

'You sound tired, Georgina,' said Mr Roland. 'You shall all have a little break at eleven.'

George frowned. She hated being called Georgina. She put her foot cautiously on Timothy to warn him not to make any more noises. Tim licked her foot.

After a while, just when the class was at its very quietest, Tim felt a great wish to scratch himself very hard on his back. He got up. He sat down again with a thump, gave a grunt, and began to scratch himself furiously. The children all began to make noises to hide the sounds that Tim was making.

George clattered her feet on the floor. Julian began to cough, and let one of his books slip to the ground. Dick jiggled the table and spoke to Mr Roland.

'Oh dear, this sum is so hard; it really is! I keep doing it and doing it, and it simply *won't* come right!'

'Why all this sudden noise?' said Mr Roland in surprise. 'Stop tapping the floor with your feet, Georgina.'

Tim settled down quietly again. The children gave a sigh of relief. They became quiet, and Mr Roland told Dick to come to him with his Maths book.

The tutor took it, and stretched his legs out under the table, leaning back to speak to Dick. To his enormous surprise his feet struck something soft and warm – and then something nipped him sharply on the ankle! He drew in his feet with a cry of pain.

The children stared at him. He bent down and looked under the table. 'It's that dog,' he said, in disgust. 'The brute snapped at my ankles. He has made a hole in my trousers. Take him out, Georgina.'

Georgina said nothing. She sat as though she had not heard.

'She won't answer if you call her Georgina,' Julian reminded him.

'She'll answer me whatever I call her,' said Mr Roland, in a low and angry voice. 'I won't have that dog in here. If you don't take him out this very minute, Georgina, I will go to your father.'

George looked at him. She knew perfectly well that if she didn't take Tim out, and Mr Roland went to her father, he would order Timothy to live in the garden kennel, and that would be dreadful. There was absolutely nothing to be done but obey. Red in the face, a huge frown almost hiding her eyes, she got up and spoke to Tim.

'Come on, Tim! I'm not surprised you bit him. I would, too, if I were a dog!'

'There is no need to be rude, Georgina,' said Mr Roland, angrily.

The others stared at George. They wondered how she dared to say things like that. When she got fierce it seemed as if she didn't care for anyone at all!

'Come back as soon as you have put the dog out,' said Mr Roland.

George scowled, but came back in a few minutes. She felt caught. Her father was friendly with Mr Roland, and knew how difficult George was – if she behaved as badly as she felt she would like to, it would be Tim who would suffer, for he would certainly be banished from the house. So for Tim's sake George obeyed the tutor – but from that moment she disliked him and resented him bitterly with all her fierce little heart.

The others were sorry for George and Timothy, but

they did not share the little girl's intense dislike of the new tutor. He often made them laugh. He was patient with their mistakes. He was willing to show them how to make paper darts and ships, and to do funny little tricks. Julian and Dick thought these were fun, and stored them up to try on the other boys when they went back to school.

After lessons that morning the children went out for half an hour in the frosty sunshine. George called Tim.

'Poor old boy!' she said. 'What a shame to turn you out of the room! Whatever did you snap at Mr Roland for? I think it was a very good idea, Tim – but I really don't know what made you!'

'George, you can't play about with Mr Roland,' said Julian. 'You'll only get into trouble. He's tough. He won't stand much from any of us. But I think he'll be quite a good sport if we get on the right side of him.'

'Well, get on the right side of him if you like,' said George, in rather a sneering voice. 'I'm not going to. If I don't like a person, I don't – and I don't like *him*.'

'Why? Just because he doesn't like Tim?' asked Dick.

'Mostly because of that – but because he makes me feel prickly down my back,' said George. 'I don't like his nasty mouth.'

'But you can't see it,' said Julian. 'It's covered with his moustache and beard.'

'I've seen his lips through them,' said George, obstinately. 'They're thin and cruel. You look and see. I don't like thin-lipped people. They are always spiteful and hard. And I don't like his cold eyes either. You can suck up to him all you like. *I* shan't.'

Julian refused to get angry with the stubborn little girl. He laughed at her. 'We're not going to suck up to him,' he said. 'We're just going to be sensible, that's all. You be sensible too, George, old thing.'

But once George had made up her mind about something nothing would alter her. She cheered up when she heard that they were all to go Christmas shopping on the bus that afternoon – without Mr Roland! He was going to watch an experiment that her father was going to show him.

'I will take you into the nearest town and you shall shop to your hearts' content,' said Aunt Fanny to the children. 'Then we will have tea in a tea-shop and catch the six o'clock bus home.'

This was fun. They caught the afternoon bus and rumbled along the deep country lanes till they got to the town. The shops looked very colourful and bright. The children had brought their money with them, and were very busy indeed, buying all kinds of things. There were so many people to get presents for!

'I suppose we'd better get something for Mr Roland, hadn't we?' said Julian.

'I'm going to,' said Anne.

'Fancy buying Mr *Roland* a present!' said George, in her scornful voice.

'Why shouldn't she, George?' asked her mother, in surprise. 'Oh dear, I hope you are going to be sensible about him, and not take a violent dislike to the poor man. I don't want him to complain to your father about you.'

'What are you going to buy for Tim, George?' asked Julian, changing the subject quickly.

'The largest bone the butcher has got,' said George. 'What are *you* going to buy him?'

'I guess if Tim had money, he would buy us each a present,' said Anne, taking hold of the thick hair round Tim's neck, and pulling it lovingly. 'He's the best dog in the world!'

George forgave Anne for saying she would buy Mr
Roland a present, when the little girl said that about
Tim! She cheered up again and began to plan what she
would buy for everyone.

They had a fine tea, and caught the six o'clock bus
back. Aunt Fanny went to see if the cook had given the
two men their tea. She came out of the study beaming.

'Really, I've never seen your uncle so jolly,' she said
to Julian and Dick. 'He and Mr Roland are getting on
like a house on fire. He has been showing your tutor
quite a lot of his experiments. It's nice for him to have
someone to talk to that knows a little about these
things.'

Mr Roland played games with the children that
evening. Tim was in the room, and the tutor tried
again to make friends with him, but the dog refused to
take any notice of him.

'As sulky as his little mistress!' said the tutor, with a
laughing look at George, who was watching Tim
refuse to go to Mr Roland, and looking rather pleased
about it. She gave the tutor a scowl and said nothing.

'Shall we ask him whether "VIA OCCULTA" really
does mean "Secret Way" or not, tomorrow?' said
Julian to Dick, as they undressed that night. 'I'm just
longing to know if it does. What do you think of Mr
Roland, Dick?'

'I don't really quite know,' said Dick. 'I like lots of
things about him, but then I suddenly don't like him at
all. I don't like his eyes. And George is quite right
about his lips. They are so thin there's hardly anything
of them at all.'

'I think he's all right,' said Julian. 'He won't stand
any nonsense, that's all. I wouldn't mind showing him
the whole piece of rag and asking him to make out its
meaning for us.'

'I thought you said it was to be a proper secret,' said Dick.

'I know – but what's the use of a secret we don't know the meaning of ourselves?' said Julian. 'I'll tell you what we *could* do – ask him to explain the words to us, and not show him the bit of linen.'

'But we can't read some of the words ourselves,' said Dick. 'So that's no use. You'd have to show him the whole thing, and tell him where we got it.'

'Well, I'll see,' said Julian, getting into bed.

The next day there were lessons again from half-past nine to half-past twelve. George appeared without Tim. She was angry at having to do this, but it was no good being defiant and refusing to come to lessons without Tim. Now that he had snapped at Mr Roland, he had definitely put himself in the wrong, and the tutor had every right to refuse to allow him to come. But George looked very sulky indeed.

In the Latin lesson Julian took the chance of asking what he wanted to know. 'Please, Mr Roland,' he said, 'could you tell me what "VIA OCCULTA" means?'

'"VIA OCCULTA"' said Mr Roland, frowning. 'Yes – it means "Secret Path" or, "Secret Road". A hidden way – something like that. Why do you want to know?'

All the children were listening eagerly. Their hearts thumped with excitement. So Julian had been right. That funny bit of rag contained directions for some hidden way, some secret path – but where to! Where did it begin, and end?

'Oh – I just wanted to know,' said Julian. 'Thank you, sir.'

He winked at the others. He was as excited as they were. If only they could make out the rest of the markings, they might be able to solve the mystery. Well – perhaps he would ask Mr Roland in a day or two. The secret must be solved somehow.

'The "Secret Way",' said Julian to himself, as he worked out a problem in geometry. 'The "Secret Way". I'll find it somehow.'

7 Directions for the Secret Way

For the next day or two the four children did not really have much time to think about the Secret Way, because Christmas was coming near, and there was a good deal to do.

There were Christmas cards to draw and paint for their mothers and fathers and friends. There was the house to decorate. They went out with Mr Roland to find sprays of holly, and came home laden.

'You look like a Christmas card yourselves,' said Aunt Fanny, as they walked up the garden path, carrying the red-berried holly over their shoulders. Mr Roland had found a group of trees with tufts of mistletoe growing from the top branches, and they had brought some of that too. Its berries shone like pale green pearls.

'Mr Roland had to climb the tree to get this,' said Anne. 'He's a good climber – as good as a monkey.'

Everyone laughed except George. She never laughed at anything to do with the tutor. They all dumped their loads down in the porch, and went to wash. They were to decorate the house that evening.

'Is Uncle going to let his study be decorated too?' asked Anne. There were all kinds of strange instruments and glass tubes in the study now, and the children looked at them with wonder whenever they ventured into the study, which was very seldom.

'No, my study is certainly not to be messed about,'

said Uncle Quentin, at once. 'I wouldn't hear of it.'

'Uncle, why do you have all these funny things in your study?' asked Anne, looking round with wide eyes.

Uncle Quentin laughed. 'I'm looking for a secret formula!' he said.

'What's that?' said Anne.

'You wouldn't understand,' said her uncle. 'All these "funny things" as you call them, help me in my experiments, and I put down in my book what they tell me — and from all I learn I work out a secret formula, that will be of great use when it is finished.'

'You want to know a secret formula, and we want to know a secret way,' said Anne, quite forgetting that she was not supposed to talk about this.

Julian was standing by the door. He frowned at Anne. Luckily Uncle Quentin was not paying any more attention to the little girl's chatter. Julian pulled her out of the room.

'Anne, the only way to stop you giving away secrets is to sew up your mouth, like Brer Rabbit wanted to do to Mister Dog!' he said.

Joanna the cook was busy baking Christmas cakes. An enormous turkey had been sent over from Kirrin Farm, and was hanging up in the larder. Timothy thought it smelt glorious, and Joanna was always shooing him out of the kitchen.

There were boxes of crackers on the shelf in the sitting-room, and mysterious parcels everywhere. It was very, very Christmassy! The children were happy and excited.

Mr Roland went out and dug up a little spruce fir tree. 'We must have a Christmas tree,' he said. 'Have you any tree-ornaments, children?'

'No,' said Julian, seeing George shake her head.

'I'll go into the town this afternoon and get some for you,' promised the tutor. 'It will be fun dressing the tree. We'll put it in the hall, and light candles on it on Christmas Day after tea. Who's coming with me to get the candles and the ornaments?'

'I am!' cried three children. But the fourth said nothing. That was George. Not even to buy tree-ornaments would the obstinate little girl go with Mr Roland. She had never had a Christmas tree before, and she was very much looking forward to it – but it was spoilt for her because Mr Roland bought the things that made it so beautiful.

Now it stood in the hall, with coloured candles in holders clipped to the branches, and bright shining ornaments hanging from top to bottom. Silver strands of frosted string hung down from the branches like icicles, and Anne had put bits of white cotton-wool here and there to look like snow. It really was a lovely sight to see.

'Beautiful!' said Uncle Quentin, as he passed through the hall, and saw Mr Roland hanging the last ornaments on the tree. 'I say – look at the fairy doll on the top! Who's that for? A good girl?'

Anne secretly hoped that Mr Roland would give her the doll. She was sure it wasn't for George – and anyway, George wouldn't accept it. It was such a pretty doll, with its gauzy frock and silvery wings.

Julian, Dick and Anne had quite accepted the tutor now as teacher and friend. In fact, everyone had, their uncle and aunt too, and even Joanna the cook. George, of course, was the only exception, and she and Timothy kept away from Mr Roland, each looking as sulky as the other whenever the tutor was in the room.

'You know, I never knew a dog could look so

sulky!' said Julian, watching Timothy. 'Really, he scowls almost like George.'

'And I always feel as if George puts her tail down like Tim, when Mr Roland is in the room,' giggled Anne.

'Laugh all you like,' said George, in a low tone. 'I think you're beastly to me. I know I'm right about Mr Roland. I've got a feeling about him. And so has Tim.'

'You're silly, George,' said Dick. 'You haven't *really* got a Feeling – it's only that Mr Roland will keep calling you Georgina and putting you in your place, and that he doesn't like Tim. I dare say he can't help disliking dogs. After all, there was once a famous man called Lord Roberts who couldn't bear cats.'

'Oh well, cats are different,' said George. 'If a person doesn't like dogs, especially a dog like our Timothy, then there really *must* be something wrong with him.'

'It's no use arguing with George,' said Julian. 'Once she's made up her mind about something, she won't budge!'

George went out of the room in a huff. The others thought she was behaving rather stupidly.

'I'm surprised really,' said Anne. 'She was so jolly last term at school. Now she's gone all strange, rather like she was when we first knew her last summer.'

'I do think Mr Roland has been decent digging up the Christmas tree and everything,' said Dick. 'I still don't like him awfully much sometimes, but I think he's a sport. What about asking him if he can read that old linen rag for us – I don't think I'd mind him sharing our secret, really.'

'I would *love* him to share it,' said Anne, who was busy doing a marvellous Christmas card for the tutor. 'He's most awfully clever. I'm sure he could tell us what the Secret Way is. Do let's ask him.'

'All right,' said Julian. 'I'll show him the piece of linen. It's Christmas Eve tonight. He will be with us in the sitting-room, because Aunt Fanny is going into the study with Uncle Quentin to wrap up presents for all of us!'

So, that evening, before Mr Roland came in to sit with them, Julian took out the little roll of linen and stroked it out flat on the table. George looked at it in surprise.

'Mr Roland will be here in a minute,' she said. 'You'd better put it away quickly.'

'We're going to ask him if he can tell us what the old Latin words mean,' said Julian.

'You're not!' cried George, in dismay. 'Ask him to share our secret! How ever can you?'

'Well, we want to know what the secret is, don't we?' said Julian. 'We don't need to tell him where we got this or anything about it except that we want to know what the markings mean. We're not exactly sharing the secret with him – only asking him to use his brains to help us.'

'Well, I never thought you'd ask *him*,' said George. 'And he'll want to know simply everything about it, you just see if he won't! He's terribly snoopy.'

'Whatever do you mean?' said Julian, in surprise. 'I don't think he's a bit snoopy.'

'I saw him yesterday snooping round the study when no one was there,' said George. 'He didn't see me outside the window with Tim. He was having a real poke round.'

'You know how interested he is in your father's work,' said Julian. 'Why shouldn't he look at it? Your father likes him too. You're just seeing what horrid things you can find to say about Mr Roland.'

'Oh shut up, you two,' said Dick. 'It's Christmas Eve. Don't let's argue or quarrel or say beastly things.'

Just at that moment the tutor came into the room. 'All as busy as bees?' he said. his mouth smiling beneath its moustache. 'Too busy to have a game of cards, I suppose?'

'Mr Roland, sir,' began Julian, 'could you help us with something? We've got an old bit of linen here with odd markings on it. The words seem to be in some sort of Latin and we can't make them out.'

George gave an angry exclamation as she saw Julian push the piece of linen over towards the tutor. She went out of the room and shut the door with a bang. Tim was with her.

'Our sweet-tempered Georgina doesn't seem to be very friendly tonight,' remarked Mr Roland, pulling the bit of linen towards him. 'Where in the world did you get this? What an odd thing!'

Nobody answered. Mr Roland studied the roll of linen, and then gave an exclamation. 'Ah – I see why you wanted to know the meaning of those Latin words the other day – the ones that meant "hidden path", you remember. They are at the top of this linen roll.'

'Yes,' said Dick. All the children leaned over towards Mr Roland, hoping he would be able to unravel a little of the mystery for them.

'We just want to know the meaning of the words, sir,' said Julian.

'This is really very interesting,' said the tutor, puzzling over the linen. 'Apparently there are directions here for finding the opening or entrance of a secret path or road.'

'That's what we thought!' cried Julian, excitedly. 'That's exactly what we thought. Oh sir, do read the directions and see what you make of them.'

'Well, these eight squares are meant to represent wooden boards or panels, I think,' said the tutor, pointing to the eight rough squares drawn on the linen. 'Wait a minute – I can hardly read some of the words. This is most fascinating. *Solum lapideum – paries ligneus* – and what's this? – *cellula* – yes, *cellula!*'

The children hung on his words. 'Wooden panels!' That must mean panels somewhere at Kirrin Farmhouse.

Mr Roland frowned down at the old printed words. Then he sent Anne to borrow a magnifying glass from her uncle. She came back with it, and the four of them looked through the glass, seeing the words three times as clearly now.

'Well,' said the tutor at last, 'as far as I can make out the directions mean this: a room facing east; eight wooden panels, with an opening somewhere to be found in that marked one; a stone floor – yes, I think that's right, a stone floor, and a cupboard. It all sounds most extraordinary and very thrilling. Where *did* you get this from?'

'We just found it,' said Julian, after a pause. 'Oh Mr Roland, thanks awfully. We could never have made it out by ourselves. I suppose the entrance to the Secret Way is in a room facing east then.'

'It looks like it,' said Mr Roland, poring over the linen roll again. 'Where did you say you found this?'

'We didn't say,' said Dick. 'It's a secret really, you see.'

'I think you might tell me,' said the tutor, looking at Dick with his brilliant blue eyes. 'I can be trusted with secrets. You've no idea how many strange secrets I know.'

'Well,' said Julian, 'I don't really see why you shouldn't know where we found this, Mr Roland. We found it at Kirrin Farmhouse, in an old tobacco pouch. I suppose the Secret Way begins somewhere there! I wonder where and wherever can it lead to?'

'You found it at Kirrin Farmhouse!' exclaimed Mr Roland. 'Well, well – I must say that seems to be an interesting old place. I shall have to go over there one day.'

Julian rolled up the piece of linen and put it into his pocket. 'Well, thank you, sir,' he said. 'You've solved a bit of the mystery for us but set another puzzle! We must look for the entrance of the Secret Way after Christmas, when we can walk over to Kirrin Farmhouse.'

'I'll come with you,' said Mr Roland. 'I may be able to help a little. That is – if you don't mind me having a little share in this exciting secret.'

'Well – you've been such a help in telling us what the words mean,' said Julian, 'we'd like you to come if you want to, sir.'

'Yes, we *would*,' said Anne.

'We'll go and look for the Secret Way, then,' said Mr Roland. 'What fun we shall have, tapping round the panels, waiting for a mysterious dark entrance to appear!'

'I don't suppose George will go,' Dick murmured to Julian. 'You shouldn't have said Mr Roland could go with us, Ju. That means that old George will have to be left out of it. You know how she hates that.'

'I know,' said Julian, feeling uncomfortable. 'Don't let's worry about that now though. George may feel different after Christmas. She can't keep up this kind of behaviour for ever!'

8 What happened on Christmas night

It was great fun on Christmas morning. The children awoke early and tumbled out of bed to look at the presents that were stacked on chairs near-by. Squeals and yells of delight came from everyone.

'Oh! a railway station! Just what I wanted! Who gave me this marvellous station?'

'A new doll – with eyes that shut! I shall call her Betsy-May. She looks just like a Betsy-May!'

'I say – what a whopping great book – all about aeroplanes. From Aunt Fanny! How decent of her!'

'Timothy! Look what Julian has given you – a collar with big brass studs all round – you *will* be grand. Go and lick him to say thank you!'

'Who's this from? I say, who gave me this? Where's the label? Oh – from Mr Roland. How decent of him! Look, Julian, a pocket-knife with three blades!'

So the cries and exclamations went on, and the four excited children and the equally-excited dog spent a glorious hour before a late Christmas breakfast, opening all kinds and shapes of parcels. The bedrooms were in a fine mess when the children had finished!

'Who gave you that book about dogs, George?' asked Julian, seeing rather a nice dog-book lying on George's pile.

'Mr Roland,' said George, rather shortly. Julian

wondered if George was going to accept it. He rather
thought she wouldn't. But the little girl, defiant and
obstinate as she was, had made up her mind not to
spoil Christmas Day by being 'difficult'. So, when the
others thanked the tutor for their things she too added
her thanks, though in rather a stiff little voice.

George had not given the tutor anything, but the
others had, and Mr Roland thanked them all very
heartily, appearing to be very pleased indeed. He told
Anne that her Christmas card was the nicest he had
ever had, and she beamed at him with joy.

'Well, I must say it's nice to be here for Christmas!'
said Mr Roland, when he and the others were sitting
round a loaded Christmas table, at the mid-day dinner.
'Shall I carve for you, Mr Quentin? I'm good at that!'

Uncle Quentin handed him the carving knife and
fork gladly. 'It's nice to have you here,' he said warmly. 'I must say you've settled in well – I'm sure we all
feel as if we've known you for ages!'

It really was a jolly Christmas Day. There were no
lessons, of course, and there were to be none the next
day either. The children gave themselves up to the
enjoyment of eating a great deal, sucking sweets, and
looking forward to the lighting of the Christmas tree.

It looked beautiful when the candles were lighted.
They twinkled in the darkness of the hall, and the
bright ornaments shone and glowed. Tim sat and
looked at it, quite entranced.

'He likes it as much as we do,' said George. And
indeed Tim had enjoyed the day just as much as any of
them.

They were all tired out when they went to bed.
'I shan't be long before I'm asleep,' yawned Anne.
'Oh, George – it's been fun, hasn't it? I did like the
Christmas tree.'

'Yes, it's been lovely,' said George, jumping into bed. 'Here comes Mother to say good-night. Basket, Tim, basket!'

Tim leapt into his basket by the window. He was always there when George's mother came into say good-night to the girls but as soon as she had gone downstairs, the dog took a flying leap and landed on George's bed. There he slept, his head curled round her feet.

'Don't you think Tim ought to sleep downstairs tonight?' said George's mother. 'Joanna says he ate such an enormous meal in the kitchen that she is sure he will be sick.'

'Oh *no*, Mother!' said George, at once. 'Make Tim sleep downstairs on Christmas night? Whatever would he think?'

'Oh, very well,' said her mother, with a laugh. 'I might have known it was useless to suggest it. Now to sleep quickly, Anne and George – it's late and you are all tired.'

She went into the boys' room and said good-night to them too. They were almost asleep.

Two hours later everyone else was in bed. The house was still and dark. George and Anne slept peacefully in their small beds. Timothy slept too, lying heavily on George's feet.

Suddenly George awoke with a jump. Tim was growling softly! He had raised his big shaggy head and George knew that he was listening.

'What is it, Tim?' she whispered. Anne did not wake. Tim went on growling softly. George sat up and put her hand on his collar to stop him. She knew that if he awoke her father, he would be cross.

Timothy stopped growling now that he had roused George. The girl sat and wondered what to do. It

wasn't any good waking Anne. The little girl would be
frightened. Why was Tim growling? He never did that
at night!

'Perhaps I'd better go and see if everything is all
right,' thought George. She was quite fearless, and the
thought of creeping through the still, dark house did
not disturb her at all. Besides she had Tim! Who could
be afraid with Tim beside them!

She slipped on her dressing-gown. 'Perhaps a log
has fallen out of one of the fire-places and a rug is
burning,' she thought, sniffing as she went down the
stairs. 'It would be just like Tim to smell it and warn
us!'

With her hand on Tim's head to warn him to be
quite quiet, George crept softly through the hall to the
sitting-room. The fire was quite all right there, just a
red glow. In the kitchen all was peace too. Tim's feet
made a noise there, as his claws rattled against the
linoleum.

A slight sound came from the other side of the
house.

Tim growled quite loudly, and the hairs on the back
on his neck rose up. George stood still. Could it
possibly be burglars?

Suddenly Timothy shook himself free from her
fingers and leapt across the hall, down a passage, and
into the study beyond! There was the sound of an
exclamation, and a noise as if someone was falling
over.

'It *is* a burglar!' said George, and she ran to the
study. She saw a torch shining on the floor, dropped
by someone who was even now struggling with Tim.

George switched on the light, and then looked with
the greatest astonishment into the study. Mr Roland
was there in his dressing-gown, rolling on the floor,

trying to get away from Timothy, who, although not biting him, was holding him firmly by his dressing-gown.

'Oh – it's you, George! Call your beastly dog off!' said Mr Roland, in a low and angry voice. 'Do you want to rouse all the household?'

'Why are you creeping about with a torch?' demanded George.

'I heard a noise down here, and came to see what it was,' said Mr Roland, sitting up and trying to fend off the angry dog. 'For goodness' sake, call your beast off.'

'Why didn't you put on the light?' asked George, not attempting to take Tim away. She was very much enjoying the sight of an angry and frightened Mr Roland.

'I couldn't find it,' said the tutor. 'It's on the wrong side of the door, as you see.'

This was true. The switch was an awkward one to find if you didn't know it. Mr Roland tried to push Tim away again, and the dog suddenly barked.

'Well – he'll wake everyone!' said the tutor, angrily. 'I didn't want to rouse the house. I thought I could find out for myself if there was anyone about – a burglar perhaps. Here comes your father!'

George's father appeared, carrying a large poker. He stood still in astonishment when he saw Mr Roland on the ground and Timothy standing over him.

'What's all this?' he exclaimed. Mr Roland tried to get up, but Tim would not let him. George's father called to him sternly.

'Tim! Come here, sir!'

Timothy glanced at George to see if his mistress agreed with her father's command. She said nothing. So Timothy took no notice of the order and merely made a snap at Mr Roland's ankles.

'That dog's mad!' said Mr Roland, from the floor. 'He's already bitten me once before, and now he's trying to do it again!'

'Tim! Will you come here, sir!' shouted George's father. 'George, that dog is really disobedient. Call him off at once.'

'Come here, Tim!' said George, in a low voice. The dog at once came to her, standing by her side with the hairs on his neck still rising up stiffly. He growled softly as if to say, 'Be careful, Mr Roland, be careful!'

The tutor got up. He was very angry indeed. He spoke to George's father.

'I heard some sort of noise and came down with my torch to see what it was,' he said. 'I thought it came from your study, and knowing you kept your valuable books and instruments here, I wondered if some thief was about. I had just got down, and into the room, when that dog appeared from somewhere and got me down on the ground! George came along too, and would not call him off.'

'I can't understand your behaviour, George; I really can't,' said her father, angrily. 'I hope you are not going to behave stupidly, as you used to behave before your cousins came last summer. And what is this I hear about Tim biting Mr Roland before?'

'George had him under the table during lessons,' said Mr Roland. 'I didn't know that, and when I stretched out my legs, they touched Tim, and he bit me. I didn't tell you before, sir, because I didn't want to trouble you. Both George and the dog have tried to annoy me ever since I have been here.'

'Well, Tim must go outside and live in the kennel,' said George's father. 'I won't have him in the house. It will be a punishment for him, and a punishment for

you too, George. I will not have this kind of behaviour. Mr Roland has been extremely kind to you all.'

'I won't let Tim live outside,' said George furiously. 'It's such cold weather, and it would simply break his heart.'

'Well, his heart must be broken then,' said her father. 'It will depend entirely on your behaviour from now on whether Tim is allowed in the house at all these holidays. I shall ask Mr Roland each day how you have behaved. If you have a bad report, then Tim stays outside. Now you know! Go back to bed but first apologise to Mr Roland!'

'I won't!' said George, and choked by feelings of anger and dismay, she tore out of the room and up the stairs. The two men stared after her.

'Let her be,' said Mr Roland. 'She's a very difficult child – and has made up her mind not to like me, that's quite plain. But I shall be very glad to know that that dog isn't in the house. I'm not at all certain that Georgina wouldn't set him on me, if she could!'

'I'm sorry about all this,' said George's father. 'I wonder what the noise was that you heard? – a log falling in the grate I expect. Now – what am I to do about that tiresome dog tonight? Go and take him outside, I suppose!'

'Leave him tonight,' said Mr Roland. 'I can hear noises upstairs – the others are awake by now! Don't let's make any more disturbance tonight.'

'Perhaps you are right,' said George's father, thankfully. He didn't at all want to tackle a defiant little girl and an angry big dog in the middle of a cold night!

The two men went to bed and slept. George did not sleep. The others had been awake when she got upstairs, and she had told them what had happened.

'George! You really are an idiot!' said Dick. 'After all, why shouldn't Mr Roland go down if he heard a noise! *You* went down! Now we shan't have darling old Tim in the house this cold weather!'

Anne began to cry. She didn't like hearing that the tutor she liked so much had been knocked down by Tim, and she hated hearing that Tim was to be punished.

'Don't be a baby,' said George. '*I'm* not crying, and it's *my* dog!'

But, when everyone had settled down again in bed, and slept peacefully, George's pillow was very wet indeed. Tim crept up beside her and licked the salt tears off her cheek. He whined softly. Tim was always unhappy when his little mistress was sad.

9 A hunt for the Secret Way

There were no lessons the next day. George looked rather pale, and was very quiet. Tim was already out in the yard-kennel, and the children could hear him whining unhappily. They were all upset to hear him.

'Oh, George, I'm awfully sorry about it all,' said Dick. 'I wish you wouldn't get so fierce about things. You only get yourself into trouble – and poor old Tim.'

George was full of mixed feelings. She disliked Mr Roland so much now that she could hardly bear to look at him – and yet she did not dare to be openly rude and rebellious because she was afraid that if she was, the tutor would give her a bad report, and perhaps she would not be allowed even to *see* Timothy. It was very hard for a defiant nature like hers to force herself to behave properly.

Mr Roland took no notice of her at all. The other children tried to bring George into their talks and plans, but she remained quiet and uninterested.

'George! We're going over to Kirrin Farmhouse today,' said Dick. 'Coming? We're going to try and find the entrance to the Secret Way. It must start somewhere there.'

The children had told George what Mr Roland had said about the piece of marked linen. They had all been thrilled about this, though the excitements of

Christmas Day had made them forget about it for a while.

'Yes – of course I'll come,' said George, looking more cheerful. 'Timothy can come too. He wants a walk.'

But when the little girl found that Mr Roland was also going, she changed her mind at once. Not for anything would she go with the tutor! No – she would go for a walk alone with Timothy.

'But, George, think of the excitement we'll have trying to find the Secret Way,' said Julian, taking hold of her arm. George wrenched it away.

'I'm not going if Mr Roland is,' she said, obstinately, and the others knew that it was no good trying to coax her.

'I shall go alone with Tim,' said George. 'You go off together with your dear Mr Roland!'

She set out with Timothy, a lonely little figure going down the garden path. The others stared after her. This was horrid. George was being more and more left out, but what could they do about it?

'Well, children, are you ready?' asked Mr Roland. 'You start off by yourselves, will you? I'll meet you at the farmhouse later. I want to run down to the village first to get something.'

So the three children set off by themselves, wishing that George was with them. She was nowhere to be seen.

Old Mr and Mrs Sanders were pleased to see the three children, and sat them down in the big kitchen to eat ginger buns and drink hot milk.

'Well, have you come to find a few more secret things?' asked Mrs Sanders, with a smile.

'May we try?' asked Julian. 'We're looking for

a room that's facing east, with a stone floor, and panelling!'

'All the rooms downstairs have stone floors,' said Mrs Sanders. 'You hunt all you like, my dears. You won't do any damage, I know. But don't go into the room upstairs with the cupboard that has a false back, will you, or the one next to it! Those are the rooms the two artists have.'

'All right,' said Julian, rather sorry that they were unable to fiddle about with the exciting cupboard again. 'Are the artists here, Mrs Sanders? I'd like to talk to them about pictures. I hope one day I'll be an artist too.'

'Dear me, is that so?' said Mrs Sanders. 'Well, well – it's always a marvel to me how people make any money at painting pictures.'

'It isn't making money that artists like, so much as the painting of the pictures,' said Julian, looking rather wise. That seemed to puzzle Mrs Sanders even more. She shook her head and laughed.

'They're peculiar folk!' she said. 'Ah well – you go along and have a hunt for whatever it is you want to find. You can't talk to the two artists today though, Master Julian – they're out.'

The children finished their buns and milk and then stood up, wondering where to begin their search. They must look for a room or rooms facing east. That would be the first thing to do.

'Which side of the house faces east, Mrs Sanders?' asked Julian. 'Do you know?'

'The kitchen faces due north,' said Mrs Sanders. 'So east will be over there,' she pointed to the left.

'Thanks,' said Julian. 'Come on, everyone!' The three children went out of the kitchen, and turned to the left. There were three rooms there – a kind of scullery, not much used now, a tiny room used as a den by old Mr Sanders, and a room that had once been a drawing-room, but which was now cold and unused.

'They've all got stone floors,' said Julian.

'So we'll have to hunt through all of the three rooms,' said Anne.

'No, we won't,' said Julian. 'We shan't have to look in this scullery, for one thing!'

'Why not?' asked Anne.

'Because the walls are of stone, silly, and we want panelling,' said Julian. 'Use your brains, Anne!'

'Well, that's one room we needn't bother with, then,' said Dick. 'Look – both this little room and the drawing-room have panelling, Julian. We must search in both.'

'There must be some reason for putting *eight* squares of panelling in the directions,' said Julian, looking at the roll of linen again. 'It would be a good idea to see whether there's a place with eight squares only – you know, over a window, or something.'

It was tremendously exciting to look round the two rooms! The children began with the smaller room. It was panelled all the way round in dark oak, but there was no place where only eight panels showed. So the children went into the next room.

The panelling there was different. It did not look so old, and was not so dark. The squares were rather a different size, too. The children tried each panel, tapping and pressing as they went, expecting at any moment to see one slide back as the one in the hall had done.

But they were disappointed. Nothing happened at all. They were still in the middle of trying when they heard footsteps in the hall, and voices. Somebody looked into the drawing-room. It was a man, thin and tall, wearing glasses on his long nose.

'Hallo!' he said. 'Mrs Sanders told me you were treasure-hunting, or something. How are you getting on?'

'Not very well,' said Julian, politely. He looked at the man, and saw behind him another one, younger, with rather screwed-up eyes and a big mouth. 'I suppose you are the two artists?' he asked.

'We are!' said the first man, coming into the room. 'Now, just exactly what are you looking for?'

Julian did not really want to tell him, but it was difficult not to. 'Well – we're just seeing if there's a sliding panel here,' he said at last. 'There's one in the hall, you know. It's exciting to hunt round.'

'Shall we help?' said the first artist, coming into the room. 'What are your names? Mine's Thomas, and my friend's name is Wilton.'

The children talked politely for a minute or two, not at all wanting the two men to help. If there was anything to be found, *they* wanted to find it. It would spoil everything if grown-ups solved the puzzle!

Soon everyone was tap-tap-tapping round the wooden panels. They were in the middle of this when a voice hailed them.

'Hallo! My word, we *are* all busy!'

The children turned, and saw their tutor standing in the doorway, smiling at them. The two artists looked at him.

'Is this a friend of yours?' asked Mr Thomas.

'Yes – he's our tutor, and he's very nice!' said Anne, running to Mr Roland and putting her hand in his.

'Perhaps you will introduce me, Anne,' said Mr Roland, smiling at the little girl.

Anne knew how to introduce people. She had often seen her mother doing it. 'This is Mr Roland,' she said to the two artists. Then she turned to Mr Roland. 'This is Mr Thomas,' she said, waving her hand towards him, 'and the other one is Mr Wilton.'

The men half-bowed to one another and nodded. 'Are you staying here?' asked Mr Roland. 'A very nice old farmhouse, isn't it?'

'It isn't time to go yet, is it?' asked Julian, hearing a clock strike.

'Yes, I'm afraid it is,' said Mr Roland. 'I'm later meeting you than I expected. We must go in about five minutes – no later. I'll just give you a hand in trying to find this mysterious secret way!'

But no matter how any one of them pressed and tapped around the panels in either of the two rooms, they could not find anything exciting. It really was most disappointing.

'Well, we really must go now,' said Mr Roland. 'Come and say good-bye to Mrs Sanders.'

They all went into the warm kitchen, where Mrs Sanders was cooking something that smelt most delicious.

'Something for our lunch, Mrs Sanders?' said Mr Wilton. 'My word, you really are a wonderful cook!'

Mrs Sanders smiled. She turned to the children. 'Well, dearies, did you find what you wanted?' she asked.

'No,' said Mr Roland, answering for them. 'We haven't been able to find the secret way, after all!'

'The secret way?' said Mrs Sanders, in surprise. 'What do you know about that now? I thought it had all been forgotten – in fact, I haven't believed in that secret way for many a year!'

'Oh, Mrs Sanders – do you know about it?' cried Julian. 'Where is it?'

'I don't know, dear – the secret of it has been lost for

many a day,' said the old lady. 'I remember my old grandmother telling me something about it when I was smaller than any of you. But I wasn't interested in things like that when I was little. I was all for cows and hens and sheep.'

'Oh, Mrs Sanders – do, do try and remember something!' begged Dick. 'What *was* the secret way?'

'Well, it was supposed to be a hidden way from Kirrin Farmhouse to somewhere else,' said Mrs Sanders. 'I don't know where, I'm sure. It was used in the olden days when people wanted to hide from enemies.'

It was disappointing that Mrs Sanders knew so little. The children said good-bye and went off with their tutor, feeling that their morning had been wasted.

George was indoors when they got to Kirrin Cottage. Her cheeks were not so pale, now, and she greeted the children eagerly.

'Did you discover anything? Tell me all about it!' she said.

'There's nothing to tell,' said Dick, rather gloomily. 'We found three rooms facing east, with stone floors, but only two of them had wooden panelling, so we hunted round those, tapping and punching – but there wasn't anything to be discovered at all.'

'We saw the two artists,' said Anne. 'One was tall and thin and had a long nose with glasses on. He was called Mr Thomas. The other was younger, with little piggy eyes and an enormous mouth.'

'I met them out this morning,' said George. 'It must have been them. Mr Roland was with them, and they were all talking together. They didn't see me.'

'Oh, it couldn't have been the artists you saw,' said Anne, at once. 'Mr Roland didn't know them. I had to introduce them.'

'Well, I'm sure I heard Mr Roland call one of them Wilton,' said George, puzzled. 'He *must* have known them.'

'It couldn't have been the artists,' said Anne, again. 'They really didn't know Mr Roland. Mr Thomas asked if he was a friend of ours.'

'I'm sure I'm not mistaken,' said George, looking obstinate. 'If Mr Roland said he didn't know the two artists, he was telling lies.'

'Oh, you're always making out that he is doing something horrid!' cried Anne, indignantly. 'You just make up things about him!'

'Sh!' said Julian. 'Here he is.'

The door opened and the tutor came in. 'Well,' he said, 'it *was* disappointing that we couldn't find the secret way, wasn't it? Anyway, we were rather foolish to hunt about that drawing-room as we did – the panelling there wasn't really old – it must have been put in years after the other.'

'Oh – well, it's no good looking there again,' said Julian, disappointed. 'And I'm pretty sure there's nothing to be found in that other little room. We went all over it so thoroughly. Isn't it disappointing?'

'It is,' said Mr Roland. 'Well, Julian, how did you like the two artists? I was pleased to meet them – they seemed nice fellows, and I shall like to know them.'

George looked at the tutor. Could he possibly be telling untruths in such a truthful voice? The little girl was very puzzled. She felt sure it was the artists she had seen him with. But why should he pretend he didn't know them? She must be mistaken. But all the same, she felt uncomfortable about it, and made up her mind to find out the truth, if she could.

10   *A shock for George and Tim*

Next morning there were lessons again – and no
Timothy under the table! George felt very much in-
clined to refuse to work, but what would be the good
of that? Grown-ups were so powerful, and could dole
out all kinds of punishments. She didn't care how
much she was punished herself but she couldn't bear
to think that Timothy might have to share in the
punishments too.

So, pale and sullen, the little girl sat down at the
table with the others. Anne was eager to join in the
lessons – in fact she was eager to do anything to please
Mr Roland, because he had given her the fairy doll
from the top of the Christmas tree! Anne thought it
was the prettiest doll she had ever seen.

George had scowled at the doll when Anne showed
it to her. She didn't like dolls, and she certainly wasn't
going to like one that Mr Roland had chosen, and
given to Anne! But Anne loved it, and had made up her
mind to do lessons with the others, and work as well as
she could.

George did as little as she could without getting into
trouble. Mr Roland took no interest in her or in her
work. He praised the others, and took a lot of trouble
to show Julian something he found difficult.

The children heard Tim whining outside as they
worked. This troubled them very much, for Timothy
was such a companion, and so dear to them all. They

could not bear to think of him left out of everything, cold and miserable in the yard-kennel. When the ten minutes' break came, and Mr Roland went out of the room for a few minutes, Julian spoke to George.

'George! It's awful for us to hear poor old Tim whining out there in the cold. And I'm sure I heard him cough. Let me speak to Mr Roland about him. You must feel simply dreadful knowing that Tim is out there.'

'I thought I heard him cough, too,' said George, looking worried. 'I hope he won't get a cold. He simply doesn't understand why I have to put him there. He thinks I'm terribly unkind.'

The little girl turned her head away, afraid that tears might come into her eyes. She always boasted that she never cried – but it was very difficult to keep the tears away when she thought of Timothy out there in the cold.

Dick took her arm. 'Listen, George – you just hate Mr Roland, and I suppose you can't help it. But we can none of us bear Timothy being out there all alone – and it looks like snow today, which would be awful for him. Could you be awfully, awfully good today, and forget your dislike, so that when your father asks Mr Roland for your report, he can say you were very good – and then we'll ask Mr Roland if he wouldn't let Timmy come back into the house.'

'See?'

Timothy coughed again, out in the yard, and George's heart went cold. Suppose he got that awful illness called pneumonia – and she couldn't nurse him because he had to live in the kennel? She would die of unhappiness! She turned to Julian and Dick.

'All right,' she said. 'I do hate Mr Roland – but I love Timothy more than I hate the tutor – so for Tim's sake

I'll pretend to be good and sweet and hard-working. And then you can beg him to let Timothy come back.'

'Good girl!' said Julian. 'Now here he comes – so do your best.'

To the tutor's enormous surprise, George gave him a smile when he came into the room. This was so unexpected that it puzzled him. He was even more puzzled to find that George worked harder than anyone for the rest of the morning, and she answered politely and cheerfully when he spoke to her. He gave her a word of praise.

'Well done, Georgina! I can see you've got brains.'

'Thank you,' said George, and gave him another wan smile – a very watery, poor affair, compared with the happy smiles the others had been used to – but still, it *was* a smile!

At dinner-time George looked after Mr Roland most politely – passed him the salt, offered him more bread, got up to fill his glass when it was empty! The others looked at her in admiration. George had plenty of pluck. She must be finding it very difficult to behave as if Mr Roland was a great friend, when she really disliked him so much!

Mr Roland seemed very pleased, and appeared to be quite willing to respond to George's friendliness. He made a little joke with her, and offered to lend her a book he had about a dog. George's mother was delighted to find that her difficult daughter seemed to be turning over a new leaf. Altogether things were very much happier that day.

'George, you go out of the room before your father comes in to ask Mr Roland about your behaviour tonight,' said Julian. 'Then, when the tutor gives you a splendid report, we will all ask if Timothy can come back. It will be easier if you are not there.'

'All right,' said George. She was longing for this difficult day to be over. It was very hard for her to pretend to be friendly, when she was not. She could never never do it, if it wasn't for Timothy's sake!

George disappeared out of the room just before six o'clock, when she heard her father coming. He walked into the room and nodded to Mr Roland.

'Well? Have your pupils worked well today?' he asked.

'Very well indeed,' said Mr Roland. 'Julian has really mastered something he didn't understand today. Dick has done well in Latin. Anne has written out a French exercise without a single mistake!'

'And what about George?' asked Uncle Quentin.

'I was coming to Georgina,' said Mr Roland, looking round and seeing that she was gone. 'She has worked better than anyone else today! I am really pleased with her. She has tried hard – and she has really been polite and friendly. I feel she is trying to turn over a new leaf.'

'She's been a brick today,' said Julian, warmly. 'Uncle Quentin, she has tried awfully hard, she really has. And, you know, she's terribly unhappy.'

'Why?' asked Uncle Quentin in surprise.

'Because of Timothy,' said Julian. 'He's out in the cold, you see. And he's got a dreadful cough.'

'Oh, Uncle Quentin, please do let poor Timmy come indoors,' begged Anne.

'Yes, please do,' said Dick. 'Not only for George's sake, because she loves him so, but for us too. We hate to hear him whining outside. And George does deserve a reward, Uncle – she's been marvellous today.'

'Well,' said Uncle Quentin, looking doubtfully at the three eager faces before him, 'well – I hardly know what to say. If George is going to be sensible – and the weather gets colder – well . . .'

He looked at Mr Roland, expecting to hear him say something in favour of Timothy. But the tutor said nothing. He looked annoyed.

'What do you think, Mr Roland?' asked Uncle Quentin.

'I think you should keep to what you said and let the dog stay outside,' said the tutor. 'George is spoilt, and needs firm handling. You should really keep to your decision about the dog. There is no reason to give way about it just because she tried to be good for once!'

The three children stared at Mr Roland in surprise and dismay. It had never entered their heads that he would not back them up!

'Oh, Mr Roland, you *are* horrid!' cried Anne. 'Oh do, do say you'll have Timothy back.'

The tutor did not look at Anne. He pursed up his mouth beneath its thick moustache and looked straight at Uncle Quentin.

'Well,' said Uncle Quentin, 'perhaps we had better see how George behaves for a whole week. After all – just one day isn't much.'

The children stared at him in disgust. They thought he was weak and unkind. Mr Roland nodded his head.

'Yes,' he said, 'a week will be a better test. If Georgina behaves well for a whole week, we'll have another word about the dog. But at present I feel it would be better to keep him outside.'

'Very well,' said Uncle Quentin, and went out of the room. He paused to look back. 'Come along into my study sometime,' he said. 'I've got a bit further with my formula. It's at a very interesting stage.'

The three children looked at one another but said nothing. How mean of the tutor to stop Uncle

Quentin from having Timothy indoors again! They all felt disappointed in him. The tutor saw their faces.

'I'm sorry to disappoint you,' he said. 'But I think if you'd been bitten by Timothy once and snapped at all over when he got you on the floor, you would not be very keen on having him in either!'

He went out of the room. The children wondered what to say to George. She came in a moment later, her face eager. But when she saw the gloomy looks of the other three, she stopped short.

'Isn't Tim to come in?' she asked, quickly. 'What's happened? Tell me!'

They told her. The little girl's face grew dark and angry when she heard how the tutor had put his foot down about Timothy, even when her father had himself suggested that the dog might come indoors.

'Oh, what a beast he is!' she cried. 'How I do hate him! I'll pay him back for this. I will, I will, I will!'

She rushed out of the room. They heard her fumbling in the hall, and then the front door banged.

'She's gone out into the dark,' said Julian. 'I bet she's gone to Timmy. Poor old George. Now she'll be worse than ever!'

That night George could not sleep. She lay and tossed in her bed, listening for Timothy. She heard him cough. She heard him whine. He was cold, she knew he was. She had put plenty of fresh straw into his kennel and had turned it away from the cold north wind – but he must feel the bitter night terribly, after sleeping for so long on her bed!

Timothy gave such a hollow cough that George could bear it no longer. She must, she simply must, get up and go down to him. 'I shall bring him into the house for a little while and rub his chest with some of that stuff Mother uses for herself when she's got a cold on her chest,' thought the girl. 'Perhaps that will do him good.'

She quickly put a few clothes on and crept downstairs. The whole house was quiet. She slipped out into the yard and undid Tim's chain. He was delighted to see her and licked her hands and face lovingly.

'Come along into the warm for a little while,' whispered the little girl. 'I'll rub your poor chest with some oil I've got.'

Timmy pattered behind her into the house. She took him to the kitchen – but the fire was out and the room was cold. George went to look at the other rooms.

There was quite a nice fire still in her father's study. She and Tim went in there. She did not put on the light, because the firelight was fairly bright. She had with her the little bottle of oil from the bathroom cupboard. She put it down by the fire to warm.

Then she rubbed the dog's hairy chest with the oil, hoping it would do him good. 'Don't cough now if you can help it, Tim,' she whispered. 'If you do, someone may hear you. Lie down here by the fire, darling, and get nice and warm. Your cold will soon be better.'

Timothy lay down on the rug. He was glad to be out of his kennel and with his beloved mistress. He put his head on her knee. She stroked him and whispered to him.

The firelight glinted on the curious instruments and glass tubes that stood around on shelves in her father's study. A log shifted a little in the fire and settled lower, sending up a cloud of sparks. It was warm and peaceful there.

The little girl almost fell asleep. The big dog closed his eyes too, and rested peacefully, happy and warm. George settled down with her head on his neck.

She awoke to hear the study clock striking six! The room was cold now, and she shivered. Goodness! Six o'clock! Joanna the cook would soon be awake. She must not find Timmy and George in the study!

'Tim darling! Wake up! We must put you back into your kennel,' whispered George. 'I'm sure your cold is better, because you haven't coughed once since you've been indoors. Get up – and don't make a noise. Sh!'

Tim stood up and shook himself. He licked George's hand. He understood perfectly that he must be quite quiet. The two of them slipped out of the study, went into the hall and out of the front door.

In a minute or two Timothy was on the chain, and in his kennel, cuddled down among the straw. George wished she could cuddle there with him. She gave him a pat and slipped back indoors again.

She went up to bed, sleepy and cold. She forgot that she was partly dressed and got into bed just as she was. She was asleep in a moment!

In the morning Anne was most amazed to find that George had on vest, knickers, jeans and jersey, when she got out of bed to dress.

'Look!' she said. 'You're half-dressed! But I *saw* you undressing last night.'

'Be quiet,' said George. 'I went down and let Tim in last night. We sat in front of the study fire and I rubbed him with oil. Now don't you dare to say a word to anyone! Promise!'

Anne promised – and she faithfully kept her word. Well, well – to think that George dared to roam about like that all night – what an extraordinary girl she was!

11   Stolen papers

'George, don't behave fiercely today, will you?' said Julian, after breakfast. 'It won't do you or Timothy any good at all.'

'Do you suppose I'm going to behave well when I know perfectly well that Mr Roland will never let me have Tim indoors all these holidays?' said George.

'Well – they said a week,' said Dick. 'Can't you try for a week?'

'No. At the end of a week Mr Roland will say I must try for another week,' said George. 'He's got a real dislike for poor Tim. And for me too. I'm not surprised at that, because I know that when I try to be horrid, I really *am* horrid. But he shouldn't hate poor Timmy.'

'Oh George – you'll spoil the whole hols if you are silly, and keep getting into trouble,' said Anne.

'Well, I'll spoil them then,' said George, the sulky look coming back on her face.

'I don't see why you have to spoil them for *us*, as well as for yourself,' said Julian.

'They don't need to be spoilt for you,' said George. 'You can have all the fun you want – go for walks with your dear Mr Roland, play games with him in the evening, and laugh and talk as much as you like. You don't need to take any notice of me.'

'You are a funny girl, George,' said Julian, with a sigh. 'We like you, and we hate you to be unhappy – so

how can we have fun if we know you're miserable –
and Timmy too?'

'Don't worry about *me*,' said George, in rather a
choky voice. 'I'm going out to Tim. I'm not coming in
to lessons today.'

'George! But you must!' said Dick and Julian
together.

'There's no "must" about it,' said George. 'I'm just
not coming. I won't work with Mr Roland till he says I
can have Timothy indoors again.'

'But you know you can't do things like that – you'll
be told off or something,' said Dick.

'I shall run away if things get too bad,' said George,
in a shaky voice. 'I shall run away with Tim.'

She went out of the room and shut the door with a
bang. The others stared after her. What could you do
with a person like George? Anyone could rule her with
kindness and understanding – but as soon as she came
up against anyone who disliked her, or whom she
disliked, she shied away like a frightened horse – and
kicked like a frightened horse, too!

Mr Roland came into the sitting-room, his books in
his hand. He smiled at the three children.

'Well? All ready for me, I see. Where's Georgina?'

Nobody answered. Nobody was going to give
George away!

'Don't you know where she is?' asked Mr Roland in
surprise. He looked at Julian.

'No, sir,' said Julian, truthfully. 'I've no idea where
she is.'

'Well – perhaps she will come along in a few
minutes,' said Mr Roland. 'Gone to feed that dog of
hers, I suppose.'

They all settled down to work. The time went on
and George did not come in. Mr Roland glanced at the

clock and made an impatient clicking noise with his tongue.

'Really, it's too bad of Georgina to be so late! Anne, go and see if you can find her.'

Anne went. She looked in the bedroom. There was no George there. She looked in the kitchen. Joanna was there, making cakes. She gave the little girl a hot piece to eat. She had no idea where George was.

Anne couldn't find her anywhere. She went back and told Mr Roland. He looked angry.

'I shall have to report this to her father,' he said. 'I have never had to deal with such a rebellious child before. She seems to do everything she possibly can to get herself into trouble.'

Lessons went on. Break came, and still George did not appear. Julian slipped out and saw that the yard-kennel was empty. So George had gone out with Timmy! What a row she would get into when she got back!

No sooner had the children settled down after break to do the rest of the morning's lessons, than a big disturbance came.

Uncle Quentin burst in looking upset and worried.

'Have any of you children been into my study?' he asked.

'No, Uncle Quentin,' they all answered.

'You said we weren't to,' said Julian.

'Why?' Has something been broken?' asked Mr Roland.

'Yes – the test-tubes I set yesterday for an experiment have been broken – and what is worse, three most important pages of my book have gone,' said Uncle Quentin. 'I can write them out again, but only after a great deal of work. I can't understand it. Are you *sure*, children, that none of you has been meddling with things in my study?'

'Quite sure,' they answered. Anne went very red – she suddenly remembered what George had told her. George said she had taken Timmy into Uncle Quentin's study last night, and rubbed his chest with oil! But George couldn't possibly have broken the test-tubes, and taken pages from her father's book!

Mr Roland noticed that Anne had gone red.

'Do you know anything about this, Anne?' he asked.

'No, Mr Roland,' said Anne, blushing even redder, and looking very uncomfortable indeed.

'Where's George?' suddenly said Uncle Quentin.

The children said nothing, and it was Mr Roland who answered:

'We don't know. She didn't come to lessons this morning.'

'Didn't come to lessons! Why not?' demanded Uncle Quentin, beginning to frown.

'She didn't say,' said Mr Roland dryly. 'I imagine she was upset because we were firm about Timothy last night, and this is her way of being defiant.'

'The naughty girl!' said George's father, angrily. 'I don't know what's come over her lately. Fanny! Come here! Did you know that George hasn't been in to her lessons today?'

Aunt Fanny came into the room. She looked very worried. She had a little bottle in her hand. The children wondered what it was.

'Didn't come in to lessons!' repeated Aunt Fanny. 'How extraordinary! Then where is she?'

'I don't think you need to worry about her,' said Mr Roland, smoothly. 'She's probably gone off with Timothy in a fit of temper. What is very much more important, is the fact that your work appears to have been spoilt by someone. I only hope it is not George, who has been spiteful enough to get back at you for not allowing her to have her dog in the house.'

'Of *course* it wasn't George!' cried Dick, angry that anyone should even think such a thing of his cousin.

'George would never, never do a thing like that,' said Julian.

'No, she never would,' said Anne, sticking up valiantly for her cousin, although a horrid doubt was in her mind. After all – George *had* been in the study last night!

'Quentin, I am sure George would not even *think* of such a thing,' said Aunt Fanny. 'You will find those pages somewhere – and as for the test-tubes that were broken, well, perhaps the wind blew the curtain against them, or something! When did you last see those pages?'

'Last night,' said Uncle Quentin. 'I read them over again, and checked my figures to make sure they were right. Those pages contain the very heart of my formula! If they got into anyone else's hands, they could use my secret. This is a terrible thing for me! I *must* know what has happened to them.'

'I found this in your study, Quentin,' said Aunt Fanny, and she held up the little bottle she carried. 'Did you put it there? It was in the fender.'

Uncle Quentin took the bottle and stared at it. 'Camphorated oil!' he said. 'Of course I didn't take it there. Why should I?'

'Well – who took it there, then?' asked Aunt Fanny, puzzled. 'None of the children has a cold – and anyway, they wouldn't think of the camphorated oil, and take it into the study to use! It's most extraordinary!'

Everyone was astonished. Why should a bottle of

camphorated oil appear in the study fender?

Only one person could think why. It suddenly came into Anne's mind in a flash. George had said she had taken Timmy into the study, and rubbed him with oil! He had had a cough, that was why. And she had left the oil in the study. Oh dear, oh dear – now what would happen? What a pity George had forgotten the oil!

Anne went very red again as she looked at the oil. Mr Roland, whose eyes seemed very sharp this morning, looked hard at the little girl.

'Anne! You know something about that oil!' he said suddenly. 'What do you know? Did you put it there?'

'No,' said Anne. 'I haven't been into the study. I said I hadn't.'

'Do you know anything about the oil?' said Mr Roland, again. 'You *do* know something.'

Everyone stared at Anne. She stared back. This was simply dreadful. She could not give George away. She could *not*. George was in quite enough trouble as it was, without getting into any more. She pursed up her little mouth and did not answer.

'Anne!' said Mr Roland, sternly. 'Answer when you are spoken to.'

Anne said nothing. The two boys stared at her, guessing that it was something to do with George. They did not know that George had brought Timothy in the night before.

'Anne, dear,' said her aunt, gently. 'Tell us if you know something. It might help us to find out what has happened to Uncle Quentin's papers. It is very, very, important.'

Still Anne said nothing. Her eyes filled with tears. Julian squeezed her arm.

'Don't bother Anne,' he said to the grown-ups. 'If

she thinks she can't tell you, she's got some very good reason.'

'I think she's shielding George,' said Mr Roland. 'Is that it, Anne?'

Anne burst into tears. Julian put his arms round his little sister, and spoke again to the three grown-ups.

'*Don't* bother Anne! Can't you see she's upset?'

'We'll let George speak for herself, when she thinks she will come in,' said Mr Roland. 'I'm sure she knows how that bottle got there – and if she put it there herself she must have been into the study – and she's the only person that *has* been there.'

The boys could not think for one moment that George would do such a thing as spoil her father's work. Anne feared it, and it upset her. She sobbed in Julian's arms.

'When George comes in, send her to me in my study,' said Uncle Quentin, irritably. 'How can a man work when these upsets go on? I was always against having children in the house.'

He stamped out, tall, cross and frowning. The children were glad to see him go. Mr Roland shut the books on the table with a snap.

'We can't do any more lessons this morning,' he said. 'Put on your things and go out for a walk till dinner-time.'

'Yes, do,' said Aunt Fanny, looking white and worried. 'That's a good idea.'

Mr Roland and their aunt went out of the room. 'I don't know if Mr Roland thinks he's coming out with us,' said Julian, in a low voice, 'but we've got to get out first and give him the slip. We've got to find George and warn her what's up.'

'Right!' said Dick. 'Dry your eyes, Anne darling. Hurry and get your things. We'll slip out of the garden door before Mr Roland comes down. I bet George has gone for her favourite walk over the cliffs. We'll meet her!' The three children threw on their outdoor things and crept out of the garden door quietly. They raced down the garden path, and out of the gate before Mr Roland even knew they were gone! They made their way to the cliffs, and looked to see if George was coming.

'There she is – and Timothy, too!' cried Julian, pointing. 'George! George! Quick, we've got something to tell you!'

12   *George in trouble*

'What's the matter?' asked George, as the three children tore up to her. 'Has something happened?'

'Yes, George. Someone has taken three most important pages out of your father's book!' panted Julian. 'And broken the test-tubes he was making an experiment with. Mr Roland thinks you might have had something to do with it!'

'The beast!' said George, her blue eyes deepening with anger. 'As if I'd do a thing like that! Why should he think it's me, anyway?'

'Well, George, you left that bottle of oil in the study fender,' said Anne. 'I haven't told anyone at all what you told me happened last night – but somehow Mr Roland guessed you had something to do with the bottle of oil.'

'Didn't you tell the boys how I got Timmy indoors?' asked George. 'Well, there's nothing much to tell, Julian. I just heard poor old Tim coughing in the night, and I half-dressed, went down, and took him into the study, where there was a fire. Mother keeps a bottle of oil that she used to rub her chest with when she has a cough – so I thought it might do Timmy's cold good, too. I got the oil and rubbed him well – and we both fell asleep by the fire till six o'clock. I was sleepy when I woke up, and forgot the oil. That's all.'

'And you didn't take any pages from the book Uncle

Quentin is writing, and you didn't break anything in the study, did you?' said Anne.

'Of course not, silly,' said George, indignantly. 'How can you ask me a thing like that? You must be mad.'

George never told a lie, and the others always believed her, whatever she said. They stared at her, and she stared back.

'I wonder who could have taken those pages then?' said Julian. 'Maybe your father will come across them, after all. I expect he put them into some safe place and then forgot all about them. And the test-tubes might easily have over-balanced and broken themselves. Some of them look very shaky to me.'

'I suppose I shall get into trouble now for taking Tim into the study,' said George.

'And for not coming into lessons this morning,' said Dick. 'You really are an idiot, George. I never knew anyone like you for walking right into trouble.'

'Hadn't you better stay out a bit longer, till everyone has calmed down a bit?' said Anne.

'No,' said George at once. 'If I'm going to get into a row, I'll get into it now! *I'm* not afraid!'

She marched over the cliff path, with Timmy running round her as usual. The others followed. It wasn't nice to think that George was going to get into such trouble.

They came to the house and went up the path.

Mr Roland saw them from the window and opened the door. He glanced at George.

'Your father wants to see you in the study,' said the tutor. Then he turned to the others, looking annoyed.

'Why did you go out without me? I meant to go with you.'

'Oh did you, sir? I'm sorry,' said Julian, politely, not

looking at Mr Roland. 'We just went out on the cliff a little way.'

'Georgina, did you go into the study last night?' asked Mr Roland, watching George as she took off her hat and coat.

'I'll answer my father's questions, not yours,' said George.

'What you want is a good telling off,' said Mr Roland. 'And if I were your father I'd give it to you!'

'You're not my father,' answered George. She went to the study door and opened it. There was no one there.

'Father isn't here,' said George.

'He'll be there in a minute,' said Mr Roland. 'Go in and wait. And you others, go up and wash for lunch.'

The other three children felt almost as if they were deserting George as they went up the stairs. They could hear Timmy whining from the yard outside. He knew his little mistress was in trouble, and he wanted to be with her.

George sat down on a chair, and gazed at the fire, remembering how she had sat on the rug there with Tim last night, rubbing his hairy chest. How silly of her to have forgotten the bottle of oil!

Her father came into the room, frowning and angry. He looked sternly at George.

'Were you in here last night, George?' he asked.

'Yes, I was,' answered George at once.

'What were you doing in here?' asked her father. 'You know you children are forbidden to come into my study.'

'I know,' said George. 'But you see Timmy had a dreadful cough, and I couldn't bear it. So I crept down about one o'clock and let him in. This was the only room that was really warm, so I sat here and rubbed his chest with the oil Mother uses when she has a cold.'

'Rubbed the dog's chest with camphorated oil!' exclaimed her father, in amazement. 'What a mad thing to do! As if it would do him any good.'

'It didn't seem mad to me,' said George. 'It seemed sensible. And Timmy's cough is much better today. I'm sorry for coming into the study. I didn't touch a thing, of course.'

'George, something very serious has happened,' said her father, looking gravely at her. 'Some of my test-tubes with which I was doing an important experiment, have been broken – and, worse than that, three pages of my book have gone. Tell me on your honour that you know nothing of these things.'

'I know nothing of them,' said George, looking her father straight in the eyes. Her own eyes shone very blue and clear as she gazed at him. He felt quite certain that George was speaking the truth. She could know nothing of the damage done. Then where were those pages?

'George, last night when I went to bed at eleven o'clock, everything was in order,' he said. 'I read over those three important pages and checked them once more myself. This morning they are gone.'

'Then they must have been taken between eleven o'clock and one o'clock,' said George. 'I was here from that time until six.'

'But *who* could have taken them?' said her father. 'The window was fastened, as far as I know. And nobody knows that those three pages were so important but myself. It is most extraordinary.'

'Mr Roland probably knew,' said George, slowly.

'Don't be absurd,' said her father. 'Even if he did realise they were important, he would not have taken

them. He's a very decent fellow. And that reminds
me – why were you not at lessons this morning,
George?'

'I'm not going to do lessons any more with Mr
Roland,' said George. 'I simply hate him!'

'George! I will *not* have you talking like this!' said
her father. 'Do you want me to say you are to lose Tim
altogether?'

'No,' said George, feeling shaky about the knees.
'And I don't think it's fair to keep trying to force me to
do things by threatening me with losing Timothy. If –
if – you do a thing like that – I'll – I'll run away or
something!'

There were no tears in George's eyes. She sat bolt
upright on her chair, gazing defiantly at her father.
How difficult she was! Her father sighed, and remembered that he too in his own childhood had been called
'difficult'. Perhaps George took after him. She could
be so good and sweet – and here she was being
perfectly impossible!

Her father did not know what to do with George.
He thought he had better have a word with his wife.
He got up and went to the door.

'Stay here. I shall be back in a moment. I want to
speak to your mother about you.'

'Don't speak to Mr Roland about me, will you?' said
George, who felt quite certain that the tutor would
urge terrible punishments for her and Timmy. 'Oh,
Father, if only Timothy had been in the house last
night, sleeping in my room as usual, he would have
heard whoever it was that stole your secret – and he
would have barked and roused the house!'

Her father said nothing, but he knew that what
George had said was true. Timmy wouldn't have let
anyone get into the study. It was funny he hadn't

barked in the night, if anyone from outside had climbed in at the study window. Still, it was the other side of the house. Maybe he had heard nothing.

The door closed. George sat still on her chair, gazing up at the mantelpiece, where a clock ticked away the time. She felt very miserable. Everything was going wrong, every single thing!

As she gazed at the panelled overmantel, she counted the wooden panels. There were eight. Now, where had she heard of eight panels before? Of course – in that Secret Way. There were eight panels marked on the roll of linen. What a pity there had not been eight panels in a wooden over-mantel at Kirrin Farmhouse!

George glanced out of the window, and wondered if it faced east. She looked to see where the sun was – it was not shining into the room – but it did in the early morning – so it must face east. Fancy – here was a room facing east and with eight wooden panels. She wondered if it had a stone floor.

The floor was covered with a large thick carpet. George got up and went to the wall. She pulled up the edge of the carpet there – and saw that the floor underneath was made of large flat stones. The study had a stone floor too!

She sat down again and gazed at the wooden panels, trying to remember which one in the roll of linen was marked with a cross. But of course it couldn't be a room in Kirrin Cottage – it must be in Kirrin Farmhouse where the Secret Way began.

But just suppose it *was* Kirrin Cottage! Certainly the directions had been found in Kirrin Farmhouse – but that was not to say that the Secret Way had to begin there, even though Mrs Sanders seemed to think it did.

George was feeling excited. 'I must tap round about

those eight panels and try to find the one that is marked on the linen roll,' she thought. 'It may slide back or something, and I shall suddenly see the entrance opening!'

She got up to try her luck – but at that moment the door opened again and her father came in looking very grave.

'I have been talking to your mother,' he said. 'She agrees with me that you have been very disobedient, rude and defiant. We can't let behaviour like that pass, George. You will have to be punished.'

George looked anxiously at her father. If only her punishment had nothing to do with Timothy! But, of course, it had.

'You will go to bed for the rest of the day, and you will not see Timothy for three days,' said her father. 'I will get Julian to feed him and take him for a walk. If you persist in being defiant, Timothy will have to go away altogether. I am afraid, strange as it may seem, that that dog has a bad influence on you.'

'He hasn't, he hasn't!' cried George. 'Oh, he'll be so miserable if I don't see him for three whole days.'

'There's nothing more to be said,' said her father. 'Go straight upstairs to bed, and think over all I have said to you, George. I am very disappointed in your behaviour these holidays. I really did think the influence of your three cousins had made you into a normal, sensible girl. Now you are worse then you have ever been.'

He held open the door and George walked out, holding her head high. She heard the others having their dinner in the dining-room. She went straight upstairs and undressed. She got into bed and thought miserably of not seeing Tim for three days. She couldn't bear it! Nobody could possibly know how much she loved Timothy!

Joanna came up with a tray of dinner. 'Well, it's a pity to see you in bed,' she said cheerfully. 'Now you be a sensible girl and behave properly and you'll soon be downstairs again.'

George picked at her dinner. She did not feel at all hungry. She lay back on the bed, thinking of Tim and thinking of the eight panels over the mantelpiece. Could they possibly be the ones shown in the Secret Way directions? She gazed out of the window and thought hard.

'Golly, it's snowing!' she said suddenly, sitting up. 'I thought it would when I saw that leaden sky this morning. It's snowing hard! It will be quite thick by tonight – inches deep. Oh, poor Timothy. I hope Julian will see that his kennel is kept clear of the drifting snow.'

George had plenty of time to think as she lay in bed. Joanna came and took the tray away. No one else came to see her. George felt sure the other children had been forbidden to go up and speak to her. She felt lonely and left-out.

She thought of her father's lost pages. Could Mr Roland have taken them? After all, he was very interested in her father's work and seemed to understand it. The thief must have been someone who knew which were the important pages. Surely Timothy would have barked if a thief had come in from outside, even though the study was the other side of the house. Timmy had such sharp ears.

'I think it must have been someone *in*side the house,' said George. 'None of us children, that's certain – and not Mother or Joanna. So that only leaves Mr Roland. And I did find him in the study that other night when Timmy woke me by growling.'

She sat up in bed suddenly. 'I believe Mr Roland had Timothy put out of the house because he wanted to go poking round the study again and was afraid Tim would bark!' she thought. 'He was so very insistent that Tim should go out of doors – even when everyone else begged for me to have him indoors. I believe – I really do believe – that Mr Roland is the thief!'

The little girl felt very excited. Could it be that the tutor had stolen the pages – and broken those important test-tubes? How she wished that the others would come and see her, so that she could talk things over with them!

13   Julian has a surprise

The three children downstairs felt very sorry for George. Uncle Quentin had forbidden them to go up and see her.

'A little time for thinking out things all alone may do George good,' he said.

'Poor old George,' said Julian. 'It's too bad, isn't it? I say – look at the snow!'

The snow was falling very thickly. Julian went to the window and looked out. 'I shall have to go and see that Timmy's kennel is all right,' he said. 'We don't want the poor old fellow to be snowed up! I expect he is wondering what the snow is!'

Timothy was certainly very puzzled to see every-where covered with soft white stuff. He sat in his kennel and stared out at the falling flakes, his big brown eyes following them as they fell to the ground. He was puzzled and unhappy. Why was he living out here by himself in the cold? Why didn't George come to him? Didn't she love him any more? The big dog was very miserable, as miserable as George!

He was delighted to see Julian. He jumped up at the boy and licked his face. 'Good old Tim!' said Julian. 'Are you all right? Let me sweep away some of this snow and swing your kennel round a bit so that no flakes fly inside. There – that's better. No, we're not going for a walk, old thing – not now.'

The boy patted the dog and fussed him a bit, then

went indoors. The others met him at the sitting-room door.

'Julian! Mr Roland is going out for a walk by himself. Aunt Fanny is lying down, and Uncle Quentin is in his study. Can't we go up and see George?'

'We were forbidden to,' said Julian, doubtfully.

'I know,' said Dick. 'But I don't mind risking it for the sake of making George feel a bit happier. It must be so awful for her, lying up there all alone, knowing she can't see Tim for days.'

'Well – let me go up, as I'm the eldest,' said Julian. 'You two stay down here in the sitting-room and talk. Then Uncle Quentin will think we're all here. I'll slip up and see George for a few minutes.'

'All right,' said Dick. 'Give her our love and tell her we'll look after Timmy.'

Julian slipped quietly up the stairs. He opened George's door and crept inside. He shut the door, and saw George sitting up in bed, looking at him in delight.

'Sh!' said Julian. 'I'm not supposed to be here!'

'Oh Julian!' said George joyfully. 'How good of you to come. I was so lonely. Come this side of the bed. Then if anyone comes in suddenly, you can duck down and hide.'

Julian went to the other side of the bed. George began to pour out to him all she had been thinking of.

'I believe Mr Roland is the thief, I really do!' she said. 'I'm not saying that because I hate him, Julian, really I'm not. After all, I *did* find him snooping round the study one afternoon – and again in the middle of the night. He may have got to hear of my father's work, and come to see if he could steal it. It was just lucky for him that we needed a tutor. I'm sure he stole those pages, and I'm sure he wanted Timmy out of the house so that he could do his stealing without Tim hearing him and growling.'

'Oh, George – I don't think so,' said Julian, who really could not approve of the idea of the tutor doing such a thing. 'It all sounds so far-fetched and un-believable.'

'Lots of unbelievable things happen,' said George. 'Lots. And this is one of them.'

'Well, if Mr Roland *did* steal the pages, they must be somewhere in the house,' said Julian. 'He hasn't been out all day. They must be somewhere in his bedroom.'

'Of course!' said George, looking thrilled. 'I wish he'd go out! Then I'd search his room.'

'George, you can't do things like that,' said Julian, quite shocked.

'You simply don't know what things I can do, if I really want to,' said George, setting her mouth in a firm line. 'Oh – what's that noise?'

There was the bang of a door. Julian went cautiously to the window and peeped out. The snow had stopped falling for a time, and Mr Roland had taken the chance of going out.

'It's Mr Roland,' said Julian.

'Oooh – I could search his room now, if you'll keep watch at the window and tell me if he comes back,' said George, throwing back the bedclothes at once.

'No, George, don't,' said Julian. 'Honestly and truly, it's awful to search somebody's room like that. And anyway, I dare say he's got the pages with him. He may even be going to give them to somebody!'

'I never thought of that,' said George, and she looked at Julian with wide eyes. 'Isn't that sickening? Of course he may be doing that. He knows those two artists at Kirrin Farmhouse, for instance. They may be in the plot too.'

'Oh, George, don't be silly,' said Julian. 'You are making a mountain out of a mole-hill, talking of plots and goodness knows what! Anyone would think we were in the middle of a big adventure.'

'Well, I think we are,' said George, unexpectedly, and she looked rather solemn. 'I sort of feel it all round me – a Big Adventure!'

Julian stared at his cousin thoughtfully. Could there possibly be anything in what she said?

'Julian, will you do something for me?' said George.

'Of course,' said the boy, at once.

'Go out and follow Mr Roland,' said George. 'Don't let him see you. There's a white macintosh in the hall cupboard. Put it on and you won't be easily seen against the snow. Follow him and see if he meets anyone and gives them anything that looks like the pages of my father's book – you know those big pages he writes on. They're very large.'

'All right,' said Julian. 'But if I do, promise you won't go and search his room. You can't do things like that, George.'

'I can,' said George. 'But I won't, if you'll just follow Mr Roland for me. I'm sure he's going to hand over what he has stolen to others who are in the plot! And I bet those others will be the two artists at Kirrin Farmhouse that he pretended not to know!'

'You'll find you're quite wrong,' said Julian, going to the door. 'I'm sure I shan't be able to follow Mr Roland, anyway – he's been gone five minutes now!'

'Yes, you will, silly – he'll have left his footmarks in the snow,' said George. 'And oh, Julian – I quite forgot to tell you something else exciting. Oh dear, there isn't time now. I'll tell you when you come back, if you can come up again then. It's about the Secret Way.'

'Really?' said Julian, in delight. It had been a great
disappointment to him that all their hunting and
searching had come to nothing. 'All right – I'll try
and creep up again later. If I don't come, you'll
know I can't, and you must wait till bed-time.'

He disappeared and shut the door quietly. He
slipped downstairs, popped his head into the sitting-
room and whispered to the others that he was going
out after the tutor.

'Tell you why, later,' he said. He put the white
macintosh around him and went out into the garden.
Snow was beginning to fall again, but not yet heavily
enough to hide Mr Roland's deep footsteps. He had
had big Wellington boots on, and the footmarks
showed up well in the six-inch-deep snow.

The boy followed them quickly. The countryside
was very wintry-looking now. The sky was low and
leaden, and he could see there was much more snow to
come. He hurried on after Mr Roland, though he
could not see a sign of the tutor.

Down the lane and over the path that led across the
common went the double row of footmarks. Julian
stumbled on, his eyes glued to the foot-prints. Suddenly he heard the sound of voices and stopped. A big
gorse bush lay to the right and the voices came from
there. The boy went nearer to the bush. He heard his
tutor's voice, talking in low tones. He could not hear a
word that was said.

'Whoever can he be talking to?' he wondered. He
crept up closer to the bush. There was a hollow space
inside. Julian thought he could creep right into it,
though it would be very prickly, and peer out of the
other side. Carefully the boy crept into the prickly
hollow, where the branches were bare and brown.

He parted the prickly branches slowly and cautiously – and to his amazement he saw Mr Roland talking to the two artists from Kirrin Farmhouse – Mr Thomas and Mr Wilton! So George was right. The tutor had met them – and, as Julian watched, Mr Roland handed over to Mr Thomas a doubled-up sheaf of papers.

'They look just like pages from Uncle Quentin's book,' said Julian to himself. 'I say – this is mighty strange. It does begin to look like a plot – with Mr Roland at the centre of it!'

Mr Thomas put the papers into the pocket of his overcoat. The men muttered a few more words, which even Julian's sharp ears could not catch, and then parted. The artists went off towards Kirrin Farmhouse, and Mr Roland took the path back over the common. Julian crouched down in the hollow of the prickly gorse bush, hoping the tutor would not turn and see him. Luckily he didn't. He went straight on and disappeared into the snow, which was now falling thickly. It was also beginning to get dark and Julian, unable to see the path very clearly, hurried after Mr Roland, half-afraid of being lost in the snow-storm.

Mr Roland was not anxious to be out longer than he could help, either. He almost ran back to Kirrin Cottage. He came to the gate at last, and Julian watched him go into the house. He gave him a little time to take off his things and then, giving Timothy a pat as he went by, he went to the garden door. He took off his macintosh, changed his boots, and slipped into the sitting-room before Mr Roland had come down from his bedroom.

'What's happened?' asked Dick and Anne, seeing that Julian was in a great state of excitement. But he

could not tell them, for just then Joanna came in to lay
the tea.

Much to Julian's disappointment, he could not say a
word to the others all that evening, because one or
other of the grown-ups was always in the room.
Neither could he go up to see George. He could hardly
wait to tell his news, but it was no good, he had to.

'Is it still snowing, Aunt Fanny?' asked Anne.

Her aunt went to the front door and looked out. The
snow was piled high against the step!

'Yes,' she said, when she came back. 'It is snowing
fast and thickly. If it goes on like this we shall be
completely snowed up, as we were two winters ago!
We couldn't get out of the house for five days then.
The milkman couldn't get to us, nor the baker. Fortunately we had plenty of tinned milk, and I can bake my
own bread. You poor children, you will not be able to
go out tomorrow – the snow will be too thick!'

'Will Kirrin Farmhouse be snowed up too?' asked
Mr Roland.

'Oh yes – worse than we shall be,' said Aunt Fanny.
'But they won't mind! They have plenty of food there.
They will be prisoners just as much, and more, as we
shall.'

Julian wondered why Mr Roland had asked that
question. Was he afraid that his friends would not be
able to send those pages away by the post – or take
them anywhere by bus or car? The boy felt certain this
was the reason for the question. How he longed to be
able to talk over everything with the others.

'I'm tired!' he said, about eight o'clock. 'Let's go to
bed.'

Dick and Anne stared at him in astonishment.
Usually, as he was the eldest, he went to bed last of all.
Tonight he was actually *asking* to go! Julian winked

quickly at them, and they backed him up at once.

Dick yawned widely, and so did Anne. Their aunt put down the sewing she was doing. 'You *do* sound tired!' she said. 'I think you'd better all go to bed.'

'Could I just go out and see if Timmy is all right?' asked Julian. His aunt nodded. The boy put on his rubber boots and coat, and slipped out through the garden door into the yard. It was very deep in snow, too. Tim's kennel was half-hidden in it. The dog had trampled a space in front of the kennel door, and stood there, looking for Julian as he came out of the house.

'Poor old boy, out here in the snow all alone,' said Julian. He patted the dog, and Timmy whined. He was asking to go back with the boy.

'I wish I *could* take you back with me,' said Julian. 'Never mind, Timothy. I'll come and see you tomorrow.'

He went indoors again. The children said good-night to their aunt and Mr Roland, and went upstairs.

'Undress quickly, put on dressing-gowns and meet in George's room,' whispered Julian to the others. 'Don't make a sound or we'll have Aunt Fanny up. Quick now!'

In less than three minutes the children were undressed, and were sitting on George's bed. She was very pleased to see them. Anne slipped into bed with her, because her feet were cold.

'Julian! Did you follow Mr Roland all right?' whispered George.

'Why did he follow him?' asked Dick, who had been dying to know.

Julian told them everything as quickly as he could – all that George suspected – and how he had followed the tutor – and what he had seen. When George heard how Julian had watched him giving a sheaf of papers to the two artists, her eyes gleamed angrily.

'The thief! They must have been the lost pages! And to think my father has been so friendly to him. Oh, what can we do? Those men will get the papers away as quickly as they can, and the secret Father has been working on for ages will be used by someone else – for some other country, probably!'

'They can't get the papers away,' said Julian. 'You've no idea how thick the snow is now, George. We shall be prisoners here for a few days, if this snow goes on, and so will the people in Kirrin Farmhouse. If they want to hide the papers, they will have to hide them in the farmhouse! If only we could get over there and hunt round!'

'Well, we can't,' said Dick. 'That's quite certain. We'd be up to our necks in snow!'

The four children looked gloomily at one another. Dick and Anne could hardly believe that the jolly Mr Roland was a thief – a spy perhaps, trying to steal a valuable secret from a friendly scientist. And they couldn't stop it.

'We'd better tell your father,' said Julian at last.

'No,' said Anne. 'He wouldn't believe it, would he, George?'

'He'd laugh at us and go straight and tell Mr Roland,' said George. 'That would warn him, and he mustn't be warned. He mustn't know that we guess anything.'

'Sh! Aunt Fanny's coming!' whispered Dick, suddenly. The boys slipped out of the room and into bed. Anne hopped across to her own little bed. All was peace and quiet when the children's aunt came into the bedroom.

She said good-night and tucked them up. As soon as

she had gone down, the four children met together again in George's room.

'George, tell me now what you were going to say about the Secret Way,' said Julian.

'Oh, yes,' said George. 'Well, there may be nothing in my idea at all – but in the study downstairs, there are eight wooden panels over the mantelpiece – and the floor is of stone – and the room faces east! A bit odd, isn't it? Just what the directions said.'

'Is there a cupboard there too?' asked Julian.

'No. But there is everything else,' said George. 'And I was just wondering if by any chance the entrance to the Secret Way is in this house, not in the farmhouse. After all, they both belonged to my family at one time, you know. The people living in the farmhouse years ago must have known all about this cottage.'

'Golly, George – suppose the entrance *was* here!' said Dick. 'Wouldn't it be simply marvellous! Let's go straight down and look!'

'Don't be silly,' said Julian. 'Go down to the study when Uncle Quentin is there? I'd rather meet twenty lions than face Uncle! Especially after what has happened!'

'Well, we simply MUST find out if George's idea is right; we simply must,' said Dick, forgetting to whisper.

'Shut up, idiot!' said Julian, giving him a punch. 'Do you want to bring the whole household up here?'

'Sorry!' said Dick. 'But, oh golly, this *is* exciting. It's an Adventure again.'

'Just what I said,' said George, eagerly. 'Listen, shall we wait till midnight, and then creep down to the study when everyone is asleep, and try our luck? There may be nothing in my idea at all – but we'll have to find out now. I don't believe I could go to sleep till I've tried each one of those panels over the mantelpiece to see if something happens.'

'Well, I know I can't sleep a wink either,' said Dick. 'Listen – is that someone coming up? We'd better go. Come on, Julian! We'll meet in George's room at midnight – and creep down and try out George's idea!'

The two boys went off to their own room. Neither of them could sleep a wink. Nor could George. She lay awake, and went over and over in her mind all that had happened those holidays. 'It's like a jigsaw puzzle,' she thought. 'I couldn't understand a lot of things at first – but now they are fitting together, and making a picture.'

Anne was fast asleep. She had to be awakened at midnight. 'Come on!' whispered Julian, shaking her. 'Don't you want to share in this adventure?'

14 *The Secret Way at last!*

The four children crept downstairs through the dark and silent night. Nobody made a sound at all. They made their way to the study. George softly closed the door and then switched on the light.

The children stared at the eight panels over the mantelpiece. Yes – there were exactly eight, four in one row and four in the row above. Julian spread the linen roll out on the table, and the children pored over it.

'The cross is in the middle of the second panel in the top row,' said Julian in a low voice. 'I'll try pressing it. Watch, all of you!'

He went to the fireplace. The others followed him, their hearts beating fast with excitement. Julian stood on tiptoe and began to press hard in the middle of the second panel. Nothing happened.

'Press harder! Tap it!' said Dick.

'I daren't make too much noise,' said Julian, feeling all over the panel to see if there was any roughness that might tell of a hidden spring or lever.

Suddenly, under his hands, the panel slid silently back, just as the one had done at Kirrin Farmhouse in the hall! The children stared at the space behind, thrilled.

'It's not big enough to get into,' said George. 'It can't be the entrance to the Secret Way.'

Julian got out his torch from his dressing-gown

pocket. He put it inside the opening, and gave a low exclamation.

'There's a sort of handle here – with strong wire or something attached to it. I'll pull it and see what happens.'

He pulled – but he was not strong enough to move the handle that seemed to be embedded in the wall. Dick put his hand in and the two boys then pulled together.

'It's moving – it's giving way a bit,' panted Julian. 'Go on, Dick, pull hard!'

The handle suddenly came away from the wall, and behind it came thick wire, rusty and old. At the same time a curious grating noise came from below the hearthrug in front of the fireplace, and Anne almost fell.

'Julian! Something is moving under the rug!' she said, frightened. 'I felt it. Under the rug, quick!'

The handle could not be pulled out any farther. The boys let go, and looked down. To the right of the fireplace, under the rug, something had moved. There was no doubt of that. The rug sagged down instead of being flat and straight.

'A stone has moved in the floor,' said Julian, his voice shaking with excitement. 'This handle works a lever, which is attached to this wire. Quick – pull up the rug, and roll back the carpet.'

With trembling hands the children pulled back the rug and the carpet – and then stood staring at a very strange thing. A big flat stone laid in the floor had slipped downwards, pulled in some manner by the wire attached to the handle hidden behind the panel! There was now a black space where the stone had been.

'Look at that!' said George, in a thrilling whisper.

'The entrance to the Secret Way!'

'It's here after all!' said Julian.

'Let's go down!' said Dick.

'No!' said Anne, shivering at the thought of disappearing into the black hole.

Julian flashed his torch into the black space. The stone had slid down and then sideways. Below was a space just big enough to take a man, bending down.

'I expect there's a passage or something leading from here, under the house, and out,' said Julian. 'Golly, I wonder where it leads to?'

'We simply must find out,' said George.

'Not now,' said Dick. 'It's dark and cold. I don't fancy going along the Secret Way at midnight. I don't mind just hopping down to see what it's like – but don't let's go along any passage till tomorrow.'

'Uncle Quentin will be working here tomorrow,' said Julian.

'He said he was going to sweep the snow away from the front door in the morning,' said George. 'We could slip into the study then. It's Saturday. There may be no lessons.'

'All right,' said Julian, who badly wanted to explore everything then and there. 'But for goodness' sake let's have a look and see if there *is* a passage down there. At present all we can see is a hole!'

'I'll help you down,' said Dick. So he gave his brother a hand and the boy dropped lightly down into the black space, holding his torch. He gave a loud exclamation.

'It's the entrance to the Secret Way all right! There's a passage leading from here under the house – awfully low and narrow – but I can see it's a passage. I do wonder where it leads to!'

He shivered. It was cold and damp down there.

'Give me a hand up, Dick,' he said. He was soon out of the hole and in the warm study again.

The children looked at one another in the greatest joy and excitement. This *was* an Adventure, a real Adventure. It was a pity they couldn't go on with it now.

'We'll try and take Timmy with us tomorrow,' said George. 'Oh, I say – how are we going to shut the entrance up?'

'We can't leave the rug and carpet sagging over that hole,' said Dick. 'Nor can we leave the panel open.'

'We'll see if we can get the stone back,' said Julian. He stood on tiptoe and felt about inside the panel. His hand closed on a kind of knob, set deep in a stone. He pulled it, and at once the handle slid back, pulled by the wire. At the same time the sunk stone glided to the surface of the floor again, making a slight grating sound as it did so.

'Well, it's like magic!' said Dick. 'It really is! Fancy the mechanism working so smoothly after years of not being used. This is the most exciting thing I've ever seen!'

There was a noise in the bedroom above. The children stood still and listened.

'It's Mr Roland!' whispered Dick. 'He's heard us. Quick, slip upstairs before he comes down.'

They switched out the light and opened the study door softly. Up the stairs they fled, as quietly as church mice, their hearts thumping so loudly that it seemed as if everyone in the house must hear the beat.

The girls got safely to their rooms and Dick was able to slip into his. But Julian was seen by Mr Roland as he came out of his room with a torch.

'What are you doing, Julian!' asked the tutor, in

surprise. 'Did you hear a noise downstairs? I thought I did.'

'Yes – I heard quite a lot of noise downstairs,' said Julian, truthfully. 'But perhaps it's snow falling off the roof, landing with a plop in the ground, sir. Do you think that's it?'

'I don't know,' said the tutor doubtfully. 'We'll go down and see.'

They went down, but of course there was nothing to be seen. Julian was glad they had been able to shut the panel and make the stone come back to its proper place again. Mr Roland was the very last person he wanted to tell his secret to.

They went upstairs and Julian slipped into his room. 'Is it all right?' whispered Dick.

'Yes,' said Julian. 'Don't let's talk. Mr Roland's awake, and I don't want him to suspect anything.'

The boys fell asleep. When they awoke in the morning, there was a completely white world outside. Snow covered everything and covered it deeply. Timothy's kennel could not be seen! But there were footmarks round about it.

George gave a squeal when she saw how deep the snow was. 'Poor Timothy! I'm going to get him in. I don't care what anyone says! I won't let him be buried in the snow!'

She dressed and tore downstairs. She went out to the kennel, floundering knee deep in the snow. But there was no Timmy there!

A loud bark from the kitchen made her jump. Joanna the cook knocked on the kitchen window. 'It's all right! I couldn't bear the dog out there in the snow, so I fetched him in, poor thing. Your mother says I can have him in the kitchen but you're not to come and see him.'

'Oh, good – Timmy's in the warmth!' said George, gladly. She yelled to Joanna, 'Thanks awfully! You *are* kind!'

She went indoors and told the others. They were very glad. 'And *I've* got a bit of news for *you*,' said Dick. 'Mr Roland is in bed with a bad cold, so there are to be no lessons today. Cheers!'

'Golly, that *is* good news,' said George, cheering up tremendously. 'Timmy in the warm kitchen and Mr Roland kept in bed. I do feel pleased!'

'We shall be able to explore the Secret Way safely now,' said Julian. 'Aunt Fanny is going to do something in the kitchen this morning with Joanna, and Uncle is going to tackle the snow. I vote we say we'll do lessons by ourselves in the sitting-room, and then, when everything is safe, we'll explore the Secret Way!'

'But why must we do lessons?' asked George in dismay.

'Because if we don't, silly, we'll have to help your father dig away the snow,' said Julian.

So, to his uncle's surprise, Julian suggested that the four children should do lessons by themselves in the sitting-room. 'Well, I thought you'd like to come and help dig away the snow,' said Uncle Quentin. 'But perhaps you had better get on with your work.'

The children sat themselves down as good as gold in the sitting-room, their books before them. They heard Mr Roland coughing in his room. They heard their aunt go into the kitchen and talk to Joanna. They heard Timmy scratching at the kitchen door – then paws pattering down the passage – then a big, inquiring nose came round the door, and there was old Timmy, looking anxiously for his beloved mistress!

'Timmy!' squealed George, and ran to him. She flung her arms round his neck and hugged him.

'You act as if you hadn't seen Tim for a year,' said Julian.

'It seems like a year,' said George. 'I say, there's my father digging away like mad. Can't we go to the study now? We ought to be safe for a good while.'

They left the sitting-room and went to the study. Julian was soon pulling the handle behind the secret panel. George had already turned back the rug and the carpet. The stone slid downward and sideways. The Secret Way was open!

'Come on!' said Julian. 'Hurry!'

He jumped down into the hole. Dick followed, then Anne, then George. Julian pushed them all into the narrow, low passage. Then he looked up. Perhaps he had better pull the carpet and rug over the hole, in case anyone came into the room and looked around. It took him a few seconds to do it. Then he bent down and joined the others in the passage. They were going to explore the Secret Way at last!

15   An exciting journey and hunt

Timothy had leapt down into the hole when George had jumped. He now ran ahead of the children, puzzled at their wanting to explore such a cold, dark place. Both Julian and Dick had torches, which threw broad beams before them.

There was not much to be seen. The Secret Way under the old house was narrow and low, so that the children were forced to go in single file, and to stoop almost double. It was a great relief to them when the passage became a little wider, and the room a little higher. It was very tiring to stoop all the time.

'Have you any idea where the Secret Way is going?' Dick asked Julian. 'I mean – is it going towards the sea, or away from it?'

'Oh, not towards the sea!' said Julian, who had a very good sense of direction. 'As far as I can make out the passage is going towards the common. Look at the walls – they are rather sandy in places, and we know the common has sandy soil. I hope we shan't find that the passage has fallen in anywhere.'

They went on and on. The Secret Way was very straight, though occasionally it would round a rocky part in a curve.

'Isn't it dark and cold?' said Anne, shivering. 'I wish I had put on a coat. How many miles have we come, Julian?'

'Not even one, silly!' said Julian. 'Hallo – look here – the passage has fallen in a bit there!'

Two bright torches shone in front of them and the children saw that the sandy roof had fallen in. Julian kicked at the pile of sandy soil with his foot.

'It's all right,' he said. 'We can force our way through easily. It isn't much of a fall, and it's mostly sand. I'll do a bit of kicking!'

After some trampling and kicking, the roof-fall no longer blocked the way. There was now enough room for the children to climb over it, bending their heads low to avoid knocking them against the top of the passage. Julian shone his torch forward, and saw that the way was clear.

'The Secret Way is very wide just here!' he said suddenly, and flashed his torch around to show the others.

'It's been widened out to make a sort of little room,' said George. 'Look, there's a kind of bench at the back, made out of the rock. I believe it's a resting-place.'

George was right. It was very tiring to creep along the narrow passage for so long. The little wide place with its rocky bench made a very good resting-place. The four tired children, cold but excited, huddled together on the funny seat and took a welcome rest. Timmy put his head on George's knee. He was delighted to be with her again.

'Well, come on,' said Julian, after a few minutes. 'I'm getting awfully cold. I do wonder where this passage comes out!'

'Julian – do you think it could come out at Kirrin Farmhouse?' asked George, suddenly. 'You know what Mrs Sanders said – that there was a secret passage leading from the farmhouse somewhere. Well, this may be the one – and it leads to Kirrin Cottage!'

'George, I believe you're right!' said Julian. 'Yes – the two houses belonged to your family years ago! And in the old days there were often secret passages joining houses, so it's quite plain this secret way joins them up together! Why didn't I think of that before?'

'I say!' squealed Anne, in a high, excited voice, 'I say! I've thought of something too!'

'What?' asked everyone.

'Well – if those two artists have got Uncle's papers, we may be able to get them away before the men can send them off by post, or take them away themselves!' squeaked Anne, so thrilled with her idea that she could hardly get the words out quickly enough. 'They're prisoners at the farmhouse because of the snow, just as we were at the cottage.'

'*Anne!* You're right!' said Julian.

'Clever girl!' said Dick.

'I *say* – if we *could* get those papers again – how wonderful it would be!' said George. Timmy joined in the general excitement, and jumped up and down in joy. Something had pleased the children, so he was pleased too!

'Come on!' said Julian, taking Anne's hand. 'This is thrilling. If George is right, and this Secret Way comes out at Kirrin Farmhouse somewhere, we'll somehow hunt through those men's rooms and find the papers.'

'You said that searching people's rooms was a shocking thing to do,' said George.

'Well, I didn't know then all I know now,' said Julian. 'We're doing this for your father – and maybe for our country too, if his secret formula is valuable. We've got to set our wits to work now, to outwit dangerous enemies.'

'Do you really think they are dangerous?' asked Anne rather afraid.

'Yes, I should think so,' said Julian. 'But you needn't worry, Anne, you've got me and Dick and Tim to protect you.'

'I can protect her too,' said George, indignantly.

'You're fiercer than any boy I know!' said Dick.

'Come on,' said Julian, impatiently. 'I'm longing to get to the end of this passage.'

They all went on again, Anne following behind Julian, and Dick behind George. Timmy ran up and down the line, squeezing by them whenever he wanted to. He thought it was a very peculiar way to spend a morning!

Julian stopped suddenly, after they had gone a good way. 'What's up?' asked Dick, from the back. 'Not another roof-fall, I hope!'

'No – but I think we've come to the end of the passage!' said Julian, thrilled. The others crowded as close to him as they could. The passage certainly had come to an end. There was a rocky wall in front of them, and set firmly in it were iron staples intended for footholds. These went up the wall and when Julian turned his torch upwards, the children saw that there was a square opening in the roof of the passage.

'We have to climb up this rocky wall now,' said Julian, 'go through that dark hole there, keep on climbing – and goodness knows where we come out! I'll go first. You wait here, everyone, and I'll come back and tell you what I've seen.'

The boy put his torch between his teeth, and then pulled himself up by the iron staples set in the wall. He set his feet on them, and then climbed up through the square dark hole, feeling for the staples as he went.

He went up for a good way. It was almost like going up a chimney shaft, he thought. It was cold and smelt musty.

Suddenly he came to a ledge, and he stepped on to it. He took his torch from his teeth and flashed it around him.

There was a stone wall behind him, at the side of him and stone above him. The black hole up which he had come, yawned by his feet. Julian shone his torch in front of him, and a shock of surprise went through him.

There was no stone wall in front of him, but a big wooden door, made of black oak. A handle was set about waist-high; Julian turned it with trembling fingers. What was he going to see?

The door opened outwards, over the ledge, and it was difficult to get round it without falling back into the hole. Julian managed to open it wide, squeezed round it without losing his footing, and stepped beyond it, expecting to find himself in a room.

But his hand felt more wood in front of him! He shone his torch round, and found that he was up against what looked like yet another door. Under his searching fingers it suddenly moved sideways, and slid silently away!

And then Julian knew where he was! 'I'm in the cupboard at Kirrin Farmhouse – the one that has a false back!' he thought. 'The Secret Way comes up behind it! How clever! Little did we know when we played about in this cupboard that not only did it have a sliding back, but that it was the entrance to the Secret Way, hidden behind it!'

The cupboard was now full of clothes belonging to the artists. Julian stood and listened. There was no sound of anyone in the room. Should he just take a

quick look round, and see if those lost papers were anywhere about?

Then he remembered the other four, waiting
patiently below in the cold. He had better go and tell
them what had happened. They could all come and
help in the search.

He stepped into the space behind the sliding back.
The sliding door slipped across again, and Julian was
left standing on the narrow ledge, with the old oak
door wide open to one side of him. He did not bother
to shut it. He felt about his feet, and found the iron
staples in the hole below him. Down he went, clinging with his hands and feet, his torch in his teeth
again.

'Julian! What a time you've been! Quick, tell us all
about it!' cried George.

'It's most terribly thrilling,' said Julian. 'Absolutely
super! Where do you suppose all this leads to? Into the
cupboard at Kirrin Farmhouse – the one that's got a
false back!'

'Golly!' said Dick.

'I *say!*' said George.

'Did you go into the room?' cried Anne.

'I climbed as far as I could and came to a big oak
door,' said Julian. 'It has a handle this side, so I swung
it wide open. Then I saw another wooden door in front
of me – at least, I thought it was a door, I didn't know it
was just the false back of that cupboard. It was quite
easy to slide back and I stepped through, and found
myself among a whole lot of clothes hanging in the
cupboard! Then I hurried back to tell you.'

'Julian! We can hunt for those papers now,' said
George, eagerly. 'Was there anyone in the room?'

'I couldn't *hear* anyone,' said Julian. 'Now what I
propose is this – we'll all go up, and have a hunt round

those two rooms. The men have the room next to the cupboard one too.'

'Oh good!' said Dick, thrilled at the thought of such an adventure. 'Let's go now. You go first, Ju. Then Anne, then George and then me.'

'What about Tim?' asked George.

'He can't climb, silly,' said Julian. 'He's a simply marvellous dog, but he certainly can't climb, George. We'll have to leave him down here.'

'He won't like that,' said George.

'Well, we can't carry him up,' said Dick. 'You won't mind staying here for a bit, will you, Tim, old fellow?'

Tim wagged his tail. But, as he saw the four children mysteriously disappearing up the wall, he put his big tail down at once. What! Going without him? How could they?

He jumped up at the wall, and fell back. He jumped again and whined. George called down in a low voice.

'Be quiet, Tim dear! We shan't be long.'

Tim stopped whining. He lay down at the bottom of the wall, his ears well-cocked. This adventure was becoming more and more peculiar!

Soon the children were on the narrow ledge. The old oak door was still wide open. Julian shone his torch and the others saw the false back of the cupboard. Julian put his hands on it and it slid silently sideways. Then the torch shone on coats and dressing-gowns!

The children stood quite still, listening. There was no sound from the room. 'I'll open the cupboard door and peep into the room,' whispered Julian. 'Don't make a sound!'

The boy pushed between the clothes and felt for the outer cupboard door with his hand. He found it, and pushed it slightly. It opened a little and a shaft of daylight came into the cupboard. He peeped cautiously into the room.

There was no one there at all. That was good. 'Come on!' he whispered to the others. 'The room's empty!'

One by one the children crept out of the clothes cupboard and into the room. There was a big bed there, a wash-stand, chest of drawers, small table and two chairs. Nothing else. It would be easy to search the whole room.

'Look, Julian, there's a door between the two rooms,' said George, suddenly. 'Two of us can go and hunt there and two here – and we can lock the doors that lead on to the landing, so that no one can come in and catch us!'

'Good idea!' said Julian, who was afraid that at any moment someone might come in and catch them in their search. 'Anne and I will go into the next room, and you and Dick can search this one. Lock the door that opens on to the landing, Dick, and I'll lock the one in the other room. We'll leave the connecting-door open, so that we can whisper to one another.'

Quietly the boy and girl slipped through the connecting-door into the second room, which was very like the first. That was empty too. Julian went over to the door that led to the landing, and turned the key in the lock. He heard Dick doing the same to the door in the other room. He heaved a big sigh. Now he felt safe!

'Anne, turn up the rugs and see if any papers are hidden there,' he said. 'Then look under the chair-cushions and strip the bed to see if anything is hidden under the mattress.'

Anne set to work, and Julian began to hunt too. He started on the chest of drawers, which he thought would be a very likely place to hide things in. The children's hands were shaking, as they felt here and there for the lost papers. It was so terribly exciting.

They wondered where the two men were. Down in the warm kitchen, perhaps. It was cold up here in the bedrooms, and they would not want to be away from the warmth. They could not go out because the snow was piled in great drifts round Kirrin Farmhouse!

Dick and George were searching hard in the other room. They looked in every drawer. They stripped the bed. They turned up rugs and carpet. They even put their hands up the big chimney-place!

'Julian? Have you found anything?' asked Dick in a low voice, appearing at the door between the two rooms.

'Not a thing,' said Julian, rather gloomily. 'They've hidden the papers well! I only hope they haven't got them on them – in their pockets, or something!'

Dick stared at him in dismay. He hadn't thought of that. 'That *would* be sickening!' he said.

'You go back and hunt *everywhere* – simply *everywhere!*' ordered Julian. 'Punch the pillows to see if they've stuck them under the pillow-case!'

Dick disappeared. Rather a lot of noise came from his room. It sounded as if he were doing a good deal of punching!

Anne and Julian went on hunting too. There was simply nowhere that they did not look. They even turned the pictures round to see if the papers had been stuck behind one of them. But there was nothing to be found. It was bitterly disappointing.

'We can't go without finding them,' said Julian, in desperation. 'It was such a bit of luck to get here like this, down the Secret Way – right into the bedrooms! We simply *must* find those papers!'

'I say,' said Dick, appearing again, 'I can hear voices! Listen!'

All four children listened. Yes – there were men's voices – just outside the bedroom doors!

16   The children are discovered

'What shall we do?' whispered George. They had all tiptoed to the first room, and were standing together, listening.

'We'd better go down the Secret Way again,' said Julian.

'Oh no, we . . .' began George, when she heard the handle of the door being turned. Whoever was trying to get in, could not open the door. There was an angry exclamation, and then the children heard Mr Wilton's voice. 'My door seems to have stuck. Do you mind If I come through your bedroom and see what's the matter with this handle?'

'Come right along!' came the voice of Mr Thomas. There was the sound of footsteps going to the outer door of the second room. Then there was the noise of a handle being turned and shaken.

'What's this!' said Mr Wilton, in exasperation. 'This won't open, either. Can the doors be locked?'

'It looks like it!' said Mr Thomas.

There was a pause. Then the children distinctly heard a few words uttered in a low voice. 'Are the papers safe? Is anyone after them?'

'They're in your room, aren't they?' said Mr Thomas. There was another pause. The children looked at one another. So the men *had* got the papers – and what was more, they *were* in the room! The very room the children stood in! They looked round it eagerly, racking their brains to think of some place they had not yet explored.

'Quick! Hunt round again while we've time,' whispered Julian. 'Don't make a noise.'

On tiptoe the children began a thorough hunt once more. How they searched! They even opened the pages of the books on the table, thinking that the papers might have been slipped in there. But they could find nothing.

'Hi, Mrs Sanders!' came Mr Wilton's voice. 'Have you by any chance locked these two doors? We can't get in!'

'Dear me!' said the voice of Mrs Sanders from the stairs. 'I'll come along and see. I certainly haven't locked any doors!'

Once again the handles were turned, but the doors would not open. The men began to get very impatient.

'Do you suppose anyone is in our rooms?' Mr Wilton asked Mrs Sanders.

She laughed.

'Well now, who would be in your rooms? There's only me and Mr Sanders in the house, and you know as well as I do that no one can come in from outside, for we're quite snowed up. I don't understand it – the locks of the doors must have slipped.'

Anne was lifting up the wash-stand jug to look underneath, at that moment. It was heavier than she thought, and she had to let it down again suddenly. It struck the marble wash-stand with a crash, and water slopped out all over the place!

Everyone outside the door heard the noise. Mr Wilton banged on the door and rattled the handle.

'Who's there? Let us in or you'll be sorry! What are you doing in there?'

'Idiot, Anne!' said Dick. 'Now they'll break the door down!'

That was exactly what the two men intended to do! Afraid that someone was mysteriously in their room, trying to find the stolen papers, they went quite mad, and began to put their shoulders to the door, and heave hard. The door shook and creaked.

'Now you be careful what you're doing!' cried the indignant voice of Mrs Sanders. The men took no notice. There came a crash as they both tried out their double strength on the door.

'Quick! We must go!' said Julian. 'We mustn't let the men know how we got here, or we shan't be able to come and hunt another time. Anne, George, Dick – get back to the cupboard quickly!'

The children raced for the clothes cupboard. 'I'll go first and help you down,' said Julian. He got out on to the narrow ledge and found the iron foot-holds with his feet. Down he went, torch held between his teeth as usual.

'Anne, come next,' he called. 'And Dick, you come third, and give a hand to Anne if she wants it. George is a good climber – she can easily get down herself.'

Anne was slow at climbing down. She was terribly excited, rather frightened, and so afraid of falling that she hardly dared to feel for each iron staple as she went down.

'Buck up, Anne!' whispered Dick, above her. 'The men have almost got the door down!'

There were tremendous sounds coming from the bedroom door. At any moment now it might break down, and the men would come racing in. Dick was thankful when he could begin to climb down the wall! Once they were all out, George could shut the big oak door, and they would be safe.

George was hidden among the clothes in the cupboard, waiting her turn to climb down. As she stood
there, trying in vain to go over any likely hiding-place
in her mind, her hands felt something rustly in the
pocket of a coat she was standing against. It was a
macintosh coat, with big pockets. The little girl's
heart gave a leap.

Suppose the papers had been left in the pocket of the
coat the man had on when he took them from Mr
Roland? That was the only place the children had not
searched – the pockets of the coats in the cupboard!
With trembling fingers the girl felt in the pocket where
the rustling was.

She drew out a sheaf of papers. It was dark in the
cupboard, and she could not see if they were the ones
she was hunting for, or not – but how she hoped they
were! She stuffed them up the front of her jersey, for
she had no big pocket, and whispered to Dick:

'Can I come now?'

CRASH! The door fell in with a terrific noise, and the
two men leapt into the room. They looked round. It
was empty! But there was the water spilt on the
wash-stand and on the floor. Someone must be there
somewhere!

'Look in the cupboard!' said Mr Thomas.

George crept out of the clothes cupboard and on to
the narrow ledge, beyond the place where the false
back of the cupboard used to be. It was still hidden
sideways in the wall. The girl climbed down the hole a
few steps and then shut the oak door which was now
above her head. She had not enough strength to close it
completely, but she hoped that now she was safe!

The men went to the cupboard and felt about in the
clothes for anyone who might possibly be hiding
there. Mr Wilton gave a loud cry.

'The papers are gone! They were in this pocket! There's not a sign of them. Quick, we must find the thief and get them back!'

The men did not notice that the cupboard seemed to go farther back than usual. They stepped away from it now that they were sure no one was there, and began to hunt round the room.

By now all the children except George were at the bottom of the hole, standing in the Secret Way, waiting impatiently for George to come down. Poor George was in such a hurry to get down that she caught her clothing on one of the staples, and had to stand in a very dangerous position trying to disentangle it.

'Come on, George, for goodness' sake!' said Julian.

Timothy jumped up at the wall. He could feel the fear and excitement of the waiting children, and it upset him. He wanted George. Why didn't she come? Why was she up that dark hole? Tim was unhappy about her.

He threw back his head and gave such a loud and mournful howl that all the children jumped violently.

'Shut up, Tim!' said Julian.

Tim howled again, and the weird sound echoed round and about in a strange manner. Anne was terrified, and she began to cry. Timothy howled again and again. Once he began to howl it was difficult to stop him.

The men in the bedroom above heard the extraordinary noise, and stopped in amazement.

'Whatever's that?' said one.

'Sounds like a dog howling in the depths of the earth,' said the other.

'Funny!' said Mr Wilton. 'It seems to be coming from the direction of that cupboard.'

He went over to it and opened the door. Tim chose
that moment to give a specially mournful howl, and
Mr Wilton jumped. He got into the cupboard and felt
about at the back. The oak door there gave way
beneath his hand, and he felt it open.

'There's something weird here,' called Mr Wilton.
'Bring my torch off the table.'

Tim howled again and the noise made Mr Wilton
shiver! Tim had a peculiarly horrible howl. It came
echoing up the hole, and burst out into the cupboard.

Mr Thomas got the torch. The men shone it at the
back of the cupboard, and gave an exclamation.

'Look at that! There's a door here! Where does it lead
to?'

Mrs Sanders, who had been watching everything in
surprise and indignation, angry that her door should
have been broken down, came up to the cupboard.

'My!' she said. 'I knew there was a false back to that
cupboard – but I didn't know there was another door
behind it too! That must be the entrance to the Secret
Way that people used in the old days.'

'Where does it lead to?' rapped out Mr Wilton.

'Goodness knows!' said Mrs Sanders. 'I never took
much interest in such things.'

'Come on, we must go down,' said Mr Wilton,
shining his torch into the square black hole, and
seeing the iron foot-holds set in the stone. 'This is
where the thief went. He can't have got far. We'll go
after him. We've got to get those papers back!'

It was not long before the two men had swung
themselves over the narrow ledge and down into the
hole, feeling with their feet for the iron staples. Down
they went and down, wondering where they were
coming to. There was no sound below them. Clearly
the thief had got away!

George had got down at last. Tim almost knocked her over in his joy. She put her hand on his head. 'You old silly!' she said. 'I believe you've given our secret away! Quick, Ju – we must go, because those men will be after us in a minute. They could easily hear Tim's howling!'

Julian took Anne's hand. 'Come along, Anne,' he said. 'You must run as fast as you can. Hurry now! Dick, keep with George.'

The four of them hurried down the dark, narrow passage. What a long way they had to go home! If only the passage wasn't such a long one! The children's hearts were beating painfully as they made haste, stumbling as they went.

Julian shone his light steadily in front of him, and Dick shone his at the back. Half-leading, half-dragging Anne, Julian hurried along. Behind them they heard a shout.

'Look! There's a light ahead! That's the thief! Come on, we'll soon get him!'

17 Good old Tim!

'Hurry, Anne. Do hurry!' shouted Dick, who was just behind.

Poor Anne was finding it very difficult to get along quickly. Pulled by Julian and pushed by Dick, she almost fell two or three times. Her breath came in loud pants, and she felt as if she would burst.

'Let me have a rest!' she panted. But there was no time for that, with the two men hurrying after them! They came to the piece that was widened out, where the rocky bench was, and Anne looked longingly at it. But the boys hurried her on.

Suddenly the little girl caught her foot on a stone and fell heavily, almost dragging Julian down with her. She tried to get up, and began to cry.

'I've hurt my foot! I've twisted it! Oh, Julian, it hurts me to walk.'

'Well, you've just *got* to come along, darling,' said Julian, sorry for his little sister, but knowing that they would all be caught if he was not firm. 'Hurry as much as you can.'

But now it was impossible for Anne to go fast. She cried with pain as her foot hurt her, and hobbled along so slowly that Dick almost fell over her. Dick cast a look behind him and saw the light of the men's torches coming nearer and nearer. Whatever were they to do?

'I'll stay here with Tim and keep them off,' said George, suddenly. 'Here, take these papers, Dick! I believe they're the ones we want, but I'm not sure till we get a good light to see them. I found them in a pocket of one of the coats in the cupboard.'

'Golly!' said Dick, surprised. He took the sheaf of papers and stuffed them up his jersey, just as George had stuffed them up hers. They were too big to go into his trouser pockets. 'I'll stay with you, George, and let the other two go on ahead.'

'No. I want the papers taken to safety, in case they are my father's,' said George. 'Go on, Dick! I'll be all right here with Tim. I shall stay here just where the passage curves round this rocky bit. I'll make Tim bark like mad.'

'Suppose the men have got revolvers?' said Dick, doubtfully. 'They might shoot him.'

'I bet they haven't,' said George. '*Do* go, Dick! The men are almost here. There's the light of their torch.'

Dick sped after the stumbling Anne. He told Julian what George had suggested. 'Good for George!' said Julian. 'She really is marvellous – not afraid of anything! She will keep the men off till I get poor old Anne back.'

George was crouching behind the rocky bit, her hand on Tim's collar, waiting. 'Now, Tim!' she whispered. 'Bark your loudest. Now!'

Timothy had been growling up till now, but at George's command he opened his big mouth and barked. How he barked! He had a simply enormous voice, and the barks went echoing all down the dark and narrow passage. The hurrying men, who were near the rocky piece of the passage, stopped.

'If you come round this bend, I'll set my dog on you!' cried George.

'It's a child shouting,' said one man to another. 'Only a child! Come on!'

Timothy barked again, and pulled at his collar. He was longing to get at the men. The light of their torch shone round the bend. George let Tim go, and the big dog sprang joyfully round the curve to meet his enemies.

They suddenly saw him by the light of their torch, and he was a very terrifying sight! To begin with, he was a big dog, and now that he was angry all the hairs on the back of his neck had risen up, making him look even more enormous. His teeth were bared and glinted in the torch-light.

The men did not like the look of him at all. 'If you move one step nearer I'll tell my dog to fly at you!' shouted George. 'Wait, Tim, wait! Stand there till I give the word.'

The dog stood in the light of the torch, growling deeply. He looked an extremely fierce animal. The men looked at him doubtfully. One man took a step forward and George heard him. At once she shouted to Tim.

'Go for him, Tim, go for him!'

Tim leapt at the man's throat. He took him completely by surprise and the man fell to the ground with a thud, trying to beat off the dog. The other man helped.

'Call off your dog or we'll hurt him!' cried the second man.

'It's much more likely he'll hurt *you*!' said George, coming out from behind the rock and enjoying the fun. 'Tim, come off.'

Tim came away from the man he was worrying, looking up at his mistress as if to say, 'I was having *such* a good time! Why did you spoil it?'

'Who are you?' said the man on the ground.

'I'm not answering any of your questions,' said

George. 'Go back to Kirrin Farmhouse, that's my advice to you. If you dare to come along this passage I'll set my dog on to you again – and next time he'll do more damage.'

The men turned and went back the way they had come. They neither of them wanted to face Tim again. George waited until she could no longer see the light of their torch, then she bent down and patted Timothy.

'Brave, good dog!' she said. 'I love you, darling Tim, and you don't know how proud I am of you! Come along – we'll hurry after the others now. I expect those two men will explore this passage some time tonight, and won't they get a shock when they find out where it leads to, and see who is waiting for them!'

George hurried along the rest of the long passage, with Tim running beside her. She had Dick's torch, and it did not take her long to catch the others up. She panted out to them what had happened, and even poor Anne chuckled in delight when she heard how Tim had flung Mr Wilton to the ground.

'Here we are,' said Julian, as the passage came to a stop below the hole in the study floor. 'Hallo – what's this?'

A bright light was shining down the hole, and the rug and carpet, so carefully pulled over the hole by Julian, were now pulled back again. The children gazed up in surprise.

Uncle Quentin was there, and Aunt Fanny, and when they saw the children's faces looking up at them from the hole, they were so astonished that they very nearly fell down the hole too!

'Julian! Anne! What in the wide world are you doing down there?' cried Uncle Quentin. He gave them each a hand up, and the four children and Timothy were at last safe in the warm study. How good it was to feel warm again! They got as near the fire as they could.

'Children – what *is* the meaning of this?' asked Aunt Fanny. She looked white and worried. 'I came into the study to do some dusting, and when I stood on that bit of the rug, it seemed to give way beneath me. When I pulled it up and turned back the carpet, I saw that hole – and the hole in the panelling too! And then I found that all of you had disappeared, and went to fetch your uncle. What *has* been happening – and where does that hole lead to?'

Dick took the sheaf of papers from under his jersey and gave them to George. She took them and handed them to her father. 'Are these the missing pages?' she asked.

Her father fell on them as if they had been worth more than a hundred times their weight in gold. 'Yes! Yes! They're the pages – all three of them! Thank goodness they're back. They took me three years to bring to perfection, and contained the heart of my secret formula. George, where did you get them?'

'It's a very long story,' said George. 'You tell it all, Julian, I feel tired.'

Julian began to tell the tale. He left out nothing. He told how George had found Mr Roland snooping about the study – how she had felt sure that the tutor had not wanted Timmy in the house because the dog gave warning of his movements at night – how George had seen him talking to the two artists, although he had said he did not know them. As the tale went on, Uncle Quentin and Aunt Fanny looked more and more amazed. They simply could not believe it all.

But after all, there were the missing papers, safely back. That was marvellous. Uncle Quentin hugged the papers as if they were a precious baby. He would not put them down for a moment.

George told the bit about Timmy keeping the men off the escaping children. 'So you see, although you made poor Tim live out in the cold, away from me, he really saved us all, and your papers too,' she said to her father, fixing her brilliant blue eyes on him.

Her father looked most uncomfortable. He felt very guilty for having punished George and Timothy. They had been right about Mr Roland and he had been wrong.

'Poor George,' he said, 'and poor Timmy. I'm sorry about all that.'

George did not bear malice once anyone had owned themselves to be in the wrong. She smiled at her father.

'It's all right,' she said. 'But don't you think that as I was punished unfairly, Mr Roland might be punished well and truly? He deserves it!'

'Oh, he shall be, certainly he shall be,' promised her father. 'He's up in bed with a cold, as you know. I hope he doesn't hear any of this, or he may try to escape.'

'He can't,' said George. 'We're snowed up. You could ring up the police, and arrange for them to come here as soon as ever they can manage it, when the snow has cleared. And I rather think those other two men will try to explore the Secret Way as soon as possible, to get the papers back. Could we catch them when they arrive, do you think?'

'Rather!' said Uncle Quentin, though Aunt Fanny looked as if she didn't want any more exciting things to happen! 'Now look here, you seem really frozen all of you, and you must be hungry too, because it's almost lunch-time. Go into the dining-room and sit by the fire, and Joanna shall bring us all a hot lunch. Then we'll talk about what to do.'

Nobody said a word to Mr Roland, of course. He lay in bed, coughing now and then. George had slipped up and locked his door. She wasn't going to have him wandering out and overhearing anything!

They all enjoyed their hot lunch, and became warm and cosy. It was nice to sit there together, talking over their adventure, and planning what to do.

'I will telephone to the police, of course,' said Uncle Quentin. 'And tonight we will put Timmy into the study to give the two artists a good welcome if they arrive!'

Mr Roland was most annoyed to find his door locked that afternoon when he took it into his head to dress and go downstairs. He banged on it indignantly. George grinned and went upstairs. She had told the other children how she had locked the door.

'What's the matter, Mr Roland?' she asked, in a polite voice.

'Oh, it's you, George, is it?' said the tutor. 'See what's the matter with my door, will you? I can't open it.'

George had pocketed the key when she had locked the door. She answered Mr Roland in a cheerful voice.

'Oh Mr Roland, there's no key in your door, so I can't unlock it. I'll see if I can find it!'

Mr Roland was angry and puzzled. He couldn't understand why his door was locked and the key gone. He did not guess that everyone knew about him now. Uncle Quentin laughed when George went down and told him about the locked door.

'He may as well be kept a prisoner,' he said. 'He can't escape now.'

That night, everyone went to bed early, and Timmy

was left in the study, guarding the hole. Mr Roland
had become more and more angry and puzzled when
his door was not unlocked. He had shouted for Uncle
Quentin, but only George had come. He could not
understand it. George, of course, was enjoying herself. She made Timothy bark outside Mr Roland's
door, and this puzzled him too, for he knew that
George was not supposed to see Timmy for three
days. Wild thoughts raced through his head. Had that
fierce, impossible child locked up her father and
mother and Joanna, as well as himself? He could not
imagine what had happened.

In the middle of the night Timmy awoke everyone
by barking madly. Uncle Quentin and the children
hurried downstairs, followed by Aunt Fanny, and the
amazed Joanna. A fine sight met their eyes!

Mr Wilton and Mr Thomas were in the study
crouching behind the sofa, terrified of Timothy, who
was barking for all he was worth! Timmy was standing by the hole in the stone floor, so that the two men
could not escape down there. Artful Timmy! He had
waited in silence until the men had crept up the hole
into the study, and were exploring it, wondering
where they were – and then the dog had leapt to the
hole to guard it, preventing the men from escaping.

'Good evening, Mr Wilton, good evening, Mr
Thomas,' said George, in a polite voice. 'Have you
come to see our tutor Mr Roland?'

'So this is where he lives!' said Mr Wilton. 'Was it
you in the passage today?'

'Yes – and my cousins,' said George. 'Have you
come to look for the papers you stole from my father?'

The two men were silent. They knew they were
caught. Mr Wilton spoke after a moment.

'Where's Mr Roland?'

'Shall we take these men to Mr Roland, Uncle?' asked Julian, winking at George. 'Although it's in the middle of the night I'm sure he would love to see them.'

'Yes,' said his uncle, jumping at once to what the boy meant to do. 'Take them up. Timmy, you go too.'

The men followed Julian upstairs, Timmy close at their heels. George followed too, grinning. She handed Julian the key. He unlocked the door and the men went in, just as Julian switched on the light. Mr Roland was wide awake and gave an exclamation of complete amazement when he saw his friends.

Before they had time to say a word Julian locked the door again and threw the key to George.

'A nice little bag of prisoners,' he said. 'We will leave old Tim outside the door to guard them. It's impossible to get out of that window, and anyway, we're snowed up if they could escape that way.'

Everyone went to bed again, but the children found it difficult to sleep after such an exciting time. Anne and George whispered together and so did Julian and Dick. There was such a lot to talk about.

Next day there was a surprise for everyone. The police did arrive after all! The snow did not stop them, for somewhere or other they had got skis and had come skimming along valiantly to see the prisoners! It was a great excitement for everyone.

'We won't take the men away, sir, till the snow has gone,' said the Inspector. 'We'll just put the handcuffs on them, so that they don't try any funny tricks. You keep the door locked too, and that dog outside. They'll be safe there for a day or two. We've taken them enough food till we come back again. If they go a bit short, it will serve them right!'

The snow melted two days later, and the police

took away Mr Roland and the others. The children watched.

'No more lessons *these* hols!' said Anne gleefully.

'No more shutting Timothy out of the house,' said George.

'You were right and we were wrong, George,' said Julian. 'You were fierce, weren't you?—but it's a jolly good thing you were!'

'She *is* fierce, isn't she?' said Dick, giving the girl a sudden hug. 'But I rather like her when she's fierce, don't you, Julian? Oh George, we do have marvellous adventures with you! I wonder if we'll have any more?'

They will – there isn't a doubt of that!

The Enid Blyton Newsletter

Would you like to receive The Enid Blyton Newsletter? It has lots of news about Enid Blyton books,
videos, plays, etc. There are also puzzles and a page for
your letters. It is published three times a year and is free
for children who live in the United Kingdom and
Ireland.

If you would like to receive it for a year, please write
to: The Enid Blyton Newsletter, PO Box 357,
London, WC2N 6QB, sending your name and
address. (UK and Ireland only)

A complete list of the FAMOUS FIVE
ADVENTURES *by Enid Blyton*

1 FIVE ON A TREASURE ISLAND
2 FIVE GO ADVENTURING AGAIN
3 FIVE RUN AWAY TOGETHER
4 FIVE GO TO SMUGGLER'S TOP
5 FIVE GO OFF IN A CARAVAN
6 FIVE ON KIRRIN ISLAND AGAIN
7 FIVE GO OFF TO CAMP
8 FIVE GET INTO TROUBLE
9 FIVE FALL INTO ADVENTURE
10 FIVE ON A HIKE TOGETHER
11 FIVE HAVE A WONDERFUL TIME
12 FIVE GO DOWN TO THE SEA
13 FIVE GO TO MYSTERY MOOR
14 FIVE HAVE PLENTY OF FUN
15 FIVE ON A SECRET TRAIL
16 FIVE GO TO BILLYCOCK HILL
17 FIVE GET INTO A FIX
18 FIVE ON FINNISTON FARM
19 FIVE GO TO DEMON'S ROCKS
20 FIVE HAVE A MYSTERY TO SOLVE
21 FIVE ARE TOGETHER AGAIN

A complete list of the SECRET SEVEN ADVENTURES *by Enid Blyton*

1 THE SECRET SEVEN
2 SECRET SEVEN ADVENTURE
3 WELL DONE SECRET SEVEN
4 SECRET SEVEN ON THE TRAIL
5 GO AHEAD SECRET SEVEN
6 GOOD WORK SECRET SEVEN
7 SECRET SEVEN WIN THROUGH
8 THREE CHEERS SECRET SEVEN
9 SECRET SEVEN MYSTERY
10 PUZZLE FOR THE SECRET SEVEN
11 SECRET SEVEN FIREWORKS
12 GOOD OLD SECRET SEVEN
13 SHOCK FOR THE SECRET SEVEN
14 LOOK OUT SECRET SEVEN
15 FUN FOR THE SECRET SEVEN